SEP 3 1975

Wallace
Blue meadow

BLUE MEADOW

By Mary Wallace

BLUE MEADOW
THE BRIGHT WINDOWS
BRENDAN
REASON FOR GLADNESS
PETER AND THE ROCK

BLUE MEADOW

by
Mary Wallace

AF

WILLIAM MORROW & COMPANY, INC.
NEW YORK   1975

1 2 3 4 5   79 78 77 76 75

Library of Congress Cataloging in Publication Data

Wallace, Mary Longstreet (date)
    Blue Meadow.
    I. Title.
PZ4.W188Bl   [PS3573.A4268]   813'.5'4   74-20600
ISBN 0-688-02887-X

Book design: Helen Roberts

To my grandchildren

Part I

(1)

Shaded by oaks, the innyard was a cool and pleasant place to while away a summer afternoon. Those who had more pressing though perhaps not better uses for their time, and could little afford to while away any of it, were envious of the four who had a thoroughly proper excuse—waiting to meet the coach from Philadelphia.

None of the four could complain that the coach was late, since it had no fixed time of arrival. They were told by villagers that last week it rolled up to the Westbridge Inn at three in the afternoon; the week before, at five; but sometimes did not arrive until dark, and sometimes not at all, depending upon the nature of the delay, which could be merely a horse losing a shoe, but could also be a broken axle, or even an act of God whereby a bridge was washed out or a ford made temporarily uncrossable. But they were enjoying the wait. The inn was a focal point for news, and as the postrider had come some hours ago, bringing copies of the *Pennsylvania Packet* as well as Ben Franklin's *Gazette*, on that June day in 1775 it was also

3

a focal point for the airing of views, no less loud and lively for being generally in agreement.

During lulls in the discussion of great affairs, smaller and more personal matters were introduced. The four divulged that the coach was bringing them, respectively, a visiting sister-in-law, a young son returning from school, an Irish chambermaid, and two crates of chickens. The chickens would continue their journey by oxcart, as would the sister-in-law. The boy would ride home behind his father on the broad back of a Flanders plow horse. The chambermaid, by what at first seemed an incongruity but on second thought not an incongruity at all, since she must have been sent for by a gentleman of substantial means, would be transported in a vehicle that caught the admiring eye of everyone who set foot in the yard, and as a conversation piece outranked the meeting of the Second Continental Congress.

In the city, where private carriages were becoming fairly numerous, a simple two-wheeled homemade one-horse chaise would have drawn little attention; but in the crossroads hamlet of Westbridge it was a rare sight. Moreover, it was a work of art, to which long hours of cutting and shaping and fitting and joining and smoothing and polishing had been devoted by someone who had fashioned his masterpiece not only with painstaking care and skill but surely with tenderness for every piece of wood his hands transformed into spoke or shaft or spring or body. And between the shafts was a fine young lightweight chestnut mare of obviously excellent breeding.

Many were the admiring comments and many the questions put to the young man—or, more accurately, boy, for they estimated his age to be no more than seventeen—who had come driving this handsome ve-

4

hicle into the yard, and who had not gone into the inn or sought any form of diversion, but seemed content to spend his time swishing a fly whisk of oak leaves over the mare's forward parts which her tail could not reach. He was dressed as a farmer, in homespun trousers, work frock, and shirt, all somewhat too large; he wore heavy cowhide shoes without buckles; and his hair was cut too short to be drawn back and tied. Some of the questioners noted that he had a look of quality, but by his poor attire they assumed he was a servant. He answered their questions courteously but in no more words than the minimum number required, from which it appeared that he himself had no very great interest in the matter; yet the more observant plainly saw that his eyes were alight with pleasure.

Perhaps twenty times his answers established that the chaise had been constructed at Blue Meadow Farm, and that all materials used had come from the premises, except the iron for the tires, which had been purchased; but the tires, too, had been made and fitted and put on at home.

"Blue Meadow? Out beyond the Forks, is that? Mr. Mark Stafford?"

"Marcus."

"Oh, yes. The gentleman who bought a parcel of the Findlay holding out on the West Branch. Came over in '68, built a fieldstone cottage and a big stone-end German barn the first year, and then a right grand big brick house the next. Has his own carriage maker, has he?"

The boy said no, Mr. Stafford did not have a carriage maker in his employ. The chaise had been built by someone who simply wanted to try his hand.

"You're saying the man who made this never made one before?"

"Yes, sir."

"Incredible!"

That the word was not to be taken literally was manifest in a renewed round of comment and renewed scrutiny from front and back, right and left, top and bottom.

The boy smiled and went on swishing flies.

An elderly Quaker, not hesitating to go on his knees in order to inspect the under parts, remained so a moment longer, looking closely at the near wheel; but as the position was becoming uncomfortable he rose rather stiffly, assisted by one of the company, without having satisfied himself upon one important detail. He brushed his breeches, adjusted his hat, and turned to ask, "Does thee know of what wood the hubs are made?"

"The Indian name is tupelo. It's also called black gum."

"And can thee tell me why black gum was used instead of black locust?"

By its tone the question implied that some perfectly sound reason must have determined the choice; and the boy, eager to explain why one wood had been preferred to another, now forgot to guard his tongue.

"Sir, the irregular grain makes it very strong and hard. So hard it can be used for plowshares. Therefore I thought it the best possible wood for the hubs."

"*Thee* thought!"

Every eye turned from the chaise to focus in amazement upon the fly-swishing boy in shabby mud-colored rough linen homespun.

"*Thee* built this?"

Modestly to disclaim any extraordinary ability, he admitted, "It took me two years, sir."

6

But the old Quaker gentleman shrewdly appraised the answer.

"Thee means—working on it in thy spare time?"

"Yes, sir."

"Thee could do well for thyself in the trade, lad."

The boy said nothing.

"Thee is indentured?"

"No, sir."

"Then thee prefers remaining a servant to making thy own way?"

"Mr. Stafford's way is my way, sir."

A curious gentleness as well as a curious significance in the reply drew a long probing look, and then: "Ah, yes. I have had the pleasure of meeting Mr. Marcus Stafford on two occasions, and now it comes to me, thee is not a servant at all, as we supposed. Thee is Mr. Stafford's younger son. Will thee deny it?"

"No, sir."

"The Lord has blessed him," the old man said. "But"—sternly and shaking a finger—"thee should not lead others into error, young man."

Had the announcement that the Philadelphia coach was in sight not been shouted into the yard at that moment, young Richard Gregory Stafford would doubtless have been lectured at length upon the sin of deceit and the virtues of openness and honesty; and would—perhaps—have reflected upon the good man's words and formed a righteous resolve to mend his ways. As it was, in the quick exodus from the courtyard the words bounced off and were forgotten, not to be remembered until some twenty minutes later; and by that time it was too late.

In a cloud of dust the coach arrived.

The chicken crates and other articles on which or

among which the passengers had been obliged to find room for their feet had to be removed first, to permit discharge of the human cargo. Next came the schoolboy, not preceding his elders by reason of bad manners but of necessity, as he was the least tightly wedged in. Then a young woman of ponderous proportions, who (to Richard's relief, for the possibility of having to seat such bulk in his precious chaise was appalling) turned out to be the visiting sister-in-law. Then a girl, extremely pretty, and obviously of an affluent family, for there could be no doubt that her fashionable brown linen traveling dress and matching hood had come from England, and she had silver buckles on her neat little brown shoes. Then three men of the village, who disappeared at once into the inn, seeking refreshment after a long, hot, wearisome and very dry trip.

And that was all.

The driver swung his coach into the yard. The girl set her small valise on the mounting block and stood looking anxiously up and down the road. The man and boy departed on their broad-backed Flemish horse. The chicken crates were loaded into one cart, the stout woman into the other, each by the combined efforts of both farmers, who then went lumbering and creaking their respective ways. The various items of freight piled by the roadside were one by one picked up and carried off. And presently only Richard Stafford and the young lady in fine imported English linen remained.

Richard had no valid excuse for lingering. His passenger had not arrived, he had a nine-mile drive ahead, it was after six o'clock, and he should set out at once if he was to reach home before darkness made the roads even more hazardous than they were at best. But it was plain that the young lady had expected to be met, and that finding herself stranded here, alone, and perhaps still many miles from her destination, she was bewildered and frightened; and certainly no gentleman could callously drive away, leaving a maiden-in-distress abandoned by the roadside.

They looked at each other, quickly looked away, and then looked back again.

Thinking that she wanted to speak to him, but of course could not, as under no circumstances except of the direst extremity was it permissible for a young lady to speak to a strange young man, even one whose apparel attested to the fact of his being a gentleman, as his definitely did not, and thinking also that he would find it very pleasant to drive her wherever she wished to go, even if that meant not getting back to Blue Meadow that night at all, Richard decided that the proper course was for him to speak to her. Whereupon he took a step or two nearer, and putting up a hand to remove his hat before remembering that he wasn't wearing a hat, courteously addressed her.

"May I be of service to you, miss?"

The white frill of her cap showed prettily beneath her hood, and beneath the frill a curl or two of the blackest hair he had ever seen. She had also the bluest eyes, the fairest skin, the loveliest blush, and the sweetest mouth. He himself was not tall, a scant five feet nine, but she was several inches less than that, and to look down into her beautiful upturned face aroused all his most chivalrous instincts, as well as other instincts that he did not at the moment attempt to identify. Indeed, it was a moment defying analysis altogether; for it seemed to him that some strange invisible current passed between them, not merely in one direction but two. Later he would wonder if it was not in some way

9

akin to what Mr. Benjamin Franklin felt through the key at the end of his kite wire; but at the time, no such rational interpretation occurred to him.

Precisely what was passing through the girl's mind he of course could not know, but he had reason to hope that if her delicate sensibilities could accept his uncouth garb, she would not find his physical appearance otherwise repellent. He was devoid of vanity (or at any rate in careful searching of conscience had so come to consider himself), but was fully—in fact, inescapably—aware that he bore a close resemblance to his father, who, as everyone said, was a very well-favored man. His features were cut in the same pattern, he had the same spare build, the same eyes of a rather uncommonly dark gray, the same dark hair with even the same lock always tending to hang forward—unless he pushed it back, as automatically he did now, though it never stayed. Also, his father was a kind man whose gentle and benevolent disposition showed in his face and especially in his smile. Hoping that he had inherited this basic character and some outward evidence of it along with the physical features, Richard tried further to assure this enchanting young creature that his intentions were of the highest order, by adding a smile to his offer of assistance.

Her eyes filled with tears.

This unexpected response would have dismayed him had it not at the same time made her lovelier than ever, so that his senses seemed to swim in her tears, and his heart swelled with the vastness of his desire to help and protect her. Had he possessed a velvet cloak, gladly would he have laid it in the dust (there being no mud puddle) so that her exquisite little feet in the brown slippers with the silver buckles would have beneath them a substance worthy to bear their imprint;

but having only a homespun work frock which if removed would reveal the now-embarrassing details that his shirt was none too clean and that his trousers were held up—securely but inelegantly—by rawhide points knotted around the waistband in lieu of buttons long since lost, he was obliged to forgo this romantic gesture.

The girl spoke. "Do you be here to fetch me?"

Two things about her voice surprised and deeply affected him. The first, it was soft—oh, softer than the whisper of a summer breeze through the grass, or the sighing of a hearth fire just before the last embers are raked together and covered for the night. The second, it had a foreign sound, puzzlingly unlike any he had ever heard. He knew the tones and accents of German and French. This was different; very different. The softness seemed also an attribute of the words themselves. English was not her native tongue, of that he was sure. But what speech except the speech of heaven could fall so delectably upon the ear?

And he—God forgive him—had to say no, he was not here to fetch her, he was here to fetch someone else; but as that person had not come, and as he had a horse and chaise, and as she had not been met as anticipated, if she would inform him as to her destination, he would be honored and happy to drive her there.

This brought another unexpected reaction. Certainly she looked relieved and grateful, yet disappointment shadowed her reply.

"May God reward you for the goodness of your heart, *a chara*, and be it not too far beyond your own going, most thankfully do I accept your kind offer, myself being lost and alone here, and knowing not which way to turn. But I do be sorry," the soft voice said, "that our ways be not the same."

Richard experienced an unusual and startling sensation, whereby he learned that certain figures of speech were founded upon fact—one's heart *could* turn over. When his righted itself and settled back to its accustomed position, though not to its accustomed pace, he asked where she wished to go.

Instead of answering, she turned her back; but as he was by this time more or less prepared for the unexpected, and as her attractiveness from any point of view varied only in degree, he watched with interest nor refrained from speculating upon the probability that she had turned away in modesty to extract something from beneath the bodice of her dress. Facing him again, she held out a card.

"It do be written here, the place where I go."

Richard had not, after all, been prepared for the unexpected. Dumbfounded, he stared at the card, on which was written: *Mr. Marcus Aurelius Stafford, Blue Meadow Farm, two miles northwest of Willowfield, near Simon's mill.*

More sadly than anxiously, when without saying a word he continued to stare, she asked, "You cannot read either, it may be?"

"No . . . Yes . . ." Richard looked up from the card and into her eyes, those very blue eyes with the long and very black lashes. "I can read, but . . ."

"It be too far, then? You cannot take me?"

"I . . . Yes, I can take you. Yes, of course. But you can't be . . . I mean . . . Who are you?"

"Brighid Ní Ghallchobhair."

"Breednie . . . ?"

She laughed. Her laughter was like the first birdsong of morning softened by the meadow mist; like silver water running over golden sands; like fairy bells ringing in the moonlight.

12

"I say it as in Donegal. The Sasanachs say it Bridget Gallagher." The blue eyes searched his face, further increasing his confusion by seeming wistfully to search for something they did not find. "You be a Sasanach, I think?"

A note of regret in the soft voice impelled him to instant denial, and he began, "No, I'm a . . ." but checked himself on the brink of saying, "a Stafford." Had his head not been awhirl, he might then have recalled the Quaker gentleman's reprimand and been guided by it to prompt confession; but he had, in that giddy moment, little connection with the past and only a blurred awareness of the future, just enough to warn him that the bright jewel of promise so tantalizingly held before his eyes by the hand of fate could be snatched away in an instant, could vanish like the stuff of dreams, could be forever lost in the depths of cruel uncrossable seas, were he not careful. Therefore he amended his answer, saying instead, "I'm from the Stafford farm—the place where you're going. It's *you* I was sent to meet! But I thought . . ."

Again he had to check his words, for certainly it would not do to say, "I thought you were a lady." But she, first with a look of surprise, then of delight, plucked the words from his mind and garnished them with her gold and silver fairy-bells-in-the-moonlight laughter.

"You thought one in such fine clothes must be a fine rich lady. Not so, *a chara dhil.* I do be none but the poorest. In bond I was, but the Mistress freed me, and now I go in service for eighteen shillings each month and my keep. The Mistress, so generous she was, gave me this dress her daughter cast aside for disliking of the color."

"But you have silver buckles on your shoes!"

"It be so. The Mistress gave me also the shoes, and

13

thought at first to remove the buckles, but did not, knowing I was sad to leave her and thinking to dry my tears with such splendid gifts. Did she not give me these things, I would have naught but rags and my old gray shawl. But fine clothes do not make the fine lady, as now you see."

"No," Richard said. "No, that isn't what I see."

"Not so?" Her eyes questioned him, perplexed.

"No. I see . . . Bridget, you do not need the clothes to make you a lady."

"Ah, sure now"—laughter was in her voice but with it something deep and warm and tender—"though you be English, it be the Irishman's tongue you have for turning a poor *cailín's* head with sweet words. And were I in truth the fine lady, I do be thinking great cause would I have at this moment to be sorry."

"Sorry?" The world was spinning. "Why?"

"Unless you also be the fine gentleman. But as you be *buachaill aimsire*—a servant boy—better I be *cailín aimsire*, so we may be friends."

Now the world stood still, and they at its center. He had not been mistaken—the strange current had indeed passed in both directions—was still passing; he felt it in tingling little waves. But . . .

Thee should not lead others into error. . . .

The words were remembered too late. To correct the error now . . . No, he could not. As well could he crush the wings of a butterfly, or kill a singing bird with a stone, as destroy what he saw in her eyes— reflection of the lovely fragile shining thing suspended there between them on a thread of gossamer. Later, when the time was right, when the thread was joined and woven with other threads, when the shining thing became strong so it would not float away or break at a touch—then he would find a way to correct the error. Perhaps on the way home; but not now.

14

She asked his name. By every dictate of reason and conscience, he knew he should say, "Richard Stafford." Instead he said only, "Richard"; and she tried it on her tongue, softly, and said though it was a Sasanach name, she liked it.

The way home was long, but not long enough. The roads were rough, but he could wish them to be rougher, for the seat of the chaise was made for two with but few inches to spare, they were jostled together when the wheels went over bumps or dropped into ruts or hollows, and there may have been times when he purposely kept the right wheel low, making it all but impossible for her to keep her balance when the left then went over a stone.

He had a package of bread and cheese and a small flask of cider. These they shared as they went along. Plain dry bread had never before tasted like Christmas cake, or hard cider like the finest Madeira wine. She drank only a little, not liking the taste; but he drained the flask, for the road was dusty and the heat of the day not yet dispelled though the sun was far down in the west.

They talked little. Their closeness in the chaise, making them self-conscious as well as very conscious of each other, seemed a substitute for talking. Now and then Richard called her attention to things of special interest—a red fox loping across a meadow, a giant tulip tree, an eighteen-foot Conestoga wagon in a German farmyard. And now and then she asked questions about her new place of service—how many were in the family, how many servants, and was the Mistress kind?

He told her there were eight in the family: Mr. Marcus Stafford, his two sons, the wife of his older son, their three little girls, and Nurse, who was counted a family member, having also been Nurse to Mr. Stafford's own children. There were only three house servants—Cook and two maids; and four field servants, two indentured, two free, but Mr. Stafford's sons also worked, just as they did. Mr. Stafford's wife had died some years before he came to the Colonies; therefore it was Mr. Vincent Stafford's wife who managed the household. She was strict and kept everyone busy, for the house was large and there was much to do; but yes (did he hesitate?), she was kind.

"You work in the fields, Richard?" A wistful note was in her voice. "You do not be a house servant?"

"Sometimes I'm at the house," he answered, wanting to please her. "I do a little of everything. In the morning I work with the horses; in the afternoon, in the fields. We have—Mr. Stafford has—a stable of Thoroughbreds. Ten mares and a very fine stallion—Red Earl. I ride and train the colts."

She gave him an anxious look. "Does that be dangerous?"

"No. I've been riding horses all my life, Bridget. And I'm the only one"—he couldn't resist this little boast—"who rides the Earl. Or even goes in the stall with him. But that's not dangerous either. We're good friends."

"I fear you be hurt sometime."

"If I ever am," Richard boldly promised, "I'll ask them to let you take care of me."

She bent her head, but he saw color stain her cheek, soft as the petal of a red rose, and felt within himself a mounting warmth—perhaps an effect of the continuing electric currents, or perhaps the hard cider. A stretch of smooth level road lay ahead. He shook the reins and the mare went into a brisk trot.

Slowing again where the roadbed was of logs laid

across a marshy place, he asked, "Bridget, what was that name you called me?"

"Sasanach? That be Englishman."

"No, I mean the other. Twice you called me a name."

"I called you *cara*. That be friend."

"And the second time?"

"The second time—I said '*a chara dhil*.' "

"What does that mean?"

Again her color was high. "That means—dear friend."

For the next ten minutes they both were silent, looking straight ahead.

The sun had long gone down, bands of lavender cloud edged with fading gold formed a barway across the western sky, and when the road led through a forest of white pine, the great crowding trees made their own twilight. Awed and uneasy, Bridget said, "There be naught like this in Ireland." And what could be more naturally reassuring than to slip an arm around her until they were safely past the shadow of the pines?

They came to a small settlement at a crossroad—half a dozen houses, a blacksmith shop, a pottery, a tannery, a church. This was the village of Willowfield, he told her. Turning right, they went down a long hill, forded a creek, and turned again to the left, passing a grist mill where a dog ran out and barked and a man called a greeting from the doorway of a small log house. Beyond this point the road was wide and well cared for, between the mill race on one hand and a wooded hill on the other; and when the woods ended, there were rail fences enclosing hillside pastures in which horses and cattle grazed.

Richard drew rein and stopped. The stillness was very deep. In it a bird called, the liquid notes clear and sweet, somewhere along the edge of the woods they had just passed. Ahead, the afterglow was pricked by a single star.

"We are home," Richard said. And could not say it with regret, even though troubled by what he now must do; for he loved every blade of grass, every bush and tree, every rock, every spring that came flowing pure and cold from secret hidden places underground; and homecoming would be the same deep satisfaction whether he had been nine or nine hundred miles away. "This is Blue Meadow."

She looked at the green fields stretching away.

"The house, it be yet far off?"

"No, not far. Just around the bend. But . . . Bridget, there's something I must tell you."

She turned to him, waiting. The soft golden light from the west touched her cheek; and the shine in her eyes was fairer than the shine of the evening star.

Tell her, "I am Richard Stafford"? No. *This* was what he must tell her . . .

Drawing her close, he put a quick light kiss on her sweet and willing mouth.

Then he drove on.

And the error remained. Compounded, not corrected.

(2)

Twice, after sunset, Marcus Stafford walked down the carriage drive, past the barn and gatehouse and on out to the road, to stand for many minutes looking eastward. A quarter mile beyond the entrance to Blue Meadow the road swung left. He could not see beyond the bend, but he listened for the sound of iron shoes or iron tires on gravel. There was nothing.

He had instructed Richard to stay over if the coach arrived too late to let him reach home before nightfall, but had failed to specify half-after-five as the latest hour for setting out on the homeward journey. That omission now worried him. These were restless and uneasy times, infected by the fever of independence sweeping the Colonies. More than the usual number of bond servants were running away, to lose themselves in the cities or push on to the west; desperate men, some of them, known to help themselves to what they wanted on the way. By daylight the roads were safe enough; but it was unwise to travel after dark, and certainly he should not have exposed a loved son to the risk of being set upon by some ruffian who would not hesitate to rob and might not hesitate to kill.

Consoling himself with the thought that Richard's own intelligence would have told him six o'clock was the extreme limit, and that half an hour remained before dusk, Marcus returned to the house.

A bench had been placed on the east terrace, where his daughter-in-law sat utilizing the daylight that remained. Supper was over, the children were on their way to bed, Vincent had returned to the barn to see the last of the day's work completed. As far as Marcus had ever been able to observe, this was the one hour of relaxation Jane allowed herself; but even when relaxing, her hands must be busy with needle and thread, stitching a new petticoat for one of the little girls.

She moved to lay her sewing aside. "Shall I have a chair brought for you, Father?"

"No, thank you, my dear. Your skirts are not so wide that I cannot share your bench."

But she rose, saying, "Then at least I will bring you a coal for your pipe."

"You spoil me, Jane."

In answer she gave him one of her cool tight little smiles. Jane's smiles were always cool and tight, it seemed to him, though she was never without thought for his comfort and often took great pains to please him. Perhaps the greater, he reflected while awaiting her return, because she had failed to do that which would have pleased him most. She had not borne a son. Three times since she and Vincent and their little daughters came from England five years ago, she had given birth prematurely, each time a female infant either stillborn or surviving only a few minutes, and now could never have another child. By centuries of custom, the major portion of the Stafford estate passed

20

from first son to first son. Should Vincent have no son, use of lands and annual income would be his for life; but at his death the inheritance would pass to Richard and thence to Richard's son, God granting that someday he would have one. Vincent himself found this not a matter of concern; but it was a sore point, Marcus suspected, with Jane, for even though substantial dowries would be provided for her daughters, she was not reconciled to their being passed over in favor of a child of Richard's.

He suspected, further, that this accounted for her not-too-well-veiled hostility toward Richard, of whose misdeeds or sins of omission she daily complained. Richard had gone to bed, the west window of his room wide open, and had not troubled to get up and close it when a storm came; the window curtains, the rug, a chair, all were drenched. Richard had not filled the woodbox; or, in doing so, had tracked mud into the kitchen. Richard had hoed only half the garden, and that in a very negligent way. Richard was not on time for meals. Richard's careless manner of dress was a disgrace to all of them. That morning, seeing him start off for Westbridge, she had been aghast. "You are letting him go like *that?* People will take him for a servant!" But she saw no inconsistency in calling upon him to perform menial tasks for her. "It is good for a boy to be kept busy," she said then.

Jane, two years older than Vincent, was now thirty-four, still a fine-looking woman, though somewhat too thin from expending all her energies upon running the house, and lacking two front teeth (a disfigurement that perhaps explained the tightness of her smile). She was an expert manager, even with insufficient help, and after an unfortunate experience with a lazy and dishonest upstairs maid, had preferred to make out as best

21

she could without one until a girl of known dependability could be found. Well, Marcus thought comfortably, things should be easier for her now.

Returning with a hot ember in the smoking-tongs, she held it to his pipe.

"Thank you, Jane. You are a kind and thoughtful daughter."

She gave him another of those closed little smiles, laid the tongs on one of the terrace bricks, picked up her sewing, and seated herself beside him.

"Your kindness far exceeds mine, Father. I am indeed grateful to you for writing your cousin about our need for a girl. And grateful to her for so generously sending us one from her own household."

"Yes," Marcus agreed, "you will have no trouble with a girl whom Elizabeth so highly recommends."

"I hope not."

Surprised, he asked, "Surely you have no doubts?"

"As to her honesty and diligence, no. But I confess—I find myself wondering why Cousin Elizabeth is willing to give up such a paragon. A really good maid is not easy to replace, you know."

Marcus drew on his pipe before answering, "Easier in the city than out here, I suppose." But he remembered a line of his cousin's letter he had not read aloud to Jane. *Bridget is a good girl, and I feel she will be safer in the country with you.* Safer? And in what sense had Elizabeth used the word "good"? Not merely to describe an honest and diligent servant, he felt sure. He drew again on his pipe. "Elizabeth's house and family are not so large as ours. Perhaps she had more servants than she needs."

The needle continued to flash in the fading light.

"Cousin Elizabeth is a widow?"

22

"Yes. With a sixteen-year-old daughter and two sons, nineteen and twenty."

Briefly the needle paused.

"The girl is seventeen, and has been with her for a year? And was indentured, I believe you said. How unusual that Cousin Elizabeth would release her after only a year's service. Could she not have transferred the contract to you?"

"She would consider that unfair. A redemptioner should not be regarded as a slave, to be sold or passed around at will. Much better for the girl to come to us by her own consent, and be free to leave us if she so desires."

"I'm not sure I agree with you, Father. Independence in a servant is not a desirable quality, and can be very troublesome."

"Perhaps so. But human dignity is not restricted to gentlefolk, and should be respected among those of the meaner classes also."

"*You* have redemptioners," Jane pointed out.

"I have men who voluntarily entered into a contract and voluntarily abide by its terms. I'm sure you remember the young man I released because he had been seized on the waterfront and forcibly put aboard ship, and then made to sign?"

"I remember—that was what he told you. It is a wonder the others did not work upon your sympathies in the same manner."

He smiled. "You must think me very credulous."

"No, but I think you so goodhearted that people are tempted to use your goodness to their own advantage."

"Well, if it comes to that, my dear, I would rather be used unfairly by others than use others unfairly.

That young man was a silversmith. To bind him to farm labor would have been a great injustice. And to hold any man who indentured himself under duress is equivalent to being a receiver of stolen goods."

"There are few who see it that way, Father. And still fewer who would furnish such a man with the means to set himself up, as you did—twenty sovereigns so he could feed and house and clothe himself, and two hundred Spanish silver dollars to convert to plate."

"I remind you, Jane, he not only discharged his debt in full but made us a gift of a very handsome silver tankard."

"Yes, he proved himself worthy. I pray that all to whom you extend kindness may do the same." Jane held her work closer. "I suppose I should not wonder at the tone of Cousin Elizabeth's letter, which seemed to indicate an almost affectionate regard for this girl. No doubt willingness to acknowledge what you term 'human dignity,' even in persons of mean condition, is a family trait."

"Indeed, I hope so. I would not have my sons judge a man's worth solely by his condition in life. Many of low birth have acquired wealth and risen to high place here, and I dare say many of gentle birth have fared poorly. And it would be especially ill of us to despise the Irish poor, since we ourselves have helped make them so, by two centuries of persecution. I have met Irish, both men and women, of obviously noble blood, yet in rags and servitude."

"I shall hope," Jane replied dryly, "that we do not find ourselves with an Irish princess making our beds. Especially if she is comely."

"Would we hold comeliness against her?"

"Not in itself. But . . . Cousin Elizabeth has two young sons, did you say?"

24

The question, weighted with suggestion, hung between them for a moment, while she made her fine neat stitches and he drew thoughtfully on his pipe. Presently he said, "Jane, my dear, the light is very poor. You are straining your eyes."

"Yes." She made the needle secure and folded the material. "I must stop. Are you still expecting Richard back this evening?"

"For another ten minutes. After that, I will assume the coach arrived late and he is waiting until tomorrow."

"Richard has a vague concept of time," Jane said. "He would be very apt to imagine he could leave Westbridge at seven and still reach home before dark. Vincent spoke of riding out to meet him."

"No, that won't be necessary. We will trust Richard's judgment." Thinking that the firmness of the answer may have seemed a rebuke, Marcus tempered it by adding with a smile, "He might risk his own safety, but he would not risk his chaise." And then remembered that the chaise, too, was a sore point with Jane, who had been able to think of a hundred better ways for Richard to spend his spare time, if indeed the luxury of spare time could sensibly be permitted him at all.

With all there was to be done, in Jane's opinion the building of a chaise represented foolish indulgence of a foolish whim. If any of them needed or wanted to go anywhere, they rode horseback. What use had they for a chaise? And wasn't it understood that here in this raw new land they could not expect to live as they had lived in England? That even though the Staffords were gentlemen, with six hundred rich acres and a fine house full of fine things, they nevertheless chose to work as farmers, side by side with hired hands and redemptioners, in order that the farm be made to support them and not they the farm?

She saw as proper, of course, that her father-in-law devoted himself solely to overseeing the labor of others; but if Vincent spent every minute of the day in actual physical labor, then certainly Richard, fourteen years his junior, should be required to do the same. If at times between the plowing and planting and cultivating and harvesting of the crops he could be spared from field work, or from clearing woodland for new fields, or from tending the cattle, or training the horses, there were innumerable and unending household chores, all far more important than something done merely for his own pleasure.

Or he should be made to continue his studies, which, since his coming to the Colonies, had consisted only of an hour's tutoring each day by his father, during the first few years, and had long ago ceased entirely. Other gentlemen's sons were shipped off to England, or at least attended the Academy in Philadelphia; but Richard had begged not to be sent away from Blue Meadow, and his father had heeded his pleas instead of compelling him to acquire formal education suitable to his rank.

The fact that Richard worked long hours, willingly and good-naturedly, at everyone's beck and call, including hers, and that his services would have been sorely missed, counted little with Jane, who made large issues of small ones, and in magnifying Richard's faults blinded herself to the very qualities that made him indispensable to all of them. Vincent, to whom most of her complaints were voiced, sometimes felt obliged on her behalf to give Richard a clout on the shoulder for daydreaming or careless performance of a task; but he was fond of his young brother, and felt that a little free time for the pursuit of pleasure was in fairness due him, especially as the pursuit took so harmless and in fact so commendable a form. Building a chaise, even though the condition of the roads made its usefulness questionable, was certainly a great deal worthier, he told his wife, than cockfighting or gaming or other pursuits that he would not offend her ears by naming; but his defense served only to make her look upon the chaise-building with increased disfavor, for she took it ill that he supported Richard against her.

Had Richard lost interest in the enterprise, or found it too difficult, or turned out a clumsy makeshift, she would have had the satisfaction of reminding them that she had disapproved all along. As it was, she could say only that it was a pity his skills had not been put to less frivolous use—construction of needed farm implements, for example. Then, in a typically feminine reversal, she had that morning complained that the chaise was much too fine to take to Westbridge to fetch home a servant girl, and had been annoyed with Vincent for saying reasonably that as it was Richard's chaise it was Richard's prerogative to use it if he wished.

In the silence that followed mention of the chaise, Marcus caught the sounds he had earlier listened for —the grating of iron tires and the mare's quick light trot. More relieved than he cared to show (for he had not been as certain of Richard's good judgment as he wished Jane to believe), he said only, "Here they come now," and rising, went down from the terrace to meet them.

Smoothly and lightly, its polished spokes catching the last of the afterglow, the chaise swung around the curve to the foot of the terrace steps. The girl was nearest him as it drew up and stopped; but because his primary concern had been for his son, whose safe return was now the primary basis for his relief and pleasure, he at first looked past her.

"You timed it nicely, Richard."

"Thank you, sir. The coach didn't come until almost six."

"I am glad it was no later," Marcus said. "I was afraid that if you had to put up at the inn, you would spend a sleepless night worrying about your chaise."

"No, sir." Richard smiled. "I would have spent the night *in* it."

Marcus gave back the same smile, one they often traded, of understanding and affection. "Then I was right about the sleeplessness, at least."

Aware that the girl's eyes were fixed upon his face, he now looked at her. Enough daylight remained to let him see that she was young, lovely, and expensively though plainly dressed. For only a second she met his eyes before lowering her own in—as he then thought—shyness and confusion. Had she not done so, he might have asked, "And who is this young lady?" for his immediate assumption was that the servant girl had not come, and that Richard had given transport to someone coming to visit the Spensers or the Findlays or one of the other families some miles farther along. But the look he caught in that brief second told him his mistake. Even so, a certain quality he found as recognizable in a human being as in a horse or any other animal made him frame his question with only slight alteration.

"And can this young lady be Bridget Gallagher?"

"Yes, sir," Richard answered, getting quickly out of the chaise and going to stand at the mare's head.

Marcus offered his hand. "Will you step down, my dear?"

The hand she slipped into his was trembling. With

28

the other she gathered her skirts, but then hesitated.

"Jump," he suggested. "Don't be afraid. I'll steady you . . . There now. That was easy, wasn't it?"

Faintly she whispered, "*Buidheachas.*" But she was trembling from head to foot, and kept her eyes on the ground.

Marcus reached into the chaise for her bag, and then, putting a fatherly arm around her shoulders, guided her toward the steps. Any frightened young thing would similarly have won his compassion; but he had, as well, a distinct reluctance to turn her over to Jane.

Coldly appraising, Jane's eyes covered their approach. She rose as they reached her. Disapproval was in the look she gave the girl, and a bitterly incredulous, *What was your cousin thinking of?* in the look she gave Marcus. The girl saw neither, but only the bricks at her feet.

"So this is Bridget."

"Yes. A most pleasing addition to our household."

"That remains to be seen. I am not accustomed to servants who have the insolence to dress beyond their station."

"Now, it is a traveling dress, Jane, and in no way unbecoming." Marcus withdrew his arm, but not before offering the comfort of a little added pressure. "We can count ourselves fortunate that Elizabeth sent us a young woman for whom she has such high regard."

"I am afraid, Father, that Cousin Elizabeth's generosity, however commendable in itself, is not to our benefit. Nor to the girl's. Assuming, of course, that the clothes were acquired through her generosity and not by other means . . . Where did you get this fine dress, Bridget, and shoes with silver buckles?"

The answer, barely audible, was gibberish to Jane's

ears. Impatiently she said, "I don't understand you. Can you not speak English?"

"*Is féidir liom* . . . Yes, I speak the English."

"Then do so from now on, when you are spoken to. Bring your bag and come inside."

Marcus, turning again toward the drive, saw that Richard had not yet started for the barn but was standing at the foot of the stone steps as if about to come up—mare, chaise, and all.

"Well, Richard?"

"Sir"—there was a note very close to anguish in his son's voice—"Jane has to treat her right!"

"Jane will not mistreat her." Marcus descended the steps. "But I wish you to tell me in just what way that is a concern of yours."

"I . . . she . . ." Richard stumbled over his words and was silent.

"Did you enjoy the drive home, Richard?"

The question brought no answer. None was needed. Nor was an answer needed to the next; for Marcus, remembering the look he had caught in the girl's eyes, was able to translate it now as shock and pain, and fully to understand what caused it.

"You let her think you a servant, didn't you?"

"Yes, sir."

"That was an act of cruelty, Richard."

"Father—no. I didn't mean to be cruel. I meant to tell her, but she was so—so pleased—thinking we could be friends."

"That it was unintentional cruelty does not excuse you."

Miserable and ashamed, Richard looked at the ground.

"Did you imagine you could continue the deception?"

30

"No, sir. I thought—hoped—to let her know—somehow—without hurting her."

"It did not occur to you that she would learn the truth when she looked at me?"

"No. I—didn't think of that."

"Well, your thoughtlessness has earned you a just punishment—in the thoughts she must now be having of you. Put the mare away, Richard. Then come back. Your supper has been kept warm for you, I believe."

"I don't want anything, sir."

"Very well. Come back in any case. I have more to say to you."

(3)

Richard wandered disconsolately under the stars.

Everything was wrong. His father was displeased with him. He was displeased with himself. And Bridget despised him.

Oh, yes, she must. Though meaning to be kind, he had been cruel. He had knowingly led her into error, deceived her, trifled with her. Or so it must appear, for she did not know or would ever believe he had acted solely in the interest of preserving that bright shining thing, that jeweled cobweb of dream, that inexplicable invisible two-way current that passed between them. She believed him loose and low-principled —the Master's son making sport with a servant girl. Even if he could tell her it wasn't that way, not that way at all, she wouldn't believe him. But he couldn't tell her, for he wouldn't be allowed to have words with her. Jane would see to that.

There she was, in the same house, but she might as well be back in Ireland for all the good it would do him to have her near. Never again would he look into the depths of those sapphire eyes, or kiss that sweet warm mouth, or be called *a chara dhil.* That is, if he were unable to elude Jane's watchful eye. Or if he obeyed his father.

There were barriers, his father had reminded him, that could not be crossed; he was a gentleman, she a servant. Of course he had not told his father that the barriers, though stronger than oak posts around a fort, had already proved vulnerable to assault, had indeed melted away like snow during that long drive home. He had, naturally and understandably, refrained from mentioning the manner in which he had soothed her fears there in the gloom of the pines, and the silent eloquence of the kiss he had substituted for the words he could not bear to say. Things were bad enough; it would scarcely have been wise to reveal the full extent of his indiscretions.

Or the full extent of the restless, undefined, ineffable yearning that filled him.

He was accustomed to obeying his father without question and strictly according to the letter of the law; but he had never before found himself in a situation that brought obedience into direct conflict with his own needs. Lacking a fund of experience upon which to draw, he had no established policy in regard to disobedience, nor any absolute knowledge of its consequences. Therefore, even while sadly contemplating the barrenness of a future in which the lovely Bridget was lost to him, he was also contemplating possible avenues of approach.

For instance, she would bring hot water upstairs in the morning, leaving a pitcher of it on the lowboy beside the nursery door, and at Jane and Vincent's door, and his father's. But not, unfortunately, at his, since he had as yet no need to shave, and hot water simply for washing his face was not among the few luxuries allowed him. Not even in winter, and this was June. He washed his face and hands outside at the pump, and once in a while under cover of darkness the rest of his body (in preference to carrying water to the bathhouse), when or if necessary and when or if he thought of it. Still, he would hear her in the hall and could open his door; but that offered no promise of conversation, and was somewhat risky besides, as other doors might open at the same time.

Later in the morning, however, after everyone had gone downstairs, she would make the beds and tidy up the bedrooms. The thought of her being there in his room, in his absence, brought further clear thinking to a halt while his mind dwelt imaginatively upon such evidence, tangible and intangible, as her presence would be certain to leave. Overcoming this mental block after a minute or two, he again picked up the main thread of his cogitations.

He could arrange to forget to bring something with him from his room, and thus be obliged to return for it, having predetermined a likely hour to find her there. This would require great finesse, for if working with the colts he would be under his father's eye, or if in the fields, Vincent's. Either of them would want to know what he had forgotten, and precisely why it was of sufficient importance to make him stop what he was doing and go to the house. The trouble was, he couldn't think of a single thing of paramount importance except the clothes on his back, and these he could hardly neglect to put on, no matter how great his haste to get outside and to the business of the day at break of dawn.

Another possibility somewhat indelicately suggested itself. One of her duties would be to empty the chamberpots from the children's room and Nurse's and Jane's. (The gentlemen of the house did not have this convenience. On Bridget's behalf he now felt deeply thankful for the lack, as to think of her performing this service for anyone but little girls and ladies would have been unendurable.) The twin Houses of Necessity, each discreetly shielded by lattices over which roses climbed, were at the end of the garden path. She would, therefore, make at least one daily trip past the garden. And if he could contrive to be hoeing the vegetables at that particular time . . . But no. He could not waylay her when she was performing this duty. Blushing at the thought, he put it from him.

If there were other avenues of approach, unhappily he could not bring them to mind. But that did not mean he would not somehow devise a way; it only meant he must tax his ingenuity as well as his patience. The barriers his father had talked about did not worry him; he had already brushed those aside, at least in his own mind. The real barriers were doors, hallways, back stairs, brick walls, and of course the vigilance of those who would set themselves as guardians of every gate, shutting her in and him out.

But he had to see her. He had to tell her he had not meant to deceive her, had not meant to be cruel. He had to tell her they were friends, true friends, no matter what their respective positions in the household. He had to tell her she was sweeter than the breath of springtime, fairer than the morning star, dearer than all his dearest dreams. He had to tell her, in short, that he loved her.

Because what could this be if not love?

He knew about love. He wasn't learned; his education, though not neglected, had been somewhat more than abbreviated; but he had read a good bit of Shakespeare and the other Elizabethan playwrights and poets, not to mention some of the Greeks, and . . . Yes, he

35

knew about love as they told of it, and unquestionably this was what they were talking about. Leander had his Hero, Tristram his Iseult, Romeo his Juliet; and he, Richard, had Bridget. That all those great loves of the past ended in tragedy did not necessarily mean his would. Those lovers had much greater obstacles to contend with: the Hellespont, King Mark, and family enmity. He had only walls and closed doors, unless that other shadowy thing must be counted. But walls had windows, and doors sometimes stood open. He must deal with the visible barriers first; the invisible could wait.

In his wanderings he had gone across the meadow, up the hill, along the edge of the field at its top, down again, through the orchard, and now stood at the end of the garden, looking at the great dark shape that was the back of the house. Not entirely dark. From a small window on the second floor a faint light shone; a mere glimmer, barely enough to be seen; the glimmer of one candle.

There were two doors at the back; one near the eastern corner, leading into the summer kitchen; the other in the center, leading into the hall that ran clear through the house. The hall was twenty feet wide at the front, but became narrow at the back, where most of the space was taken up by the main staircase—three steps to a broad landing and then a graceful curve to the second floor. Behind the landing was a partition, and behind the partition the servants' stairs; and directly above the rear entrance to the central hall was a room, hardly more than a large closet, formerly used for storage but a year ago converted to quarters for an upstairs maid. That room, then—the one with the small window from which came the faint gleam of candlelight—that room must be Bridget's.

The window went dark.

From the east terrace came a call, "Richie!" That was Vincent, ready to lock up for the night. Richard moved slowly along the garden path, eyes on the window. He thought he could see a pale blur. Was she looking out? Did she see him? His heart leaped, he raised a hand . . . But the blur was gone.

"*Richard!*"

Vincent's no-nonsense voice. Quickening his step, Richard went around the corner of the house to the terrace.

"Where the devil have you been?"

"Nowhere. Just taking a walk."

"A *walk*. I'll give you all the walk you want tomorrow, with a scythe in your hands."

Vincent closed and locked and bolted the terrace doors; carefully; methodically. Five spermaceti candles burned in the room, one in a single holder, the others in a four-branched silver candelabrum. In the same careful methodical way, he snuffed out the four. Vince did everything carefully, Richard thought, watching, and probably always had, even as a boy.

Richard had no recollections of his brother as a boy. In the very earliest he could summon from the misty realm of his own beginnings, Vince was already a mature and responsible sixteen. He could not picture Vince doing the things he sometimes did: dreaming away a summer afternoon; or racing the shadows of clouds on a windy day; or climbing to the top of a tall pine, where the trunk became a thin spire swaying dizzily in even the lightest breeze. Or falling in love.

With *Jane?* That seemed highly improbable. Indeed, fantastic did not seem too strong a word. Surely Jane had never inspired within the breast of his staid, hardworking, often harassed but always master-of-any-situation brother anything like the whirling, surging, inexpressibly tender emotions Bridget inspired in him.

He had been only seven years old when Vince married, didn't really remember much about it, and knew nothing at all of the courtship that preceded it— if any did. All he remembered was that Vincent's marriage took place quite soon after their mother's death; presumably—or so he had gathered from scraps of talk overheard—because someone was needed to run the house. He remembered being glad it was Vince and not his father who supplied someone to fill this need, for he had been told stories about wicked stepmothers and was not at all eager to acquire one. The stories had never dealt with sisters-in-law who had no fondness for small boys, and who were extremely sensitive to muddy boots, torn breeches, food accidentally dropped on tablecloths, and pet toads sometimes taken into one's bedroom for companionship.

His sister-in-law began saying almost at once that he needed to be flogged. Fortunately his father did not share her opinion; but the possibility that she might in his father's absence succeed in persuading Vincent that this need existed lent added fervor to his pleas to be taken along to the Colonies. He had always been—and still was—a little afraid of Jane, so tall and cold and disapproving; and always a little sorry for Vince. Long ago he had decided that when *he* married he would choose someone gentle and gay and warm and loving, as their mother had been; not necessarily someone who could run a house, and certainly not someone with the ungentle and, it seemed to him, unwomanly conviction that boys needed to be flogged. He even wondered, sometimes, if that wasn't why Vince seemed unworried about not having any sons. After all, if he had none he couldn't be called upon to flog them.

Vincent was kind. Quick to anger, sometimes, but only when excessively burdened by the amount of work to be done and the many vexatious problems that went with it. Looking at his brother's face lighted by the remaining candle, Richard thought he looked tired. It was a good strong face, weathered and browned and deeply lined. Vincent also resembled their father, though not so closely as did he. Vince was taller and heavier; his eyes were blue instead of that "Stafford gray"; his hair, which he wore long and clubbed, as their father did, was a much lighter brown. But his features were the same. The father-and-son brother-and-brother relationships were plain.

They were cut from the same cloth, and there were times when he felt very close to Vincent, despite the fourteen years between them. Times when he could talk about things; or, better yet, when there was no need to talk. Vince had understood about the chaise; how important it was; how his heart, not only his hands, had shaped each piece and lovingly fitted one to another. Sometimes Vince had sat watching him work, out there in the shed, even on cold winter evenings when the hearth fires in the house provided much more comfortable places to sit. He had seemed to enjoy watching the dream take shape; and though his words of praise were few, that may have been why they were treasured; why "A fine piece of work, Richie," meant more than all the admiring comments in the innyard at West-bridge. And Vince was the only one who called him "Richie." As far back as he could remember, Vince was the only one.

Feeling that closeness now, he would have liked to ask, "Vince, were you ever in love?" For he was torn by this new thing within him, this strange sweet longing that was torment and joy, and the need to speak of it, to let it surface, was great. But he dared not. The word "love" could not be mentioned. His father had not used that word, but another that he was ashamed to hear. It was natural, his father had said, for a young man to lust for an attractive young woman; but he must not foster any further thoughts of her attractiveness. "A gentleman," his father had said, "does not take advantage of a servant girl without forfeiting the name of gentleman."

Take advantage? Of someone you *loved?* But it had seemed prudent to accept his father's words without attempting to explain the true nature of his regard for Bridget—the bright beautiful soaring thing it was; prudent to let it be thought a passing fancy—though *he* knew it would never pass.

But he felt a deep sadness, as if alienated from his father and brother by this new feeling which he must keep secret. Always before, he had shared his feelings, or at least confessed them—hopes or fears or uncertainties or joys or griefs. And his love of Blue Meadow. *That* was no secret. Sometimes he stood lost in contemplation of the ribbons of rich brown earth when he should have been plowing, or of swaying feathery-topped grasses that should have been falling to his scythe; but these lapses were tolerated, for his father and brother understood that he was not intentionally idle, but rapt.

Would Vincent understand *this* feeling? Longing for a sympathetic word, he began, "Vince . . ." but then stopped, not knowing what he had been about to say, for there was nothing he dared say.

Vincent looked at him, waiting.

"I—hope I didn't keep you up. I'm sorry."

"If you had made me come looking for you," Vincent answered, "I was planning to toss you in the duck pond to cool off." A smile came with the words. And wasn't it a sympathetic smile? "Come along, Richie. You'll work it off tomorrow."

So Vince had been told. And thought it just something that could be worked off swinging a scythe. Not anything important—or deep—or eternal.

Silently Richard followed his brother through the hall. The candle cast its soft golden wavering light over the polished floor and steps and mahogany banister. The house was sleeping.

He undressed in the dark. Opening his windows, west and north—the night air *couldn't* be unhealthy, he reasoned, not the warm rose-scented air of a night in June—he stood looking at the starlit fields and woods and distant hills.

This was home. This was the place he loved. On all the earth there could not be another place so fair.

A chilling thought came. Suppose, if they learned how he felt about Bridget, they sent him away. Back to England. Away from Blue Meadow, which was one, now, with his very heart and soul.

On the heels of that thought came defiance, scarcely less chilling. They couldn't. He wouldn't go. He would hide in the woods, and live there, as the Indians had.

There was a secret place deep in the woods, on a south slope. He thought no one knew about it but himself, for they had taken no timber or firewood from there, the slope being too steep for the oxen. Great rocks enclosed it on three sides, but the south side was open, so that even in winter it was warmed all day by the sun. He thought how easy it would be to lay poles across the rocks and build a roof of sticks and sod. The spaces between the rocks could be filled in the same manner, and then sealed with mud, making a good tight room. Of course he would have to have a fire in winter, and the smoke would be seen; but perhaps not, for the hill

41

was between, and the surrounding trees were tall. Food would be a problem. He could hardly make off with a musket, or risk shots being heard in any case; so he would have to depend upon snares. But . . . Snare a rabbit, and then ruthlessly destroy it in spite of its terror-filled beseeching eyes? No, stealing was a lesser crime than murder. And anyway, would coming down in the night and helping himself to something from Blue Meadow—a piece of beef, a smoked ham, a bag of corn-meal—actually be stealing? Well, if that problem arose he'd face the moral issues when the time came.

In bed, he tried to compose his thoughts by remembering the afternoon in the innyard, and how gratifying had been the admiration of his chaise. But all that was *before* the arrival of the coach, and now seemed very long ago; he couldn't fix his thoughts upon it.

All he could think of clearly was that beautiful face upturned to his, and the feel of those warm sweet lips under his own; and of this moment, when she lay sleeping behind those walls and doors that must somehow be made to open.

Bridget was not sleeping.

Frozen by nameless emotions—nameless because too mixed, too overlapping, too jumbled and confused to be separated and identified—Bridget had somehow survived that first dreadful hour in this new place, this beautiful new place already spoiled for her by heart-break before ever she set foot across the doorsill. That hour had been taken up in following the new Mistress around; being shown the room she would sleep in and the rooms she would take care of each day; being told the exact duties she must perform; being given maid's clothes to wear and having her brown traveling dress and silver-buckled shoes taken from her—"I will put

42

these away, as you will not wear them again while you are here," the Mistress had said, and she had not dared protest, nor even answer, but with bowed head had let the lovely things be carried off, perhaps never to be seen by her eyes again.

But that did not matter, did not really matter, for her anguish was already too great to let her feel the loss of a dress or a pair of shoes. Her anguish was for the loss of something she had not really had; something held before her and then cruelly snatched away. For when the chaise carried them up the curving drive to this splendid house, and someone came down the steps to meet them, she had at once known that was the Master. Very simply dressed he had been in dark coat and breeches, white stockings, plain white linen neck-cloth, and the plainest of pewter buttons on his coat. He wore no wig, nor was his hair powdered in the fashion of fine gentlemen; dark brown turning gray, his hair was simply drawn back and tied with a bit of plain dark ribbon. But the simplicity had not misled her. Unmistakably he was the Master.

It was when he stood beside the chaise, close, looking past her to Richard, that she knew. For his was the same face to which she had raised her eyes there at the inn; many years older, but the same. The eyes were the same, and the cleanly-carved features, and even the lines his smile cut beside his mouth. And that was when she knew. Richard was not a servant boy. Richard was the Master's son.

Within her in that moment of recognition, everything became locked in icy stillness. Joy and warmth fled, their places taken by numbing grief and fear. Had she not been numb, she could not have endured the next hour; the pain would have torn her heart in two.

Wordlessly she had followed the Mistress about,

automatically recording the long list of her duties, though with but one part of her mind, for the rest was too fogged for thought. She was told which rooms were used and which were not (but the spare rooms also must be dusted and aired each day); and to which ones she must carry hot water as the first of her morning tasks. All but one of the occupied rooms were on the same side of the stairs. The exception, the northwest corner, was young Mr. Richard's room, the Mistress told her, adding that he was up and out at four, as a rule, but that she must not enter unless she found the door standing open. Then at last she was left alone in a little room at the end of a narrow passage beside the back stairs. It held a bed and a chest of drawers, and had one small uncurtained window at shoulder height.

No one could look in that window; but when she had extinguished her candle, she looked out. The night was very clear and full of stars. Far off she could see a dark wooded hill, and nearby a patch of small trees—young fruit trees, she thought, by their shape. Nearer, another square patch that might be a vegetable garden. And still nearer . . .

Someone was standing on the garden path. Quickly she drew back; and began to tremble, for she knew—oh, yes, even in the dark she knew—who that was.

The coldness and the numbness left her, and tears came.

He had deceived her. He had let her think they could be friends. He had put his arm around her. He had kissed her. And all the time, all the time, he had known and she had not, that they could never be friends, that they walked in two different worlds separated by a great abyss. She had looked into his face and thought him kind and good. She had seen everything she had ever hoped to see, someday, in a young man's face; everything she dreamed of, and her heart had opened to him as a flower opens to the sun.

Now she knew it was all a cruel mistake. He was a gentleman.

At the house in Philadelphia there were two young gentlemen, brothers, who for sport had laid a bet between them as to which would know her first. They had taken turns setting themselves in wait for her, in dark halls or stairways where she must pass and where they should not have been—the two fine young gentlemen of the house, in their velvets and laces and frills. One of them, impatient when the game ran on too long, tried by force to have his way with her, and she struck and clawed and fought free of him, and then ran, unaware that her hand still clutched his lace fall. And so their mother, their kind mother, learned of their game, and sent her away, not in anger but in sorrow, to this place in the country where she would be safe from rich young gentlemen who had nothing useful to do with their time and thought only of how to amuse and indulge themselves.

Safe? But no, no, he could not, could not be like those two.

A chara dhil . . .

She felt no anger toward him for the deception. What was it she felt, then? Grief for what she had thought was hers—a bright dream on the point of coming true. Fear—but not of him. No, it was another fear— that he might try to see her, speak to her, and then she would a second time be sent away, never to see him again in all her life. And what else? What of this other thing she felt? What of her willingness when he kissed her? What of the sweet fire that went through her at his touch, and still warmed her, reaching even now into the cold emptiness where joy had been?

(4)

In the first few days of Bridget's service at Blue Meadow, Richard had not so much as one glimpse of her; and she but one of him—on Sunday morning when from an upstairs window she watched the family set out for church.

To Richard it seemed that his father and brother between them made sure of having him under surveillance at all times; and as he reasoned that the best way to induce them to relax their vigilance was to give them not the slightest cause to maintain it, he applied himself to his work with vigor and apparent wholeheartedness, leaving the house before the first gray daylight advanced enough to pale the stars, and not returning until after darkness fell—except for meals, when he was of course in their company. If from time to time his thoughts and inner longings took possession of him, the resulting absentmindedness was not out of the ordinary, since daydreaming had always been numbered among his faults.

Bridget, too, was closely supervised during those first few days, for Cousin Elizabeth Peirson's letter of

46

recommendation did not eliminate Jane's need to rely on her own observations and judgment as to the quality of her new maid, and there were few moments when she was not close at hand, a sharp eye on the bedmaking and cleaning and other activities.

But on Sunday no one worked, except to do the essential things: outside, the tending of the livestock; inside, the making of beds and the preparation and serving of meals.

The family and most of the servants attended the Anglican Church, Jane told Bridget, in Willowfield; but as she was a Roman Catholic it was not required of her to accompany them, and was impossible for her to attend a Catholic church, as there was none within forty miles. She could, therefore, stay home with Cook, who was German and a Moravian and went to church only once a month, hers being at a distance of ten miles. Or, if she wished, she could go to Willowfield with the other girls and wait while they attended the service; afterward they would remain in the village for a few hours to visit their families or friends, and would be glad to take her with them. In any case, the afternoon would be hers to spend as she pleased.

Bridget chose to stay with Cook. From an upstairs window she saw Mr. Vincent Stafford helping the three children and the Mistress and Nurse into a wagon; and the Master and Richard on horseback, waiting so they all might go together. Richard . . . But not the servant boy in homespun farm clothes. No, the Richard she saw from the window was a gentleman's son in fine English-made riding coat and breeches and polished black boots. Silently her heart called to him, as if he were the same; but through tears she watched him ride away, out of her sight and lost to her.

By Monday there was abatement of the double

vigilance, Richard's exemplary behavior having satisfied his father, and Bridget's having satisfied Jane. In consequence Bridget learned that Richard was not as lost to her as she had thought.

On the previous Saturday she had been told to put fresh linens on all the beds, and temporarily to put the soiled things in the second-floor hall closet. Now she was told to bring them down for washing. When she did so, she found Richard tending the fire under the great iron kettle behind the house, and carrying buckets of hot water to fill the washtubs that were set just outside the summer kitchen. Pretending not to see him, she put her armful of linens on a bench beside the tubs, and turned quickly to go back in the house; but he also moved quickly, and as if by accident blocked her way, setting down one of the steaming wooden pails right in front of her. Under cover of emptying the other into a tub, he spoke to her, very low but distinctly, and the words he said were, "Bridget, I love you." The other girls, who would do the washing, were not ten feet away; but his back was to them, and the splash of the water came at the same moment as his words; they did not hear. She could only hope they did not see the color rise in her cheeks as with bent head she hurried back inside. When she came down a second time, he was gone. But all day the words sang in her heart, and all night touched her dreams with the music of harp and flute and soft Irish pipes.

After that, she had frequent opportunities to watch him from the windows, though limited to a very few minutes, for she dared not risk having the Mistress come to see what was delaying her.

East of the house was the field where every morning he exercised and trained the horses. There were bar jumps and a stone wall over which he sometimes took them. It was breathtaking to see them lift in a beautiful clean arc, and even more so when now and then one refused and she feared he must be pitched off by the sudden stop, though he never was. Twice she saw him riding a big red one that she thought must be the stallion he had told her of, and twice saw it rear almost as straight as a man stands, and did not know how he could remain in the saddle; but each time he simply leaned forward close against the creature's neck until in a moment its forefeet were again on the ground and it was trotting off as docilely as if no thought was in its mind except to please him.

In the afternoons, when her work took her to the spare bedroom at the southwest corner, she saw him in the hayfields, for west of the house lay the many broad acres of hay and wheat and Indian corn. Even though far off, and though half a dozen might be working near together in the same field, she was able to pick him out at once—no other moved in quite the same way, with such lightness and natural grace. His scythe flashed in smooth rhythmic strokes, and though the sun beat down he seemed unmindful of its heat, and tireless as he moved along the swath. Once she saw him cut carefully around a clump of bright gold flowers, and saw his brother point to them but then motion him on. Tears of gratitude filled her eyes for his brother's understanding and kindness in not making him lay those brave bright flowers low with his scythe.

And one night, just before going to bed, she heard a sound against the small high window of her room, such as sleet makes striking against window glass in the cold of winter. But there could not be sleet in June; and besides, the stars were shining. She looked out.

Again someone was on the garden path, but closer, only a few short paces from the house. And again she

49

knew who it was, down there in the soft dark lighted by stars. And knew what the sound had been, for even at that moment he was scooping up a handful of fine gravel to toss against her window. She should have drawn back, even though thinking he would not see her; but she did not draw back, and when he straightened and looked up, he did see her, and let the gravel slide from his hand, and tossed her a kiss, instead.

She was a long while going to sleep that night, and had strange, lovely and disturbing dreams.

It was on the next Sunday afternoon that she first ventured away from the house.

After helping Cook with the dinner dishes she had nothing to do with her free time. For what was there to do when one could neither read nor write, nor play upon the little Irish harp that had been left behind in Donegal, nor listen to the old men's tales of Cuchulainn and Fionn MacCumhaill? Timidly she asked if it was necessary to have permission from the Mistress to go walking up the path behind the house. Cook said no, as her time was her own, and anyway the *Gnädige Frau* was off visiting at the next farm; but not to stay too long in the sun, for the day was hot.

On the hill, looking down at the meadow and the stream, the checkered pattern of green fields and wheat turning gold, the farm buildings and the big red brick house set among its sheltering trees, Bridget remembered the note in Richard's voice that first evening when he said, "We are home;" and thinking how he must love this place, she loved it too, for his sake.

Her own home was far off, far beyond the great sea. Yet had she not stood one time on a higher hill than this, looking across Donegal Bay to the west and thinking that out there somewhere, far out across that bright water, lay the place of dreams that so many had sought and none had ever found—that wandering Isle of the Blest? *This* way she had looked, as had her people for hundreds of years before her, knowing that somewhere beyond the rocks and bays of Ireland's western edge lay a fairer land than any they had ever seen, fairer than any they had come to in all the long journey from their land of origin, wherever that had been, far back in the shadowy mists of time.

She had not traveled westward in search of a dream. She had come only because she was poor, and in her father's family were too many mouths to feed from one acre of stony ground. She and her brother had come, he one year older than herself; but on shipboard he was taken by a fever, and his body dropped into the sea long before the voyage was even halfway to its end. So she came alone to this vast and lonely land.

But God had been good to her. After only one year she was free, and soon would have silver money of her own, which somehow she must send to her father, though she had no idea how. They would tell her how; that is, if she could summon the courage to ask. And if she was allowed to stay.

Fear went through her with that thought. Fear of her own weakness; for though she knew she must never speak to Richard, nor give any sign of hearing if again he spoke to her, she could not trust herself to obey the dictates of her mind against the stronger dictates of her heart. Suppose they met some time when no one else was there. Would she turn her eyes from him, then, and close her ears, and in silence hurry away?

"Bridget."

At first it seemed only some trick of the wind in the trees, making her think she heard him softly call her name. But . . .

"Bridget. Over here." He was standing at the edge

of the woods, his horse beside him, where a cart trail led out from the trees to the hilltop field. Beckoning he said, "Come slowly. Pick a few flowers. Someone may be watching you from down below."

And without hesitation, without even the briefest struggle between mind and heart, she did as she had feared she would, did not turn away but went to him. When she reached the trees he took her hand and drew her into their shelter.

"I saw you come up here," he said. "I came another way. By the road, as if I were going to the Spensers or Findlays. No one knows I came here. I had to see you, Bridget."

Then for a long moment neither of them spoke, but simply looked at each other, each seeing the unspoken thing reflected in the other's eyes. And then he put his arm around her, and held her close, and kissed her, and said as he had said before, "I love you."

"No," she pleaded, "no, you must not. I be a servant . . ."

"That doesn't matter. We are just two people. And you are everything I ever dreamed of, everything I want, everything I love."

"No, no, I cannot be."

"You *are*. But you haven't said . . . Bridget, do you love me?"

"Yes," she whispered. "So much I love you, there does not be room for aught else in my heart."

"And do you believe heaven made us for each other?"

Tears filled her eyes. "Ah, now, that I cannot. Heaven made you a gentleman, and me but a servant girl."

Confidently he answered, "I do not think there are such distinctions in heaven. In the sight of God we are

all the same. I'm sure it says so somewhere in the Bible—
the Authorized Version."

"I be not able to read the Bible."

"Well then, you will have to believe what I tell
you."

"But the laws of God and the laws of men—I think
they do not be always the same."

Richard, whose reading of the Bible had foundered
somewhere about halfway along in Genesis, supple-
mented only by Ecclesiastes and the Twenty-third
Psalm, decided against pursuing a discussion of the laws
of God, even though sure that love must be one of those
laws. Anyway, there were more intimate matters to discuss.

"Bridget, when I met you at the inn I didn't mean
to deceive you. I couldn't tell you who I was—I was
afraid to. Afraid you would let it shut us off from each
other before we had time to become friends. I didn't
mean to be cruel. Please tell me I wasn't cruel, or at least
that you forgive me."

"Cruel you could not be. And forgive you I cannot,
there being naught to forgive—unless it be the bringing
to me of great joy and this beautiful thing in my heart."

"Then you did feel it too, the first minute, just as
I did—this thing between us?"

"The very first minute—when I looked into your
face—that minute I felt it."

"That's what I hoped you'd say." Richard drew a
deep breath, looked long into her eyes, kissed her again,
and said, "Bridget, I want to marry you."

Dizzily the world rocked as they stood there together on a glorious summit higher than all the highest
mountains piled one on top of another, all the vast
reaches of infinity spread in rainbow colors below and
above and about them.

She descended first from that lofty pinnacle, smiling through tears for the dream that could never be more than a dream.

"Ah, Richard, *a rún*, we be not in heaven at all, but on earth, where men's laws say what can and cannot be. You be the Master's son, I but a servant in his house. You cannot marry a servant girl. He would not let you."

"No," Richard admitted, "not right now. But the time will come when I can marry you, Bridget."

"I think that time will not come, *a chara*. If they learn you have such thoughts, they will send me away."

"Then I will go with you."

"Not so. You would be cast off and disowned, and could never again come back to this place you love. To pay so high a price for your kind feeling toward me . . . No."

"I will pay *any* price, Bridget. I love you. I want you to be my wife."

"Great happiness does be on me for that wanting, but it cannot ever be, for you must marry one of your own station. In the kitchen they say you will one day marry the young lady on the next farm."

"No. That young lady and I are cousins, and we're friends. But that's all."

"They say she will bring with her much money and many acres of land, and all will be yours when you wed her."

"But I'm not going to wed her. I love *you*."

"I think these things do not be decided by love. It be already arranged, I hear them say."

"That's only kitchen talk, Bridget. It's far from 'arranged.' No. Unless I marry you, I will never marry anyone."

He made this passionate avowal from the depths

of his heart and believed it true; but she was older than he, not in years but in wisdom, and knew how short a time "never" can often be.

With smiling tenderness she said, "Ah, but you must, for this too I hear them say—that upon you it rests to provide a son to carry on your father's name."

"But, Bridget—*we* can have a son!"

He knew at once that he had gone too far. His tongue had run away with him, beyond any limit of propriety. He had said a totally outrageous thing. One did not before marriage—and very possibly not afterward either—speak directly and openly of such matters to a young woman. Children simply happened. To speak of them beforehand was to imply explicit knowledge of *how* they happened; and, even worse, in the full light of day to suggest an act that took place—somehow—only under the shielding cloak of night.

They looked at each other in shock.

When the shock passed, color flamed in her cheeks and she closed her eyes; did not merely lower her eyes but altogether closed them, so the black lashes lay against the rose-petal cheeks in a way that all but overwhelmed him with intense awareness of her loveliness. Being already all but overwhelmed by those strange pulsating electric currents which increased tenfold as his own moment of shock passed, he was plunged into despair by the thought that he had offended her so grossly she could no longer bear to look at him. The beautiful high mountains started to crumble.

"Please, Bridget, I didn't mean . . . " But how could he explain what he didn't mean without offending her anew? "Bridget . . ."

She opened her eyes. To his boundless relief they were filled not with tears or anger or horror, but with love and laughter. And he heard it again—the silver water running over golden sands. Warm and bright and tender, her laughter healed the self-inflicted wounds of his despair.

"*A chuisle mo chroídhe*, I do be thinking your heart leaps ahead of your reason, and your tongue ahead of both. What talk can we have of a son, when we cannot even with good sense talk of marriage, except as a night-time dream that addles our brains through coming by day? So, now. Will you not walk me a way down this path? For I be afraid to go alone among these great trees—but with you I be not afraid."

Wide enough for an oxteam, the path allowed them plenty of room to proceed three abreast, Bridget on one side, Richard's horse—Sea Mist, a fine gray gelding—on the other, and he with a hand for each. Her hand in his was so trusting—he could almost have wished for some danger against which to protect her; but as there had not been a black bear seen in the woods for the past three years, the worst he could hope for was the sudden appearance of a white-tailed deer, which might at least startle her, or a fox which might stand in the path for a moment before yielding the right of way. As it was, they met nothing more formidable than an occasional squirrel, and a broad-winged hawk that dropped down among the trees and rose again with some small forest creature in its talons. Bridget gasped and clutched his hand and cried, "Ah, the poor wee thing!" thus giving him the opportunity to offer physical comfort by tight-ening the pressure of his own hand, and philosophical comfort by explaining, "It is simply the way of nature."

The path led gradually downward to a clearing, where Richard took a coiled strip of rawhide from his pocket and tied Sea Mist to a tree, saying there was a place farther down that he wanted to show her. After walking some fifty paces along the edge of a steep slope, they left the trail and went straight down among the trees. There was little undergrowth, but here and there a fallen branch over which he assisted her with great care so she would not trip and fall, or tear her petticoat; and because of the steepness of the slope he of course kept firm hold of her hand.

Ahead were his rocks. Gray-green lichens dulled them on the north side; but on the south, caught by sunlight—for beyond that point no large trees grew, the slope becoming too nearly vertical to support them— mica crystals glittered like jewels. Within the semicircle formed by the rocks, soft grasses pushed up through the dry brown carpet of last year's leaves, and among the grasses wild columbine and other flowers of summer bloomed.

"At home I would be thinking this a fairy place," Bridget said in a hushed voice. "I would not dare set foot in such a place, for fear of the *Sluagh Sidhe* who live inside the hills."

"Nobody lives inside this hill, Bridget, unless perhaps the spirit of a Leni-Lenape Indian. But you needn't be afraid," he hastened to assure her. "They were friendly Indians, and he's a friendly spirit. He talks to me in the wind, and the rustle of leaves, and the songs of birds. Listen."

They stood very still, listening to the sounds of stillness—the sighing of the wind, the secret whisperings, the singing of unseen birds; and to the stillness itself, the far deep age-old stillness that had its beginning at the beginning of time.

"I think the Indian spirit does be lonely and sad," Bridget said softly at last, "all his friends long gone and only he remaining. He must like you to come, Richard."

"He puts up with me," Richard answered. "And perhaps *my* spirit will come back here someday; then we'll be company for each other."

"I do be glad you are young, and that day far off. But let us not talk of spirits, *a chara*. See there . . . What name do you call the flowers of red and yellow, with the faces hanging down and the little spurs pointing up?"

"Columbine. Also rock bells. Want to pick some? Or . . . No, you might be asked where you found them, and here at Blue Meadow this is the only place they grow. And—this is a secret place. *Our* secret place, now."

He looked into her eyes. Losing himself as always in those blue depths, he felt a rising tide of emotion that threatened to sweep him away as flood waters sweep away all in their path. He forced himself back to safe footing.

"Can we sit here a while, Bridget?"

"I think I must not stay too long," she answered, "or at the house Cook will wonder, and maybe ask questions. But . . . Yes, a few minutes longer I can stay."

He took off his riding coat and spread it on the ground, despite her protest—"Your fine Sunday coat, Richard!"

"It will keep your dress clean. We can't let Jane catch you with woods soil on your dress. There now."

She sat down. He dropped beside her, reclining, propped on an elbow. The leaves were warm and dry, the grass soft and fragrant. Sunlight fell in dancing patterns through the branches of twin young beech trees that formed a doorframe on the south. And the rocks hid them from all the world . . .

"So quiet," Bridget whispered. "I think there never

58

was a place so quiet. And so far it seems from any-where."

"It's a separate world, Bridget. Our world. Will you come here next Sunday? And every Sunday all summer long?"

Smiling, she promised, "If so it be I can. But I fear they find out"—the smile faded—"and then they will send me away."

"No one will find out. We'll be careful. And no matter what, they won't send you away. I won't let them. We'll come here, and I'll build us a house—right here. It will be easy."

She smiled again. "You be the sweet one, Richard, to have these thoughts. And so young . . ." Shyly she touched his cheek. "No beard you have, but skin smooth and clear as a girl's, though burned brown by the sun. I think it no wonder the Indian spirit likes you. He may be thinking you one of his own."

Her fingers touching his cheek sent a tingling sensation all through him—that same strange current, but even warmer and more delightful than before. He caught her hand and kissed it.

"There—that's the first time I ever kissed a lady's hand."

"Then you have yet to do so, for I be not a lady."

"Oh, yes, you are. And you have the hands of a lady. So soft and white and—beautiful."

"Soft they would not be, if I do much work. The Mistress in Philadelphia did not truly need me—it was only with a friend she came to the riverside when the contracts were sold; but in her kindness she bought mine from the owner of the ship, bidding much more than it was worth, I think, because she saw how frightened I was, and felt sorry for me."

59

"She saw more than that, Bridget. She saw how lovely you are."

"Ah, not so. Could you have seen me then, you would not call me lovely. A poor Irish girl in rags—so thin and weak from the sickness aboard ship—hair all in tangles—no shoes on the feet—and hands still rough, then, from the work I do at home, such work as ladies know naught of."

"But that doesn't mean anything," Richard said. "There's nothing wrong with work. My hands are rough, too. Look." He held out his hand, palm up. "Feel it."

Gently she traced the record left there by scythe and ax and hoe and plow handle. He imagined he could see little sparks pass between her finger and his palm; he did not have to imagine that he felt them.

"You be strong, Richard. Not with bigness but like the steel. From the window I watch you work, and not ever does any man do more than you, or with such ease and quickness."

Though he found these words very pleasing, conscience required that he correct the mistaken impression she had of his abilities. "It may look that way to you, Bridget, but actually the others do a great deal more of the really hard work. Most of the things I do are easy."

"But I think you do things no other can. I watch you ride the horses, and with none but you would they fly like birds!"

He laughed and admitted, "Well, yes"—for had his father not told him that false modesty is worse than conceit?—"I suppose that's what I do best. And maybe I was showing off, because I saw you at the window. But . . . Bridget, the windows are too far away. We have to see more of each other."

"Do we see more of each other, *a rún*, then I fear we no longer see each other at all."

"But we must. We belong together. There has to be a way. . . ."

"Already we have the way."

"Meeting here on Sundays? But a whole week between . . . I can't go a whole week without seeing you, Bridget; without having you close."

"I think we be close without the seeing. As in the *Gaedhilge* we would say, '*M'anam istigh thú.*'"

"How would we say it in English?"

"We would say it, 'The soul inside me be you.'"

So soft her voice, so tender her smile. So deep the pleasure of having her with him in his secret place. So enveloping the stillness, so magical the sense of being in a world apart. . . .

Love was summer sunlight. Love was the fragrance of earth and leaves; the songs of birds; the wind in the trees. Love was a cresting wave, like the sea surf when it rises in an arched wall of green shadow and sunlit foam. . . .

"Richard, I think now it be time I go."

"No, not yet. Just one minute more . . ."

Love was a touch, a caress, a silent promise spoken from heart to heart. . . .

Abruptly the silence was broken. From the clearing where Richard's horse was tied came a call: "Richard!"

Bridget, in panic, would have leaped to her feet had he not caught her by the shoulders. In an urgent whisper he said, "No—stay down! Move closer to the rocks—no one will see you." Hurriedly he put on his coat, fumbling with the buttons.

Again the call, and the sound of a horse trotting along the trail above them. Bridget sat huddled against

61

one of the great gray rocks. He knelt beside her, taking her trembling hands in his.

"Don't be afraid. It's only Meg Findlay—my cousin. She won't find us—she's going on down the trail."

"No, Richard, no! She comes again!"

The horse trotted back to the clearing. A long-drawn shout, "Hallo-o-o, Richard!"

"She waits for you," Bridget whispered. "You must go."

"But Bridget, then you'd have to go back alone. Wouldn't you be afraid to?"

"No, no . . . " Not so afraid as she was of being discovered there. The awesome loneliness of the forest, the towering crowding trees, the lurking unknown dangers . . . Nothing could be so fearful as being discovered there in the woods, with Richard, by the young lady Richard was to marry. "I be not afraid. Go, Richard. Go quickly, I beg you!"

Though unwilling to leave her, he knew she was right. Meg would wait; might even leave her horse in the clearing with his and come searching for him. There were bare places on the trail, where in the soft earth she might see their footprints. The footprints would disappear at that point directly above the rocks. She might come down. . . .

"Well—wait a minute or two after you hear us pass above. It will be safe, then, to go up—you won't be seen. Now remember—first to the right, and then, at the clearing, to the left, and that takes you straight up to the field. You'll remember, won't you? It isn't far, and there's nothing to be afraid of, nothing at all."

He added a quick kiss to these reassuring words. But he didn't want to go. It seemed wrong to go; cowardly; as if he were forsaking her. He knew it was in fact the opposite; but did she? Did she understand that his only fear was the fear of losing her? His only motive the safeguarding of the future—*their* future?

"Bridget, I don't want to leave you like this. I'm doing it because right now it seems the wisest thing to do. But I never will again. Never. I'll find a way to work things out so we can be together all our lives. . . ."

(5)

The bright day ended in a gathering of clouds across the west. After darkness fell there were flickers of lightning near the horizon, and distant mutterings of thunder; but when the wind rose it carried the storm southward, far from Blue Meadow.

Richard went early to his room. Not to sleep—he had no wish to sleep; but to be alone with his turbulent secret. And with his anxiety, which kept pushing to the surface. When his father asked, "Where did you go this afternoon?" the answer, "Riding with Meg," not only had the sound of truth but was, fortunately, indeed the truth. In other respects, however, he was less fortunate. Because his thoughts were far afield, while going about his evening chores he did some things twice and others so abstractedly that he could not remember whether he had done them at all, and had to go back to the barn to make sure, which made him late for supper. Ordinarily he was inclined to eat somewhat too quickly, and had to keep reminding himself that it was ill-mannered to do so (for if he didn't someone else would—his father or brother or, with biting sarcasm,

64

Jane); but tonight he had little disposition to do more than look at the food on his plate. His father asked if he was feeling unwell. Replying that he was quite well—just fine, in fact—he reached for his wine glass, but too hastily, with the result that instead of picking up the glass he knocked it over. The mishap turned out to be, in one way, beneficial: the ice of Jane's wrath completely encased them all, and he was permitted to sit in abashed silence throughout the rest of the meal, and immediately thereafter to retire to his room.

The anxiety persisted. He knew, of course, that Bridget had found her way safely back to the house. Or rather, he knew this to be the only reasonable assumption. He had not seen her; but if she had not returned, word of her absence would have reached him. They would be searching for her; and since he knew the woods better than anyone else did, he would have been sent to join in the search. Obviously nothing was amiss; nevertheless he would feel much better if he could satisfy himself beyond any question as to her safe return. Besides, she had been badly frightened by Meg's coming, and by being left alone in the woods. Perhaps she was still frightened. Perhaps even after reaching the open field, even after coming down to the house, and even now in her room, the fear remained. To see her at this hour was impossible (also unthinkable); but if only he could speak to her, say comforting things, tell her how much he loved her—then the fear would go.

Restlessly he paced back and forth. The far-off rumbles of thunder continued, but over Blue Meadow the moon was shining. The hour was late—ten o'clock at least. Everyone else was in bed. And asleep.

He had taken off his coat, which he was required to wear at mealtimes (a work frock not being gentlemanly), and his shoes; but that was all, for an undefined and as yet unacknowledged intention lay at the back of his mind. The intention, even in its early nebulous stage, superimposed on the anxiety a highly pleasurable excitement; and the excitement, in turn, served to clarify and strengthen the intention. If there was a risk, he dismissed it as negligible. In younger days, when he and Meg used to play at being Indians, he had learned how to steal through the woods without cracking a single dry twig under his foot. Here in the house there were of course no twigs to crack, nor leaves to rustle. If he were to go the entire length of the hall and back, no one would hear him, even if anyone was awake. But he didn't have to go the length of the hall. The distance from his room to the passage leading to the back stairs was no more than ten or twelve feet.

Opening his door, he stood looking into the hall, listening. There was no sound, and no light except that behind him—pale silver of the moon at first quarter, now dropping into the west. The half-formed intention crystallized into a firm resolve, and silently he moved forward toward the servants' stairs.

To his surprise—yet not entirely to his surprise, for somehow he had felt that she would be awake, as he was—a vertical strip of light marked the tiny bedroom. The door was a few inches ajar, a candle still lighted. To guide him? To welcome him? Had she known he would come? No, she could never have imagined he would do anything so bold—he could never have imagined it himself! But here he was, every step taking him nearer to that open door, to the candlelight, to his love.

Softly he knocked, and spoke her name very low. He couldn't see her, but he thought he heard an indrawn breath and a startled move. Then a whisper: "Richard, you should not . . ."

"I just want to know if you're all right. Are you?"

"I . . . Yes, I be all right."

"But it's late and you're not asleep. Why not, Bridget? Because of what happened this afternoon? Are you still frightened?"

"Please, not so. It be only the heat—the room too hot for sleeping. So by the candle I mend my old shawl where it be raveled. And I open the door but not much air comes."

"What about your window?"

"I think the Mistress does not wish me to open the window."

"Well, she doesn't wish you to suffocate, either. That little room, and no air . . . You'd better open the window, Bridget."

"I cannot. The sash be fastened."

"No, it's probably just stuck. Would you like me to open it for you?"

"Richard, I be in my nightdress."

A brief silence while he reflected upon this. He had once happened to catch sight of Jane in her nightdress—an astonishingly voluminous garment, more concealing than the dresses she wore in the daytime. He remembered thinking it odd that a woman would wear such a dress at night, when she was going to be under the bedcovers anyway. He himself seldom wore anything in bed—only his shirt, sometimes, on cold nights.

Cautiously he asked, "What's it like? Has it a high neck and long sleeves? Does it reach all the way to the floor? Is it rather like—well—a tent?"

Soft laughter came out to him. "It be so. But . . ."

"Then I think it's all right for me to come in. The only thing—I haven't my coat on, or shoes. Do you mind?"

Again the silvery ripple of laughter, quickly silenced—he pictured her pressing a hand to her mouth. The margin of light widened; the door opened.

Had not the sound of her voice and her laughter already established the unquestionable reality of her presence, Richard might have wondered if his eyes were conjuring up a heavenly apparition, a vision of loveliness beyond the most extravagant dreams of mortal man. Her long white nightdress was made, he later realized, of quite ordinary coarse linen; but at that moment in the soft golden light it seemed a fabric of exquisite fineness and purity, hanging from her shoulders in graceful Grecian folds. She was not wearing her housecap; the candle, set high on a chest of drawers, cast its gleam on her hair, and little loose ends of the black curls, catching that gleam, gave her a nimbus. He could only look at her; he could not speak.

"Richard, the window . . ."

The window? "Oh—yes. I'll open it, Bridget."

She stepped back to let him enter.

The room was so small, and so tucked away where you really wouldn't expect to find a room, that it seemed to him as secret as his place in the woods. And the door was so close to the chest, the chest to the bed, that two people must necessarily be in very close proximity to each other. Also, as she had said, it was hot; and that may have been why his own internal temperature seemed suddenly to heighten.

Quickly he addressed himself to the window, which he was able to open without much difficulty. Then he took a little melted tallow from the candle, rubbing it into the grooves of the frame, and raising and lowering the sash a number of times until it moved freely. But there was no stick to prop it.

"Have you anything, Bridget? Anything stiff."

"I have . . . Wait, but do not look, please."

Though puzzled by this request, he respected it and did not look. He heard her pull open a drawer. Presently she handed him an unidentifiable object, tightly rolled, with the feel of cloth, but rigid.

Curiosity got the better of him. "What is it?"

"It be stays."

His knowledge of undergarments worn by women was not extensive; but he did know from Meg of a strange and extremely uncomfortable contrivance of cloth and whalebone into which they laced themselves for the support and improvement of their figures. At parties Meg was often in an ill humor because custom demanded that a young lady be properly laced. . . . "Oh, *damn* these stays! How can I *dance* when I can't *breathe!*" He knew she refused to wear them at any other time, and he was unable to imagine Bridget ever wearing them at all. Bridget's figure needed neither support nor improvement. Besides, he had put his arm around her that very day and certainly had felt no whalebone!

"What ever do you want with stays?"

"The Mistress gives them to me with the new petticoats and other things. I do not wear them. So stiff—how could I do the work that needs the bending over?"

"Well"—Richard was laughing as he propped the window—"this is a better use than they were intended for. There you are. Now you'll be able to sleep."

He had made the little operation last as long as he could. There was nothing more to be done, no further excuse for staying. But if he released his hold on this moment, how long might it be before such a moment was his again?

"Come look, Bridget. The moon won't be full for another week, but look how bright everything is."

They stood close together, looking out at the silvered fields. The breeze from the northwest found the window; they felt its cool touch on their faces. It brought into the room all the freshness and sweetness of the night, the smell, and even the taste. They breathed it in, and it became part of them.

Richard turned his head. Not looking at the fields; looking at her. Again he saw the candlelight on her hair; and on her cheek; and in her eyes, for she also turned, raising her eyes to his. He meant only to take her hand; instead, he took her in his arms.

Perhaps it was the candlelight. Or the trapped heat not yet dispelled by the air coming in the window. Or the feel of her hair, the curls a little damp and clinging where they lay against her forehead or her neck. Or the sweet yielding of her body to his arms, her mouth to his kiss. Whatever it was, it was quick. Too quick.

He should have known. He should have guarded against that quickness; for though innocent in the ways of a man and a woman, he was far from ignorant of the ways of male and female—did he himself not handle Red Earl when he served the mares, and did he not know how in an instant that swift fire rises, and how it overpowers and puts all else aside? Yes, he knew; and perhaps even at that moment remembered—but then it was too late.

"Bridget, I love you, I want you. Do you want me? Say you do. Say you love me. Say I may have you . . . Bridget, Bridget, I must have you . . ."

Filled with shame and remorse, Richard stood looking at the guttering candle, wishing its small flame would die, wishing the room and the whole world would be plunged into darkness so he would never have to see the bitter accusation in her eyes. He had violated her; not only her body but far more despicably her trust. And he had hurt her, had forced from her a stifled little cry of pain, yet had not spared her. Now the fire and the ecstasy were gone, only shame and sorrow were left; for the beautiful thing—the shining dream—was destroyed by his carnal act. He had said, "I'm sorry, Bridget, I'm sorry," as he turned away. But she would never forgive him. He would never forgive himself.

He heard the slight creaking of the bed, and knew she was now standing behind him.

"Richard, *I* be not sorry."

At first, only the sound of the words reached him; not a bitter sound; not even reproachful. When the meaning came, he turned, dazed, and saw that she was smiling.

"Bridget"—a wild awakening of hope—"you aren't angry? You don't hate me?"

Tears made the smile brighter. "How could I be hating one I love?"

"You still love me?"

"A *mhíle ghrádh*—a thousand times over I love you."

"But I took advantage of you."

"Not so, when I be willing."

"Do you really mean—you wanted me—as I wanted you?"

"It be—how did you say?—the way of nature, *a rún*."

Very gently he kissed her. "You are good, kind, sweet . . . and so dear, so dear to me . . ."

"As you to me," she answered. "But now you must go. So late the hour—I fear I do not wake, and the Mistress will be angry."

71

"Yes, I'll go; but in the morning, early, I'll see you again."

"No. We must not be seen near together, not any time. We must not speak, or even look at each other. None must ever know."

"But Bridget! We can't just . . . I mean, it's all right for everyone to know about us now. Because now we have to be married. I'll tell my father we have to be married."

In great alarm she protested, "No, no, I beg you, tell nothing! We cannot marry, and they will send me away. Please say nothing. Please—because we cannot!"

"But we must! I have known you. My father will let us marry."

"No, Richard, no! He would not let you. We must say nothing, nothing. You be my life now—my *whole* life—I could not wish to live if they send me away—if we be parted!"

"We won't be parted. My father is kind. And more than kind. Even if I didn't want to marry you, I would have to—he would *make* me, as a matter of honor and —and decency."

But he could not persuade her. She continued to plead with him to say nothing; and helpless in the face of her fear and desperation, he consented. Though only for a time, he said; only until he could convince her that no matter how much his father might disapprove he would let them marry, because not to do so would be wrong. And meanwhile . . .

"You will come to the woods next Sunday?"

"Richard, I be afraid. Your cousin, should she find us . . ."

"Then may I come here again—at night?"

Faintly she answered, "If much you wish to, yes. But you will keep the promise to speak of us to no one?"

"I will keep my promise, Bridget. *Both* my promises—to say nothing, and to marry you. So, until next time . . ."

"*Slán agat, a rún.*"

The whisper followed him through the dark passage.

Back in his room he dropped down on the bed, just as he was, intending merely to lie there for a while, to think about what had happened and to plan a course of action—how to banish her fears, how to tell his father.

Outside, the wind sang in the trees; but he fell asleep listening to more distant music—angelic lutes accompanying the sweet chorusing voices of cherubim and seraphim and all those lovers of the past, from the open portals of heaven.

(6)

One night in July, the children's Nurse quietly died in her sleep.

At seven o'clock when Bridget came bringing a pot of tea, the jug of hot water she had brought at six was still on the lowboy beside the door; and the door was still closed, though customarily at that hour it stood open so she could enter the sitting room, which connected the old lady's bedroom and the children's, and place the tea tray on a table. Hearing footsteps within, and thinking her own may have been heard, she waited. The door was opened by ten-year-old Harriet; or, as it seemed, by all three girls, for the younger ones—Eleanor, nine, and Virginia, six—were crowding close.

Bridget smiled at them, as she always did—except when they were in their mother's company. Not to smile was very hard indeed—they were such beautiful little girls, one so like the other, fair as angels with their pale translucent skin and golden hair; but always, too, she felt anxious, thinking it not altogether good that they had a look more of the next world than of this.

"I bring your Nurse's tea," she said.

Their three voices—flutelike and as delicate as their faces—answered her, one following immediately upon the other like three measures of music sliding down the scale.

"Norrie is still sleeping," said Harriet.

"With her eyes open," said Eleanor.

"We can't wake her up," said Virginia.

To Bridget the words meant only one thing; but she did her best to hide the cold shock of understanding.

"Ah, now, perhaps she be unwell." Entering the room, Bridget quickly set down the tray. "Should you not go tell your mother, Miss Harriet?"

"No. Mama doesn't like us to come downstairs before eight o'clock. Bridget"—the child's lower lip was trembling and her eyes were filled with fear—"we want you to come wake Norrie."

"Yes," said Eleanor, "you come, Bridget."

"Come," Virginia commanded, taking her hand.

Bridget in her seventeen years had many times seen death. She had no need to touch the still figure on the bed. "Go ndeanaidh Dia trócaire ar a h-anam," she whispered, crossing herself. Then, turning to the girls: "It be best we do not try to wake her—that deep she sleeps. And best that you go now to your own room, while I fetch your mother to care for the dear lady."

Running down the back stairs, she found their mother in the kitchen. A coldly disapproving look made her slow her step.

"Why are you tearing around in that senseless manner, Bridget? What ails you?"

"Mistress—I beg pardon—but Nurse be dead."

Jane, having always found the Irish imaginative and excitable, resisted the impact of that word.

"Don't be ridiculous. She is merely sleeping."

"Mistress—pardon—no. She be dead many hours."

Cook was staring. The maids were staring. And Jane could no longer doubt that the girl knew what she was talking about.

"Go at once and tell Mr. Marcus Stafford. Be quick!"

Bridget ran from the kitchen.

Mr. Marcus Stafford was at the far end of the training field; it was to Richard she delivered her message.

"Norrie—is dead?"

The sadness of his voice and look made her tears start.

Death be cruel, she thought, watching him ride out to tell his father. Even the death of an old woman. For they loved her, they all loved her. And the poor little ones . . . Who will tell them? Who will stop their tears?

By opening their bedroom door just a crack, the girls could look into the sitting room and across to Nurse's door. They saw their mother go through that door, come rather quickly out again, and disappear into the hall. Presently they heard footsteps on the stairs; then their grandfather's voice, "When, Jane?"

"Sometime in the night, apparently."

Their mother and grandfather appeared in the sitting room, went into the bedroom, closed the door.

They knew and yet did not know. Fear of what they knew, and even greater fear of what they didn't know, kept them close to the crack, waiting, watching, only half breathing. When they saw Bridget come in, hesitantly, and pick up the tea tray, they pulled the door wide, and with one accord, moved by nameless dread and nameless need, rushed upon her, surrounding

76

her with reaching hands and whispering voices. "Bridget! Bridget!"

She put the tray down and gathered them into her arms, hugging them close, all three. "Ah, now, my dears, my pretty dears . . ."

They clung to her. Harriet knew about death. "Bridget, is she. . . ?" Eleanor knew but could not accept. "She's sleeping, isn't she? Just sleeping?" Little Virginia knew only that fear was in the room. "What's wrong with Norrie? What's wrong?"

"Now there be nothing wrong"—Bridget's back was to the other door, she did not see it open—"for all things be God's will, and therefore right, as in but a moment your mother and your good *seanathair* will explain to you."

Jane, seeing her daughters in the embrace of a servant girl, was too taken aback to summon the sharp words of rebuke so urgently called for; but Marcus, perceiving what had been asked and what so readily given, at once made the most of it.

"Bridget, my dear, will you do us all the kindness of taking the children to the third floor and remaining with them for the rest of the day? Their meals and yours will be sent up. Forget your other duties."

"Father," Jane protested, "nothing has been done . . ."

"None of us will suffer from sleeping in unmade beds tonight, Jane. You will be occupied, and the children cannot be left alone to deal with something that is hard enough for even the experienced to deal with. Their instincts have led them to seek comfort from one well qualified to give it, and for that we may thank God." He laid a hand gently on Virginia's little lace cap. "Go with Bridget now, my darlings. Do as she says—and believe what she tells you."

Willingly they obeyed. Indeed, to have compelled Virginia at that moment to do anything else would have required physical force—so tightly she clutched Bridget's hand.

On the third floor were three spare bedrooms west of the stairs, and one large room to the east—the children's schoolroom, workroom, and playroom. Here they had learned their letters, and to do sums; to knit and sew and fashion a patchwork quilt; to paint on china and on glass; to play the spinet; to weave dainty baskets of straw or willow. And here, when the prescribed daily amount of attention had satisfactorily been given to these various proper accomplishments of proper young ladies, they were permitted to amuse themselves with toys and games.

That day, going to their third floor room with Bridget, they at first did none of these things; for that day their world had fallen apart, and must be gathered together again, and rebuilt.

Sitting with them on a sofa—one on each side and Virginia on her lap—Bridget explained that their dear Nurse had gone to God; and that although they would never see her again in this world, they would someday be with her in Heaven; and that they must not grieve, for it was the reward for her goodness that so sweetly and gently her soul had left her body, and that God in His mercy had taken her to eternal rest and eternal happiness.

But the children wept.

"Why did God take her from us, when we love her?"

"What will we do without her?"

"We want her here. We *want* her!"

"And gladly would she have stayed," Bridget said, "for your sakes, though she be ever so old and ever so tired, for that much she loved you. But now you must not with your tears make her soul grieve for you. Come. Did she not hear you say your prayers at bedtime? Say them now for her, that she may rejoice in the sound of your voices speaking to God for her sake, asking that she may rest in peace."

Harriet and Eleanor said their prayers. Virginia continued to cry.

"A *pháistín*, will you not say the Our Father?"

"No. God had no right to take Norrie away. I love her."

"But many you have to love, and many who love you."

"No. *No*body else loves us. They're all too busy."

"Ah, busy or not, they love you. Your mother and father, and your grandfather . . . Did you not but just a few minutes ago hear the love in his voice and feel it in the touch of his hand? So dear you be to all of them, the precious lot of you, and well I know they be dear to you."

"Virginia loves Uncle Richard best," Harriet said.

"Does that be so?" Bridget was surprised; for even though she could easily understand how anyone must love Richard, it seemed strange that a little girl's first love would be given to any but her parents.

"Uncle Richard plays games with us sometimes," Eleanor explained, "and tells us stories, and makes things for us."

Softly Bridget said, "Now then, since he be so thoughtful of your happiness, Miss Virginia, it would be hurtful to him did he see how sorely you grieve. So will you not dry your tears, that for your Uncle Richard one sadness does not be laid upon another?"

Virginia did not dry her tears, but she became quiet, and presently slipped from Bridget's lap to cross

79

the room and take from a low shelf a beautiful little horse carved of wood. With this in her hands she returned to her place of comfort.

"It's a Shetland Island pony," Harriet said. "She would like to have a real one, but Mama won't let her, for fear she'd be hurt. So Uncle Richard made this for her."

"And he's going to make her a hobby horse," said Eleanor, "big enough to sit on."

"He made almost all the things for our babies." Harriet pointed to the doll furniture, which many times Bridget had admired while cleaning the room, never dreaming that the lovely little things were the work of Richard's hands. "Want to come look at them? Let her, Virginia. You can show them to her."

There were little tables and chairs, a chest of real drawers that opened, a cupboard with shelves on which were tiny wooden trenchers and bowls and cups and saucers. There were three beds—"We made the canopies and quilts," Harriet said—and three little birch-bark cradles. There was a spinning wheel and loom.

"Now when could your uncle do all this," Bridget asked in wonder, "so hard as he works every minute?"

"On winter evenings," Harriet said. "When it was too dreadfully cold to work out in the shed, on his chaise, Mama let him make these by the fire in the kitchen."

"But he had to sweep up the shavings," said Eleanor.

"One night he stayed up very late," Harriet remembered, "after everyone else went to bed. He fell asleep, and Cook had a terrible fright when she came down in the morning and found him lying there on the floor. And the fire had gone out, because he hadn't covered it. Mama was very angry with him."

"Mama's unkind to Uncle Richard," Virginia said.

Harriet spoke reprovingly. "No, she isn't, Virginia."

But Eleanor agreed, "Yes, she is. She treats him like a servant."

"That's only because there's so much to be done, and Mama simply hasn't enough servants for this big house."

"Then she should be *glad* to have Uncle Richard do things, instead of always finding fault with him."

"Eleanor, you ought not criticize Mama."

"Well, Mama ought not criticize people either. For instance, Cousin Margaret. She called Margaret a hoyden!"

"Mama was shocked," Harriet said, "because Margaret sometimes rides horseback astride, like a man."

"Well, but she's a *lady* just the same."

"Yes, of course. Uncle Richard's going to marry Cousin Margaret," Harriet said to Bridget. "They've been friends for years and years."

"It be good that friends marry," Bridget answered, looking down at Virginia's soft shining golden hair.

"They go riding together on Sunday afternoons. Margaret isn't the least bit afraid to jump fences or ditches or anything. She rides much too recklessly for a girl, Mama says."

Memory of that Sunday in the woods, the voice calling, the fear of being found there with Richard, filled Bridget with a cold inner trembling. She felt herself on dangerous ground, and her instinct was to run from danger; but to keep the girls talking and their minds from their loss, she said, "This I hear—that Miss Margaret Findlay be very well educated."

"Oh, she is. Her father thinks girls should be educated just the same as boys. Her brother goes to the Academy in Philadelphia; but there aren't any schools for girls anywhere near, so Margaret had a governess. Well, she still has, but she doesn't really need a governess any more, so Mistress Kershaw is coming here."

"She wasn't to come until fall," said Eleanor, "but now I guess she'll come right away. Now that . . ."

Eleanor's voice caught and broke, and Virginia began to cry.

"I don't want her to come! I want Norrie . . ."

"Ah, there now." Bridget stroked the shining hair. "You want to be educated, don't you, Miss Virginia?"

"No! I hate to learn words! I hate to do sums! I won't do it for anyone but Norrie!"

"But your Norrie wants you to."

"She doesn't! She's dead!"

"Not in your heart. A thousand times each day you will think of her, won't you, and do as she would have you do? Now, see. What would you be doing at this minute, were she here?"

"We would be downstairs having breakfast," Harriet said. "Then we would come up here and sing a morning hymn, and say the Twenty-third Psalm."

"And would you not like to do that now?"

"We could sing the Doxology. Virginia knows it —it's very short. I can play the music."

Harriet seated herself at the spinet, and after some coaxing Virginia consented to sing.

"Praise God from whom all blessing flow . . ."

High and sweet and clear the three voices blended.

"Praise Him all creatures here below,
Praise Him above, ye heavenly host . . ."

From the doorway another voice joined, deeper but as clear and true as theirs.

82

"Praise Father, Son, and Holy Ghost."

The girls whirled around. "Uncle Richard!"

Bridget tried to keep her eyes down, but could not —so much she loved the sight of him standing there, holding high a breakfast tray lest the children in the extravagance of their welcome knock it from his hands. Above their heads his eyes met hers, and in his eyes she read many things—gratitude and sorrow and joy and love.

He was in riding clothes—and so much the fine gentleman he always looked in his riding clothes—yet here he was, waiting upon his little nieces as a servant, in her place, she being the one whose duty it was to carry trays above stairs when trays were needed.

"To the four fair Princesses in the Enchanted Tower," he said, "I bring greetings. Also four bowls of porridge, a jug of cream, sugar, johnnycakes, and tea." He set the bowls on a table, each with a grand flourish. "Princess Harriet—Princess Eleanor—Princess Virginia— and Princess *Brighid Ní Ghallchobhair.*"

"Princess *who?*" the girls cried.

"*That* princess," he answered, pointing. "The one with hair as black as a raven's wing and eyes as blue as heaven. The one whose cheek is like a red, red rose blooming in the snow."

"That's Bridget! She's not a princess—she's a servant!"

"Sh-h-h." He bent down, bringing his head close to theirs and speaking low and mysteriously. "She is under a spell. *You* know her as Bridget. But shall I tell you who she really is?"

"Yes, yes!"

"Hearken, then. In truth she is the only daughter of the last High King of Ireland, who fled from the

Sasanachs and now dwells in the jeweled halls of a fairy palace underneath the hills of Donegal. Someday she will meet a prince, and marry him, and then the spell will be broken, and you will see she is a True Princess of the Blood Royal."

"He has to be a handsome prince," Eleanor said.

"Not necessarily. This particular spell can be broken by a quite ordinary everyday betwixt-and-between sort of prince. The only requirement is that he must fall in love with her at first sight. Instantaneously. Like that!" Richard snapped his fingers. "Then he'll whisk her away to his father's kingdom, where they'll live happily forever and a day."

"What's to fall in love?" Virginia asked.

"That means—the moment he looks at her he will see her as the loveliest and most important person in the world, and will know he can't live without her."

"But there aren't any princes in the Colonies."

"One will turn up. You can even summon him, if you like." From a pocket of his riding coat Richard took a stone; a strange beautiful stone, one side plain rough gray, the other a mass of pointed shining crystals, purple in color and glass smooth. "I found this on the hill. It's a magic talisman. You keep it, and every morning touch it and say, 'Bring a prince for Bridget.' Then keep watching, but be patient, for the magic may need a while to build up, and the prince may have a long way to come."

Virginia touched the stone. "Bring a prince for Bridget!"

"Now be very still," Richard said, "and listen . . . Hear that? A horse. Galloping, galloping . . . far off . . . far beyond the Seven Great Hills and the Seven Green Seas and the Seven Distant Lands . . ."

"A pure white horse? With a bridle made of gold?"

"Well . . . Maybe just a gray horse, with a plain leather bridle. Remember, don't expect a *Crown* Prince. And don't be disappointed if he isn't wearing an embroidered velvet cloak and a cloth-of-gold waistcoat and diamond-studded buckles on his boots. Personally I wouldn't be surprised to see him turn up in homespun linsey-woolsey."

"Who ever heard of a prince in linsey-woolsey!"

"Ah, but princesses don't usually dress like servant girls, either." He made them all a courtly bow. "Now, Highnesses, I must leave you."

"No, Uncle Richard, no! Stay with us! Tell us more about the prince!"

"Alas, I cannot, for I am under orders from the Queen to be back three minutes before I left. Would you have me dragged behind wild horses, drawn and quartered, boiled in oil?"

The treachery of laughter brought back Virginia's tears. She hid her face against him. "Uncle Richard, Norrie's gone. . . ."

He went down on one knee, putting an arm around her. There was no lightness in his voice now; only tenderness.

"Yes, Ginny. We loved her, and now she's gone. But the love isn't gone. We still have that, to be divided up, spread around, shared with one another. You can love your sisters more, and your mother and father, and your grandfather, and Bridget, and me—and other people too, anybody, anywhere—by dividing among us your love for Norrie. Will you do that?"

"I—don't know if I can. I'll—try."

"That's my good girl. And no more tears. You'll be sick if you cry, and you mustn't get sick—because you're guardian-in-chief of the magic stone. Now come eat your breakfast."

"Uncle Richard, if I eat my breakfast, will you come back and tell us more about Bridget and the spell and the prince?"

"If I'm allowed to," he promised, "I'll come at bedtime and tell you all about the fairy palace where Bridget's father lives. But if I can't come, you think about it anyway, and then when you fall asleep you will go there in your dreams."

He placed chairs for them at the table, seated them —Bridget first in spite of her "No, please"—stood for a moment with his hands on the back of Virginia's chair, his eyes on Bridget, and then rather abruptly turned and left them.

(7)

Nurse was laid to rest in the churchyard at Willow-field. Not in a corner, alone, but beside the three little graves already there—the infant daughters of Vincent and Jane. There, too, when the time came, other Staffords would be laid beside or around her; for she had been one of them, Marcus said, for thirty-three years, and would so remain.

Upon Richard, in such odd moments as could be spared, fell the task of making a headstone for her grave, shaping and smoothing and polishing the stone, then cutting into it her name and the dates of her birth and death. *Caroline Gray*. Beneath the name he would add, when he had time, *August 4 1700–July 17 1775*. And it was strange to chip out her name, which he had altogether forgotten or perhaps had never known. Strange to think that long ago she had been a child, a young woman, a wife . . . or had she never married? He didn't know. He knew her only as Nurse, or Norrie (it was he who first gave her that name), already an elderly woman when he was born. But long ago, to her family, to the friends of her youth, she had been Caroline.

As he was Richard.

Looking at the stone and the name, he wondered if someday far in the future anyone would puzzle over the identity of Caroline Gray, wondering who she had been and how she had come to be buried there among the Staffords. And perhaps wondering whose hand had cut those letters in the stone. Would they be able to tell that the chiseling had been done with care, or would they see only the imperfections and think it crudely and impatiently done, never knowing that the workman was accustomed to wood, not stone? He had cut the letters deep; but how long would they last, under the wind and the rain and the freezing and thawing of who knew how many winters? *Gravestones tell truth scarce forty years.* . . . But that meant stones were sometimes moved, or other bodies placed beneath them. No one would move this stone, not after it was placed in the churchyard, over the mortal remains of Caroline Gray.

In a reverie he saw other stones, shadowy row on row, and on one of them *Richard Gregory Stafford.* And he saw shadowy figures looking down, reading that name. Curiously, the shadowy figures seemed all to be himself, each in turn approaching, pausing, moving on. He heard them speak his name. "That was the first Richard," one of them said. "The first Richard Stafford of Blue Meadow Farm—my great-great-great-great-great-grandfather." How many generations would that be? How far ahead in the vast unending halls of time? Who was the speaker, so many years unborn?

There is nothing strictly immortal but immortality. . . . (The good Dr. Browne again, whom his father had made him read and reread until his mind was so

filled with those splendid echoing phrases that he sometimes heard them in his sleep.)

But wasn't *that* immortality—those shadows of the
future, pausing to read his name—his, the first Richard?
There was to be another Richard, then, and certainly
another Marcus, a Vincent, a Gregory—his children and
his children's children. One hundred—two hundred—
years from now they would still be filing past, long
after there was nothing but dust beneath the stone that
would bear his name. Would they know he had walked
these same fields, under the same sun that would shine
down on them? That he had made hay, husked corn,
split firewood, ridden horses, built a chaise? That he
had once been seventeen—and in love?

"Wake up!" A light cuff on the side of the head
brought Richard out of his reverie. "I've had my eye
on you," Vincent said, "and you haven't moved a finger
in five minutes. You think there's time to sit around
and dream?"

Richard quickly picked up his hammer and chisel;
but Vincent said, "Never mind about that now. You're
driving over to the Findlays' to fetch the girls' governess. Take a wagon, not your chaise—she'll have a
chest and other things."

In pity, Richard thought, *So soon?* For he knew the
girls weren't ready to accept a substitute for Norrie.
Unless that substitute were Bridget . . .

"Why can't you be our governess, Bridget?"

"Ah, now, how could a poor servant girl who knows
not how to read or write, be governess to young ladies?"

"But Eleanor and I already know how to read and
write. You could learn, then you could teach Virginia."

"And who would make the beds and clean the
rooms and all?"

"Mama could get someone else to do that."

89

"Not so, Miss Eleanor. And your Mama would be not pleased with such a thought. A governess of young ladies must herself be a lady, with much knowledge of all things needful for young ladies to know. What does Bridget Gallagher know of such things?"

Firmly, Virginia said, "You are a *princess* under a spell."

"If I be under a spell, a great while longer will it last. Your uncle does be saying these things but to amuse you."

"No. We can *see* you're a princess."

"Your eyes see with kindness, Miss Virginia. But you must keep clear in your mind the difference between a thing told you in playfulness and a thing told in truth."

"Uncle Richard *was* telling the truth," Virginia said stubbornly. "And I shall tell Mama."

"Ah, never tell your Mama I be a princess. That angry would she be with your Uncle Richard for putting such ideas in your head. And that angry with me—I fear not again would I be allowed to come near you."

"All right, I won't tell her *that*. But I *will* tell her we want you to be our governess. And if she won't let you," Virginia promised, "I shall get very sick and most probably shall die."

Between laughter and tears, Bridget had told Richard of this conversation; but when he asked, "Can't we make it true? Can't we let the prince come?" then there had been only tears, and, "No, Richard, no—please—we cannot."

So Mistress Kershaw came to Blue Meadow.

The arrangement should have been a satisfactory one, all around, for she was in fact an amiable woman, despite her scholarly attainments. That it bid fair to be, instead, a disastrous arrangement, was due to no one's having taken Virginia at her word.

Virginia became ill. Not immediately, and perhaps not by deliberate choice, intent, and design; but without doubt her refusal to accept Mistress Kershaw was rather more than contributory to her illness.

Harriet and Eleanor, being older and wiser, saw the unfairness of disliking Mistress Kershaw simply because she was not Norrie, and also the futility of opposing things-as-things-had-to-be. They were amenable, dutiful, and polite, as properly brought up young ladies were expected to be. Not so Virginia, who sat in hostile silence, refusing to spell words, refusing to do sums, refusing to knit, embroider, or quilt, refusing even to dance.

"I don't like her," Virginia said.

"You are a naughty and ungrateful child," Jane admonished with cold displeasure. "It isn't necessary to like her, but simply to do as she tells you. Or you shall be punished."

But, "Oh, let her alone," said Vincent, too weary at night to listen to trivial complaints. "She'll tire of sulking."

Mistress Kershaw held a position of privilege in the household. Her afternoons were spent in the schoolroom, but her mornings and evenings were spent as she pleased. She was not given to early rising, her breakfast was carried up by Bridget, she passed the hours from nine to twelve in seclusion—reading, it was to be assumed, for Richard had loaded and unloaded and toted upstairs two very large boxes of books.

The children, therefore, also had the morning to themselves; and Bridget, going up at ten to clean and tidy the schoolroom, the week after Mistress Kershaw's arrival, found Harriet at the spinet and Eleanor coaxing Virginia to try the steps of the minuet.

"This silly child will not even *try*," Eleanor said helplessly. "She won't do *any*thing. She just *sits*."

"But does the sweet lass not understand how joyful it does be to dance? And such pretty music!"

"Bridget," the two older girls asked together, "can *you* dance?"

"In Ireland there be none who cannot. And could you hear the gay tunes—such as make your feet start dancing of themselves!"

"Show us, show us!"

"Ah, now, I be here to dust and clean, not to dance."

"Oh, please. No one will know."

"But you have not the Irish music . . ."

"We have music for the Roger de Coverly." Harriet played a few bars. "Can you dance to that?"

"It be much like the music we dance to. But . . ."

"Then I'll play, and you and Eleanor will dance, and Virginia will stand at the door and tell us if anyone starts upstairs. You'll do *that*, won't you, Virginia?"

Yes, Virginia would do that.

So Bridget danced, she and Eleanor, hand in hand. And what fun it was—a gay, lively dance that brought color to Eleanor's pale cheeks and delight to all of them. Virginia, entranced, forgot to watch the stairs, and heard the footsteps barely in time to hiss, "Mistress Kershaw!" and run back to her stool. Harriet had the presence of mind to keep on playing, and Eleanor to keep on dancing alone; but had stair-climbing not been a laborious ordeal for a stout and tightly-laced middle-aged lady, Bridget would not have had time to snatch up her dustcloth and be wiping the shelves a scant second before Mistress Kershaw reached the door.

Eleanor stopped dancing, and curtsied. Harriet stopped playing, stood up, and curtsied. Virginia remained seated.

"Well!" Mistress Kershaw beamed her pleasure. "When I heard such romping above my head, I could not imagine what you young ladies were up to. How beautifully you were doing the steps, Miss Eleanor! And was the little one also dancing? I'm sure from the sounds I heard she must have been."

Mistress Kershaw smiled indulgently upon "the little one," who showed her a pale proud cameo profile and said nothing.

"Play the music again, Miss Harriet, and perhaps she will be persuaded by it in spite of herself."

While Harriet was playing and Virginia was stonily resisting persuasion, Bridget quickly finished her work and slipped away. Mistress Kershaw had taken no notice of her presence and took none of her departure. In her sight, a servant girl blended with the furniture. Certainly she made no connection between the "romping" she had heard and the Staffords' upstairs maid.

At teatime Virginia would eat nothing. At bedtime she said her head ached. In the night she woke crying for Norrie to bring her a cup of cold water. Harriet, wakened by the crying, offered her water, tepid from long hours in the pitcher. She drank thirstily, and then promptly brought it up, together with what seemed, in the dark, everything she had eaten in the past week.

Harriet had no candle, no clean bedding, nor any knowledge of what medicine Norrie used to give them when they threw up, nor where to find it even had she known what to look for.

What to do?

Eleanor was still asleep. There was no use waking her, she would be no help, more likely would make matters worse by following Virginia's example, for she too had a very queasy stomach.

Wake Mistress Kershaw? But she was there to teach them in the afternoons, not to take care of them in the night.

Wake Mama? But Mama never took care of them either, and might be cross, having to get out of bed, and light a candle, and find medicine, and change the bed linens.

Bridget? But to get Bridget would require going through not only the dark front hall but the narrow and still darker back hall—a journey far too terrifying.

No, it would have to be . . .

Harriet fled past the great yawning well of the stairs.

"Uncle Richard! Uncle Richard! Virginia's sick!"

Richard took the candle from the lowboy in the hall and went downstairs to light it at the kitchen fire. Richard found clean linen sheets, and bundled up the soiled ones and took them away. Richard brought fresh water—cool pure spring water that ran perpetually through the summer kitchen in a trough made of a halved and hollowed-out chestnut log. He let Virginia take only a few sips—"A little at a time, Ginny, so it stays down." But when he put his hand against her forehead and her burning cheeks, he lost no time waking Jane.

"Why wasn't I called at once?" Jane demanded, venting her displeasure upon Harriet. "Why did you call your uncle instead of me?"

Richard, though never in his own defense standing up to Jane, did so for the now tearful Harriet. "Because she is a kind and considerate daughter, and wanted to spare you if she could."

"Spare me? Does she imagine *you* know anything about caring for a sick child?"

"She thought the sickness was over. She didn't know Ginny has a fever."

"Oh, very well. Go see if your brother is still awake. If he is, tell him he isn't needed. Then go stir up the fire and set the kettle to boil. After that, go back to bed."

But Virginia protested, "No! I want Uncle Richard to stay here!"

"Hush, Virginia. He can't stay here. Now don't start crying or you'll be sick again." Jane stirred half a teaspoon of white powder into half a cup of water. "Drink this. It will settle your stomach and make you well."

"No! I want Norrie! I don't want to get well! I want to die!"

"Virginia, drink this."

"I won't! Not unless Uncle Richard holds the cup!"

Richard, on his way back from delivering the message to Vincent, was stopped as he passed the door.

"Somehow," Jane said coldly, "you have managed utterly to spoil this child. Come give her her medicine before you go downstairs."

Virginia drank the bitter contents of the cup. Lying weakly back against her pillows, she pleaded, "Stay with me, Uncle Richard. I think I can go to sleep, if you stay with me."

In any ordinary circumstances Jane would not have yielded; but the child's eyes were so unnaturally bright, her skin so hot and dry. If she slept she would be better in the morning, and then the preposterous situation could be dealt with.

"Oh—stay, then, if nothing else will quiet her. But only until she sleeps. Understand, Virginia? *Only* until you fall asleep."

"Yes, Mama . . . Uncle Richard, tell me about the prince. Where is he now? Has he started across the Seven Green Seas?"

Virginia was not better in the morning. Her fever seemed no higher, but neither had it abated. She slept until nine, restlessly, with much tossing and turning and little whimpering sounds of distress. When she woke, she asked at once for Richard.

With patience and reasonableness, even with gentleness, Jane explained that Richard was working and could not possibly come in to see her just then, but would come at his earliest opportunity; and that she must remain quietly in bed, and not fret or excite herself, but try to sleep again if she could.

To this patient reasonableness her perverse little daughter responded by insisting that if Richard could not come, then she wanted Bridget.

Casting patience to the winds, Jane said flatly that Bridget could not come either, would not be permitted to come even if she were not otherwise occupied, and that there was to be no more of such nonsense. But the nonsense continued, mounting from fretfulness and entreaty to hysteria.

Vincent, taking a few minutes to come to the house in the hope of assuring himself that Virginia had slept off her indisposition, learned instead that she was worse, and that they had his father to thank for it.

"I knew it was a great mistake to send the girl upstairs with them that day. They have developed an inordinate fondness for her—all of them—and now see what I have to put up with! This child should be quiet—resting—sleeping. But what is she doing? Screaming for Bridget—and a *stone!*"

"Well, if you want to keep her quiet," said Vincent, greatly exasperated by what seemed to him the irrational nature of women, "and if she wants Bridget, then for God's sake let her *have* Bridget!"

"Are you recommending that I, her mother, permit myself to be displaced by a servant?"

"I'm recommending that you put the child's health ahead of your own pride! Time enough to straighten her out when she's well again."

"Straighten her out! With that girl bewitching her on the one hand, and Richard on the other?"

"My God, Jane! You should be damned glad you've *got* Richard and the girl to bewitch her, if that means keeping her quiet. Such a puny sickly little thing as she is—you'll be straightening her out in a coffin if you let her go on like this!"

Vincent seldom chose to assert himself in differences of opinion with Jane, for he valued domestic peace above his husbandly right to dominate; but there were occasions when he didn't hesitate to lay down the law.

"Where is the girl? Call her in here!"

"*You* call her," Jane said bitterly. "If you wish to encourage your daughters in this demoralizing attachment, then take *all* the responsibility upon yourself."

Stepping into the hall, Vincent shouted, *"Bridget!"* in a voice that all but shook the house and brought her —scared half out of her wits, he supposed—from his father's room.

This was the first time he had really seen her. He was almost never on the second floor between the hours of dawn and dusk, and his only previous glimpses had

97

been of her retreating down the hall after having left his jug of hot water in the morning. Looking down at her now, and having a thoroughly masculine appreciation of feminine charms, he found himself thinking, *By God, she's a pretty thing—small wonder Richie got worked up.*

With a reassuring smile he said, "Forgive me. I didn't mean to be that loud. But Virginia is ill and calling for you, Bridget. We want you to sit with her and keep her quiet. She is very delicate—even a minor illness can be dangerous for her. We want you to stay with her day and night until she's completely recovered. You are a child's nurse, now. That is your only duty, for the present."

Jane left the room as Bridget entered; but Vincent, lingering, was touched by the scene he witnessed—his daughter's joyful weeping and her thin little white arms reaching out, and Bridget kneeling beside the bed to hold her close.

"*A chailín bheag dhílis*, you be sick, your father tells me, and now you must lie still, and rest, and not upset yourself with crying, or with such hugging and all . . ."

"Bridget—the stone! I must touch the stone!"

"Now, that can wait. One of your dear sisters will bring it to you later."

"No, Mama won't let them. They're not to come near me, or they might get sick too. And Uncle Richard said every morning. He said I must touch it every morning!"

Mystified, Vincent asked, "What is she talking about?"

Bridget, getting to her feet but looking down, cheeks aflame, answered, "She speaks of a pretty stone, Master."

"Why did Richard tell her she must touch it every morning?"

"It—be only a game, Master."

"Well, where is the stone?"

"In the schoolroom."

Vincent went to the third floor. His two older daughters were there, frozen into two little statues by the singular and apparently terrifying circumstance of his coming to the schoolroom, and even more so by his asking for the stone. Neither spoke, neither moved; as far as he could see, neither breathed. He tried to speak gently; but he was accustomed to shouting directions at field hands or oxen, and he supposed his voice had acquired an ineradicable harshness even when kept low.

"Your sister wants the stone. Would one of you be good enough to tell me where to find it?"

Now Harriet went to a toy cupboard—the cupboard Richard had made—opened the tiny door and drew forth the stone. Trembling, she placed it in his hand.

"Amethysts," he said in surprise. "Where did this come from?"

"Uncle Richard found it, Papa—on the hill."

"Why, these are good clear gems. He gave this to Virginia?"

"To all of us, Papa; but—especially to Virginia."

"And why must she touch it every morning?"

"Uncle Richard said—it's a magic stone."

"That's nonsense, of course. Do you believe nonsense?"

"No—but Virginia does."

"And what magic does she expect the stone to produce?"

Harriet was silent, looking frozen again.

Quite sternly he said, "When I ask you a question, Harriet, I want an answer. An intelligent answer, if possible, but at least a truthful one. Now speak up! What is the so-called magic?"

"A—a prince for Bridget," Harriet whispered.

"A prince for . . . ?" Well, there was no use pursuing the matter any further, Vincent decided. Not here, at any rate. *But when I get my hands on that boy . . .*

Saying nothing more, he went downstairs, gave Virginia the stone and Bridget a long look, and still without another word betook himself outside to his interrupted morning work. On the way, he glanced toward the training field where Richard was exercising Red Earl.

"Just wait, Richie," he said under his breath. *"Just you wait."*

(8)

An hour remained before dusk. The sky was clear, the day's heat still lay over the fields; but the dew was falling and no more hay could be made. Richard, having finished his evening chores, set about cutting the numeral 7 on the headstone. But again he was told to never mind about that now.

"We're taking a walk. Come along."

Surprised and apprehensive, Richard laid down his tools. To ask, "Where are we going?" would have brought no answer, as he well knew by his brother's grimly forbidding expression. In silence—and it could not be called companionable silence—they walked through the orchard and up the hill to the woods. There, beyond sight of the house, and quite alone, they stopped.

"All right," Vincent said, "now talk."

Apprehension, which had become a dark foreboding, now centered in one tight knot in Richard's stomach. "Talk—about what?"

"You know damned well what."

"No, Vince, I . . ."

Vincent slapped him; not hard, but hard enough to convey an intensely direct message.

"That's a warning. I didn't come up here to listen to evasions or lies. What's between you and the girl? And if you ask, 'What girl?' you'll get the back of my hand across your mouth!"

Richard made an instinctive move to put himself out of reach, but Vincent caught him by the shirtfront in a tight grip.

"Well, I guess you mean . . ."

"Don't do any guessing. I want the facts!"

". . . you mean Bridget. We—love each other."

"That's hog slop. Tell me what's between you!"

"I can't tell you. I promised . . ."

"You'll tell me," Vincent said, reaching for a stick, "and you'll tell me now, or I'll beat it out of you with this!"

"Vince, if you promise not to tell anyone else . . ."

"I'll promise nothing and you'll tell everything. Now talk!"

So Richard talked. He told how he fell in love with Bridget at first sight, thinking her a lady; and she with him, thinking him a servant. He told of the long drive home, and how he meant to tell her who he was, but couldn't. He told of meeting her that Sunday in the woods, and of having to leave her there alone when Margaret came. He told of going to her room that night, intending only to speak to her through the door, but then going in to open her window. And . . .

"I didn't mean it to happen, Vince. Please—that's the truth—I didn't. We were just standing there looking out the window—and then—all of a sudden . . ."

"The girl was a virgin! You know that, don't you?"

Miserably Richard admitted, "Yes."

102

"A good girl," Vincent said, "sent here *to be safe!*"

"Vince, I'm going to marry her."

"You damned young fool, you *can't* marry her!"

"Yes, I can. I have to, now that . . ."

"How many times have you gone to her room?"

"Four times."

"And how many times have you had to do with her?"

Richard didn't answer. Vincent raised his stick. *"How many?"*

"Four."

"Richie, I ought to give you the damnedest trouncing of your life . . . !"

The words and gesture were threatening; yet Vincent released him, then, and tossed the stick away. And in the words, for all their harshness, Richard heard what he so desperately wanted to hear—understanding and sympathy. In the "ought to." In the "Richie." A wild hope rose in him that his brother wasn't really angry and wouldn't be against him but on his side, would see that there was only one thing to be done, would speak for him, would help him.

"Vince, I'm sorry I've done something everyone will see as a disgrace. But I didn't want to keep it secret, and wouldn't have, if she hadn't been so frightened, so sure she'd be sent away. She begged me not to tell. So I promised, but I said only for a while—only until I could convince her everything would be all right."

"And what in the name of God makes you think it could ever be all right?"

"Why—because it has to be."

"There's no 'has to be' about it. You're a gentleman —in name, at least—and gentlemen don't marry serving maids."

103

"They do—when it's the only honorable thing."

"No point of honor is involved," Vincent said, "in an affair with anyone so far beneath you."

"But she isn't. Vince, have you ever looked at her?"

Thoughts flicked through Vincent's mind; thoughts that surprised him, not in themselves, but in that they seemed to have been lodged in his mind all day, like brook trout in a deep shadowed pool, waiting for just the right moment to flash through the shallows.

He thought of his three living daughters, so fragile, so ethereal, given to all manner of sicknesses; and of the three who had not lived. He thought of the sons he had never had. He thought of his two sisters; one still childless after ten years of marriage; the other with two children as fragile as his own. Staffords married their own kind; often their second or third cousins, but always their own kind. The line needed a good outcross; new blood; new vitality. And he thought of Bridget Gallagher as his eyes had appraised her that morning—so young and lovely, the fresh bloom on her cheeks, the look of good sound health and good sound quality—yes, quality, servant or no. And then, looking at his young brother—lean, wiry, vigorous, and a Stafford through and through—he thought: *They would have good colts, those two.*

But he said, "You are going to marry Margaret Findlay."

"No, I'm not. I couldn't, now, even if I wanted to. She wouldn't have me. Not when I tell her about Bridget."

"Richie, don't be an idiot. You know what comes with Margaret—the four hundred acres next to us and a hundred thousand pounds."

"I know, but . . . Vince, I *love* Bridget."

"Love—whatever you mean by the word—is a trap

for fools. A romantic fiction. A delusion. Forget it. You'll have a proper marriage and you'll have it soon. As to this girl—I promise you you'll never have a chance to get near her again."

"Vince, I'm going to marry her." There was firmness in Richard's voice; not defiance, just firmness. "Now or later, and no matter what anyone thinks or says or does—I'm going to marry her."

"You're going to do as you're told," Vincent said curtly. "But if she's in trouble, you needn't worry about her—I'll see that she's taken care of."

"In—trouble?"

"If she's with child. We'll know about that before long. It won't be hard to find some good honest fellow who'll be glad to marry her, with a little something on the side."

"But—if she is—it's *my* child! She can't marry anyone else if she's carrying my child! Why—it could be a son! A Stafford!"

Richard was speaking from the depths of profound shock, too impulsively to frame his protest in any words other than the first that came into his head; but had he chosen them with all deliberateness and care, he could not have chosen better.

My child. A son. A Stafford.

The thoughts that had flicked through Vincent's mind a minute earlier came back, eddied and circled and made a place for themselves—and remained. But he was not ready to acknowledge them as practical, feasible, or creditable thoughts.

"Do you think for one minute the child of a servant, even though your son, would be accepted as a Stafford? Or that you would remain in line for the inheritance if you should beget such a son?"

"Vince, I don't know anything about the inheritance. But I do know—if I have a son—even if he's never accepted as a Stafford—he'll *be* a Stafford just the same. And so will his sons be, and their sons, and theirs, on and on . . ."

Vincent's smile was barely discernible, but it was there, softening the grim look ever so little.

"You have a good idea in that 'on and on' part, Richie. But they have to be sons worthy of the name, not the produce of a servant girl. *She* has sense enough to know you can't marry her, hasn't she? That you'd be a disgrace to your family if you did?"

"Yes, she's afraid of that—afraid I'd be disowned and sent away. But . . . I wouldn't have to leave Blue Meadow, would I, Vince? I thought, if you'd let me, I could build a little house somewhere, maybe down on the other side of the woods. And I could still work here, couldn't I? As a hired hand, for just enough to live on?"

Vincent was silent, for again many thoughts were going through his mind; among them: *Richie, I'm damned if I know how we could get along without you.* And mingled with the thoughts were emotions, for he was deeply moved. *Richie, you're the nearest to a son I'll ever have. Send you away? From Blue Meadow? From me? From your father, whose hope for the future you are? He could no more think of sending you away than he could think of destroying you with his own hands* . . . But it was necessary to suppress these thoughts and feelings; for to speak of them, or even to let them surface in a look, would be to lend encouragement to the gravest folly.

Richard, seeing only the cold set expression of disfavor, pleaded, "We wouldn't bother anyone. I mean, except for my working here, we'd keep out of sight . . ."

How would Virginia feel, Vincent wondered, about their keeping out of sight? Virginia, whose small world had revolved around Nurse, and now, after the catastrophic loss of its center, was in new orbit around the two fixed stars of her choice? He could still hear the sound of her frenzied screaming. Was his little daughter to be offered as a sacrifice to the gods of class distinction? But this disturbing thought, like the others, must be suppressed.

"Are you saying that, forbidden to bring this girl to your own level, you would be willing to descend to hers?"

"Yes." The wild hope came again. "It wouldn't be any different. I'd be doing the same things—the very same things I do now."

"What you do now you do as a Stafford."

"But I would still be a Stafford."

"Perhaps so," Vincent conceded without change of expression, "but no longer a prince."

Daylight was fading. Under the trees it was even then almost gone. Richard was glad, for he didn't want to see his brother's face too clearly—the anger and the new threat—nor did he want his own consciousness of guilt to be too clearly seen.

"*A prince for Bridget,*" Vincent said in a hard voice. "It wasn't enough to play the fool yourself. You have made fools of my children. Worse than fools— innocent accomplices in your low affair with a servant girl!"

"No, Vince, please. It was only . . ."

"Only to fill their heads with arrant nonsense. Only to bewitch them into seeing the girl through your eyes, so they would aid and abet you."

"No," Richard protested in dismay. "It was only—

they felt so bad when Norrie died—it was only to distract them, to give them a fairy tale to think about instead of . . ."

"Well, you succeeded in distracting them—right out of their minds. You have also distracted their mother. Are you aware that Virginia will have no one near her except this girl? And that her life may depend on humoring her senseless demands?"

"Vince, please believe me, I didn't mean to be taken seriously. And it was only that one morning. I haven't even seen them since then, except last night, when Harriet called me."

"Why did Harriet call you instead of her mother?"

"I don't know, unless she's a little afraid of Jane. *I* always was."

"And have you told the girls that when you were their age you were afraid of their mother?"

"No, but"—Richard ventured to smile—"they've had opportunities to observe that I still am."

"They seem also to be afraid of me," Vincent said. "You find that equally understandable, for the same reason?"

"No. That's because they hardly ever see you, except on Sundays. They hardly know you. If they did . . ."

"*You* know me. And you know damned well I'd have laid that stick on you just now."

"Well, yes. I was afraid of that. But not of you."

"You make fine distinctions," Vincent said. "Too fine for me. What's the difference?"

"Why—we're brothers. I couldn't be afraid of you, Vince. We understand each other. We're—close."

"Look, *brother*. Save the milk and honey for someone who eats pap. I'm a roast-beef man. And if you have any idea in your harebrain that you can cajole me

108

into fighting your battles for you, get rid of it. Now, one more thing. Where did you pick up the amethysts?"

Richard was perplexed. "What are amethysts?"

"The stone. The 'magic' stone," Vincent said with heavy irony.

"Oh. I found it over there." Richard pointed across the hilltop field. "Part way down the slope on the other side."

"Were there more?"

"I don't know. I just happened to see it lying there. I didn't have time to look around."

"Well, sometime when you're over that way, take a look. If you find more, I'll have them cut and polished. An amethyst necklace will make a nice wedding present," Vincent said, "for Margaret."

(9)

There was no opportunity during the next few weeks for Richard to do anything so far from urgent as looking for amethysts. No opportunity to work on the headstone. And no opportunity to catch more than a rare glimpse of Bridget at a distance of some seventy or eighty yards.

Bridget, under Vincent's orders, was staying at Virginia's side twenty-four hours a day; and though her inability to perform her proper duties put an added and—Jane complained—intolerable burden upon the other girls and herself, Richard's services for any of the household chores were not available. One of the field hands could be sent in from time to time if needed, Vincent said. But not Richard. There was too much for Richard to do outside.

"And since when," Jane demanded, "has Richard become so indispensable to you? You know very well I cannot have just anybody in the house. If I must spend every minute of my time watching them, I might just as well do the work myself!"

"Then do it," Vincent replied, "or let it remain undone, as you prefer. You'll have another girl as soon as we find one. Until then, you'll have to make out as best you can."

Virginia's illness continued through the month of August. Jane suspected that it was in part feigned; but a doctor, brought from Philadelphia by Marcus, said no. The child had a low but persistent fever, could digest no solid food, and was already so wasted that only constant care of the most indulgent sort could restore her to health.

To Jane's horror, the doctor recommended that Virginia be taken outside for an hour or two every afternoon.

None of the children had ever been permitted to spend much time outdoors. They were too delicate, Jane said. Their very fair skin could not stand exposure to the sun. They would suffer heat stroke. Wet feet would give them chills. Cold winds would be fatal. On Sundays, going to church, or on rare visits to the neighbors, they were always bundled up and hooded, even in summer. The air in the Colonies was extremely bad for children, Jane was convinced; and as the high mortality rate supported her conviction, Vincent had never pushed his own idea that to be out in the sun and wind and rain and cold would do them good. "Look at Richard," he had said one time. And when Jane pointed out that Richard was a boy and boys were different, he had made the further mistake of saying, "Well, look at Margaret Findlay," which drew the caustic reply that she certainly hoped he was not suggesting that she raise her daughters as Margaret Findlay had been raised—"Like a wild Indian!" Conceding that the raising of daughters lay within the mother's province, and already having as much on his hands as he could manage, Vincent had not interfered. Until now.

Virginia would be taken outside as the doctor recommended. She would walk for a few minutes in the sunshine, would sit for an hour in the shade, where the soft wind of summer would touch her—the clean bright wind that carried only sweetness on its breath. And, "When you are well," Vincent told his pale little wisp of a daughter, "when you are strong, when you can run and jump and skip rope and roll a hoop and shout and sing—I will get you a pony." Virginia's recovery began on that day.

As often as he could, Vincent stopped by to see her when she was sitting in her little wicker chair under the beech tree on the front lawn. At best he could do so infrequently, and she remained shy in his presence; but he was able to satisfy himself that each time she showed improvement. And was able to have a word with Bridget, though she too was shy and frightened, keeping her eyes down and answering faintly when he spoke to her. Usually he confined his words to a brief expression of gratitude for the loving care she was giving Virginia; but one day he asked her questions about herself—what part of Ireland she came from, how long had her people lived there, and were they farmers, fishermen, or what?

She told him they had always lived there; that they had once been teachers, until Catholics were forbidden either to teach or be taught; and that her father, though without schooling, had learned the old tales and histories from *his* father . . . "There be many come to hear him tell the histories."

"What histories do you mean?"

"Of Ireland, Master. Of a thousand years and more. Even of the Tuatha de Danaan."

"Originally, then, were your father's people scholars?"

112

"I think they be so. Far back, some be taught in monasteries, that they may teach others."

While Vincent was reflecting upon this information for a moment in silence, she looked up as if about to ask a question, but losing courage looked quickly down again.

"If there's something you want to ask me, go ahead."

"Master, I wish to send the shillings to my father, but I do not know how this be done."

"The shillings? You mean your wages?"

"Yes, please."

"Well, that may present some difficulties, but perhaps it can be arranged through our solicitor in London. What is your father's name and where does he live?"

"Brian Séamus Ó Gallchobhair, near Ballyshannon, on the road to Pettigo, in Donegal."

He smiled. "I'll have to ask you again when I have pen and paper at hand. But I'll see what we can do about it, Bridget."

Her eyes filled with tears. "You be most kind, Master."

The devil of it was, he reflected as he walked away, that when a pretty girl's eyes filled with tears, a man was hard put to keep a level head on his shoulders.

She was not a peasant. She came of good stock. Learned men, educated in monasteries. Poor . . .

But his own mother had been poor, a daughter of the local vicar whose living had been little more than the word implied—a meager portion of the tithes paid by the Staffords and their neighbors in the parish. Not *so* poor, of course, as ever to have been obliged to indenture herself as a house servant in the Colonies. Still, the Buckinghams had not looked with unqualified approval upon Jane's marriage to a son of the vicar's

113

daughter, even though that son was a Stafford. Had Jane not been twenty-four at the time, and somewhat too willing to remain unwed, their consent might not have been given. As it was, they gave little more than their consent; but Jane was a good wife and a good housekeeper, and he had no complaint to make of the bargain, except that she had never given him a son—a failure that in justice could be considered no more her fault than his own.

Marriage was a practical matter, entered into for sound practical reasons unclouded and uncluttered by romantic fripperies. Love was something for poets to write about; a moon-madness; a midsummer night's dream. Or a daytime dream, for someone young and foolish enough. He and Jane loved each other, he supposed, but in a sensible prosaic way. Certainly he could not picture himself, even at seventeen, suddenly overwhelmed by passion for her or any other woman, to the total exclusion of sanity and the total abandonment of all restraint.

That damned young hotspur!

And yet—perhaps it wasn't wholly incomprehensible. The girl *was* fetching, and might easily turn the head of a boy who went about half the time with his head in the clouds.

While talking with Bridget, he had seen Richard come from the field with a wagonload of oats. The team and wagon stood on the barn floor, waiting; but Richard, instead of unloading and stacking the sheaves, was standing in the doorway, transfixed.

Vincent asked, "Well, are you waiting for the sheaves to take themselves off by magic?"

Ordinarily the rough tone would have been a spur to immediate activity; but Richard remained transfixed.

"Vince—you were talking to Bridget."

"Am I answerable to you for that?"

"No, but—you didn't tell her I told you—anything?"

"Get to work," Vincent said.

"Vince, you didn't, did you? It would frighten her. She might run away. . . ."

"You are equating the girl's intelligence with your own. And you flatter yourself in assuming that any words I might exchange with her would necessarily have to do with you. We discussed important matters."

"What—important matters?"

Vincent kept his face set in hard unsmiling lines. "How to send eighteen shillings to Ballyshannon. *Now* get to work!"

So the days passed, crowded with work; nothing but work from the first gray of dawn to the last hour of deepening twilight; then to bed, and then another day just like the one before. And only those infrequent, brief and too-far-off glimpses of Bridget; for Richard could not escape his brother's vigilance, and dared not even try.

Things would improve, he told himself, when the pressures of summer—the haying, the harvesting of grain—leveled off to the less demanding work of early fall. And when Virginia was better. But, as it turned out, the hoped-for improvement did not come.

No new girl was found. When Virginia was better and the constant watch could be relaxed, Bridget resumed most of her morning duties as upstairs maid, while Virginia slept. This easing of the situation for Jane meant that any chance of Richard's being sent to the house to carry firewood or fill the washtubs or move heavy furniture, vanished entirely.

Nor was that all. The amount of barn and field work that fell to his lot, far from diminishing, increased

115

when the gatehouse tenant left in the middle of September.

This was a serious loss. Not only was the gatehouse tenant a hardworking and reliable man, but his wife prepared three meals a day for the redemptioners, who lodged with them, as well as a noon meal for the by-the-day hands who came from Willowfield. A new tenant had to be found; but the finding would not be easy, as labor was scarce in the Colonies, particularly at this time of unrest and rebellion. Furthermore, the man's reason for leaving suggested that a replacement might be more than ordinarily hard to come by.

He was a Patriot; he could no longer work for Tories.

Uselessly Marcus tried to convince him that they were neutral, having no quarrel with either the Patriots or the Crown. He replied that the "skittish" were as bad as the Tories, or worse, for an honest man ought to make up his mind to be on one side or the other, not straddling the fence, ready to jump whichever way the wind blew. It was known, he said, that none on this road had joined the Militia; and since they weren't Quakers or members of any other sect opposed to bearing arms, and had come across from England only a few years ago, that was all anyone needed to know they were Tories.

Marcus could not in sincerity put up a strong argument against the allegation; for the truth was that the Staffords and Findlays and Spensers, though circumspectly keeping their opinions to themselves, were Loyalists at heart, seeing active rebellion as treason. They did not want to fight for independence. They wanted only to farm their lands and be at peace.

The emergency was met in part by Cook's bringing one of her nieces to help in the kitchen, where the field hands would now have to be fed. And fortunately, though not to the extent Richard had hoped for, the outside work did reach that no-longer-quite-so-urgent stage. This was offset by there being one less hand to do it; still, they could manage. There was the corn to be cut and shocked, the fields to be plowed and harrowed for fall planting, and then the actual corn harvest, the husking of the ears—but that, whether done at the barn or in the field, could run on into cold weather, even after the snows came, with no damage except to the hands of the huskers.

Vincent seemed in no hurry to find a new tenant for the gatehouse. He said they were making out well enough, and in any case the cottage should first be cleaned and refurbished, repairs made to the roof, which leaked around the west chimney, and a Franklin stove put in the front room, as those twenty-inch stone walls took up a great deal of heat—even with a good hearth fire going that room in winter was cold as a tomb. Also, other provision should be made for the bond servants, so that new tenants, possibly with a number of children, would not be inconveniently crowded. The men could have the room off the kitchen, there at the house, and the maids could be moved to a room on the third floor. Marcus agreed, and Richard was assigned the rainy-day task of thoroughly cleaning the interior of the cottage, and the odd-moments task of repairing the roof.

Virginia, meanwhile, was steadily improving. The prescribed period outdoors was no longer spent sitting under the beech, but walking with Bridget in the meadow or the orchard; slowly, because she tired easily; but each day the walk was a few minutes longer. She wore her housecap but no hood or other protection against the sun, which, as the days passed, gave her fair skin a delicate golden tint, almost as golden as her hair; and when the crisp air of October came along, her father noted with satisfaction that she returned from her walks with faint little patches of red on her cheeks.

From the fields or barn, Richard watched when he could, longing to join them or at least be near when they came back. It was not fear of his brother that kept him from doing so. Rather, it was the opposite: a feeling that Vincent would somehow solve the problem, if he would just be patient and wait. Vincent had not told anyone, neither his father nor Jane; of that Richard was sure. And the fact that he hadn't told meant— didn't it?—that he was still weighing the matter in his own mind. And if he was still weighing it, that had to mean he wasn't wholly opposed. And if he wasn't wholly opposed, then surely he would see that the right thing was the only thing, and surely would speak for them, surely would help.

"How is Ginny?" Richard asked almost every day; and desperately wanted to ask, "How is Bridget?" Because more than two months had passed since Vince said, "We'll soon know." And if they would know, then what of Jane? The thought of Jane's cold, sharp, suspicious eyes discovering that Bridget was with child filled him with dread.

He was on the barn floor one afternoon, helping Vincent load a cart with sacks of seed wheat to take to the field for sowing, when he saw Bridget and Virginia coming down the drive toward the barn. To his surprise, Vincent neither told him curtly to get on with his work, nor went down the barn bank to question their approach.

Richard was prepared to find Virginia looking better than he had ever seen her. He was not prepared to find Bridget pale, or to see shadows under her eyes, or faint hollows in the cheeks that had been so sweetly rounded; but she was smiling, and for just a moment raised her eyes to his—and yes, they were as blue as ever and as filled with love. If they also held an anxious pleading message—"Say nothing, Richard, please say nothing"—he had not time to answer it, nor to wonder about the paleness or the shadows. Virginia was running to him. He knelt to let her fling herself into his arms.

"Uncle Richard, you haven't come to see me—not once—and I've missed you so!"

"I'm sorry, Ginny. But you know I've been thinking about you."

"Yes, but I wanted you to come. I *needed* you!"

"He couldn't come," her father told her. "I needed him more than you did. You have Bridget." And then, after waiting a moment, "Did you come down here to ask your uncle something?"

"Yes."

"Well, time is fleeting. Why don't you ask him?"

"Uncle Richard, will you carry me up the hill?"

"Carry you—up the hill?"

"To the field on top. I've never been there—it's too far and too steep. But I want to go—Bridget says it's very beautiful—and Papa said I may, if you have time to come with us and carry me up the steep part. Have you time, Uncle Richard?"

Richard stood up slowly, his eyes on his brother's face. Nothing showed there; it was impassive as stone.

"Have I, Vince?"

"Not unless you go at once," Vincent answered brusquely. "I'll want you back here in an hour. *One hour*, understand?"

One hour? Eternity could be in an hour . . .

A wind blew across the hill. A bright wind, warmed by sunshine but carrying a reminder of the nighttime frosts that had turned the green woods scarlet and gold. The hilltop itself was gold, the dry grasses rustling under the wind.

"It's so high," Virginia said, enraptured. "It's like Heaven!"

She was walking between them, her hands in theirs; a link, not a divider.

"*Isn't* it Heaven?" Richard asked, sounding surprised.

"Why no, of course not. We're alive!"

"So we are. But sometimes we find Heaven on earth, Ginny. *I* have. Heaven is being with someone you love."

"Then I'm in Heaven too," Virginia said contentedly, "because I love you and Bridget."

They felt the love—hers, and theirs passing through her—in the tight clasp of her hands.

Richard asked, "Have you been taking good care of Bridget?"

"Why Uncle Richard, no. *She's* taking care of *me*."

"But she looks tired, Ginny." To himself: *And pale, and short of breath coming up the hill.* "Is she working too hard?"

"I don't know. Maybe she is, because Mama's cross if all the rooms aren't done before I wake up."

"I be not tired and not working too hard," Bridget said quickly. "But so hot it was, in the summer. At home in Donegal the wind from the sea brings coolness. There be nothing wrong with me, please, but only the many hot days."

"There will soon be many cold days," Richard said. "Much colder than in Ireland. How will you be then, Bridget?"

"I will be"—she faltered and turned her head away —"not mindful of the cold."

"Of course she won't mind the cold, Uncle Richard.

120

She'll be in the house with me, beside the fire. And anyway, by that time the prince will be here."

"You're still counting on the prince, Ginny?"

"Oh, yes. Only I'm not going to let him take her away. That's what I say to the stone now. 'Bring a prince for Bridget—but make him stay *here.*'"

"That's a very good addition. I'm glad you thought of it."

"Do you think he'll come soon, Uncle Richard?"

"Yes, Ginny. I think the magic is working"— Richard caught a quick agonized look from Bridget, and held it long enough to put into his own all the hope and assurance and promise he could—"and he has to come soon."

Vincent had taken the wheat sacks out to the sowers and was back for another load when Richard returned to the barn. They looked at each other, Vincent with a question in his eyes, Richard with a plea.

"Vince, I know why you let me go."

"You are discerning. All right, help get these sacks on."

In vain Richard looked for some sign, something on which to pin his hopes. His brother's face was hard and cold.

"We're planting wheat. Get busy!"

(10)

Jane stood in the doorway of her father-in-law's room, watching Bridget polish the mahogany Chippendale chest of drawers.

The girl was irritatingly slow these days, and wasn't looking well. Her face was thinner, her color poor, even her hair had lost some of its luster. A moment before, after being on her knees to wipe the cabriole legs of the chest, she had seemed affected by a slight vertigo as she stood up.

It certainly wasn't that she was overworked, Jane reasoned. Two or three hours' work in the morning and another in the evening was less than a third of what she should be doing. The rest of the time she merely sat with or walked with or waited on Virginia. A life of ease, actually, for which she received eighteen unearned shillings each month.

Apparently no one else had noticed that she was looking rather peaked; but there was no one else who saw much of her other than Virginia—unless Vincent should be counted. She had observed him in brief conversation with the girl, but it was unlikely that he

122

would notice any change—Vincent noticed only what it suited him to notice.

Well, *she* did not feel obliged to mention it to anyone. Had the girl been kept in her place, the whole situation would have been avoided. Perhaps serving in two capacities did put a strain upon her. If so, to mention it would be again to lose her services as maid altogether, Vincent being obsessed with this exaggerated idea of her importance to Virginia's welfare.

Jane noted disapprovingly that in addition to the peaked look, the girl was not as neat in regard to dress as she had been. Her bodice was laced very carelessly, very loosely . . . Or was it drawn as tight at the waist as it could be?

Cold suspicion needed only a moment to settle into cold awareness of the truth. *So that was it.*

"You aren't looking well, Bridget. Do you find your duties too burdensome?"

Bridget's hand and the polishing cloth were still. "No, Mistress."

"Perhaps you are carrying a burden we don't know about?"

Now a quick look of terror. "I . . . No, Mistress, I be well."

But inexorably Jane asked, "When do you expect your child?"

"Please, you mistake . . ."

"Don't lie. And don't faint, for I shall not be taken in by that, either." Jane allowed herself a thin smile. "Now I understand why your former mistress did us the great favor of sending you here. You are about four months with child. That fact is of course even now barely evident; but I wonder that I did not suspect, sooner, the reason for Cousin Elizabeth Peirson's generosity. Is the father one of her sons?"

Bridget, starting to say, "It be not so," broke off the words and stood trembling.

"Yes," Jane said, "the sensible thing is not to deny it. Quite possibly if you were to return to her and make the claim, she would provide for you more than adequately."

"I . . . Yes," Bridget whispered. "Yes, Mistress. To return to her—that be best. I go at once."

"You cannot go at once. You cannot go until it is convenient for someone to take you to Westbridge."

"I walk. It be not far . . ."

"Don't be ridiculous." Jane's voice sharpened as the realization came of what she had precipitated—of what the girl's abrupt departure might mean. "There's no need to go rushing off. Mr. Stafford may wish you to stay in spite of your unfortunate condition."

"No, Mistress. I cannot stay."

"You mean you will abandon Virginia, when any minute she will be calling for you?"

"There be one . . ."

Again Bridget broke off her words. *There be one I must put ahead of Virginia.* No, she must not speak those words, for then the question would be, "Who is that one?" Let the Mistress think the father of her child one of the young gentlemen in Philadelphia. Let them all think so. Let *him* think so. He was so young, and had never till that time known a woman. Perhaps he did not know how it was different with one yet a maiden . . .

"There be others to care for the little one, Mistress. Much she loves her uncle. Do you let him come to her once in a while, she will not be missing Bridget Gallagher."

"Yes," Jane said coldly, "I noticed that he was permitted to go walking with her yesterday, in spite of all the field work to be done. Very well, Bridget, if you are set on running off, I will not abase myself by trying to persuade you to stay. But I remind you—the clothes you are wearing are not yours. I will get your traveling dress for you, after breakfast, at my convenience."

Jane turned and left; proudly and stiffly, though inwardly shaken, for the matter had taken an unforeseen course. Well, she would have to think what to do. Send someone out to the field, perhaps, to tell Vincent to come in. Or his father. Ordinarily his father would be right there near the house at this hour, watching Richard ride the colts; but because the day was overcast, with rain in the wind, Vincent had wanted Richard's help in sowing the last of the wheat. But there was no immediate need to do anything. Virginia was still asleep, and in any event the girl would have to wait for her clothes. Summoning her two older daughters, Jane went down to breakfast.

It was like a ballet, Richard thought, the six of them striding abreast down the field, rhythmically tossing their handfuls of wheat, reaching into their bags, tossing again, always the same sweeping gesture, measured, as if to unheard music. Not that he had ever seen a ballet, or ever expected to; but he imagined it had to be something like this. Or like the mowing, when they marched down the field, in a diagonal line, each ten feet from the other, scythes flashing through the green or the gold.

He glanced at the sky. There would be rain, but not for another hour. Six more trips would finish the field, with time to spare for taking the hickory-peg harrow over it to cover the seed. Though perhaps Vince would have him start the harrowing while the others finished the sowing. Either way they would finish in good time, the wheat would be planted, the millions of little oval golden grains showering down on the rich brown earth of Blue Meadow. By the end of next week the green spears would be pushing up, and next summer there it would all be again—the gold sea of ripe grain bending and rippling under the wind. That was how life was—the beginning leading to the end, and the end to the beginning, a turning wheel, a great circling. You could get quite dizzy thinking about it.

You could get dizzy thinking about other things, too. Such as being a father. Just turned eighteen—*and a father!* Because even if your child was not yet born, once you planted the seed it was there, alive, growing in the warm dark like any other seed, like *this* seed, but even more miraculously. Did mothers love their children before they were born? Did fathers?

"Watch where you're going!"

Richard cast a startled glance at his brother, next to him on his right. The distance between them had noticeably dwindled. Quickly he readjusted his direction without changing his stride or the rhythmic sweep of his hand. But there might be a skip, back there; a place where the wheat would be thin and the weeds would grow. If so, Vince would remember its exact location, and in the early summer would send him out to pull the weeds—the tangible evidence of letting his feet wander along with his mind.

At the end of the field, the end nearest the buildings, his father was waiting to replenish their sowing bags from the sacks of wheat on the cart. His father still hadn't been told about Bridget. Had he been, Richard could have read in his eyes an answer of some sort to the guilty questioning look he felt sure must show in his own; but with a smile his father said, "A straight line is the shortest distance between two points, Richard," unaware of any graver wandering than that which he was guilty of in not keeping a fixed distance between himself and the other sowers.

While waiting his turn to have his bag filled, he stood looking toward the house, some five hundred feet away, wondering what Bridget was doing at that moment. He thought it must be about nine o'clock, but he didn't know, for heavy clouds hid the sun that yesterday had shed its golden light upon them, up there on the golden hill.

His eye was caught by someone running down the drive. A stranger, a ragged figure in black petticoat and gray head-shawl. "Who can that be?" he asked Vincent, who shrugged and said he didn't know. Some poor old beggar woman, Richard imagined, to whom Jane had given short shrift. Now she was gone, disappearing between the shed and the barn.

Idly he wondered why an old beggar woman would come so far out here in the country. Twice a year a peddler came, in a gypsy wagon loaded with assorted wares. And once in a while an itinerant musician or artist, or a runaway bond servant on his way to the west, or just some restless footloose vagabond wandering about the country picking up a few pence here and there for an hour's work. But women didn't walk the roads, begging. At any rate he had never seen one. It struck him as more than a little odd.

"Now keep your mind on what you're doing," Vincent warned as they lined up to start back.

So he kept his mind on what he was doing. Or tried to. For some reason he felt a vague uneasiness that kept making him want to turn and look back toward the house. Not the uneasiness of the past two months, for that was ever-present and anything but vague. This was different; of unknown origin, indefinable, and very puzzling. He searched his mind for something to which it might be attributable.

The field was a quarter-mile long; each round trip took about ten minutes. They had completed two trips and were on the return lap of the third when in his mind-searching for the cause of the uneasiness a memory sprang out at him. It came in words, clear and exact: *Did she not give me these things, I would have naught but rags and my old gray shawl.*

For a few seconds after the memory came, he automatically went on sowing wheat; it took that long to wrest himself free of the rhythm. But then . . . *"That was Bridget!"* he flung at his brother, and took off at a run.

Vincent's angry shout didn't stop him. His father's amazement didn't stop him. He had pulled the shoulder strap of his bag over his head as he ran, and not heeding his father's, "Richard!" tossed the bag into the cart as he passed.

Never before had he been so glad that he could run so fast—faster than anyone else around—no one could overtake him. His horse was in the paddock. Running into the barn he snatched his bridle from its hook, ran out again, vaulted the fence, slipped the bridle on, gathered up the reins, and gave a spring that put him astride the gray's back. The fence was four feet high; Sea Mist could clear five. Wheeling about, Richard put him to it, and over they went, clean and free.

From the corner of his eye as he turned at a gallop down the drive, he saw Vincent and his father approaching. They may have been calling to him to stop. If they were he didn't hear, nor would have heeded. He heard only the pounding of Sea Mist's hoofs on the hard ground, and the name *Bridget, Bridget,* repeated over and over in the pounding of his heart.

He turned toward Willowfield. A hundred yards ahead, the stub of a dead tree had fallen across the road. There was room to pass, by keeping close against one bank; but Sea Mist arched across the tree with no slowing of his stride. The road swept in a wide curve to the left; they swept with it. Fences and hedges flashed by. A dog ran barking from the mill, pursued them, but soon was left behind. Now they were a mile beyond Blue Meadow. The road swung right, to the ford. Still at full speed they splashed across; for beyond the ford, halfway up the hill, was the hurrying figure in draggled black skirt and gray shawl.

The sound of the galloping reached her, she looked back, then tried to run; but it was too late for running, she could not run as Sea Mist could. Moving to the side of the road, out of his way, she pulled her shawl across her face. Did she think he would not know her, would go racing past, no thought in his mind that this poor beggar girl could be Bridget, his own, his beloved?

Drawing rein, he came to a sliding stop beside her, dropped to the ground, took her in his arms.

"Bridget, Bridget . . . Suppose I hadn't seen you, suppose someone else had picked you up, suppose I had never found you . . ."

Tears were running down her cheeks. He pushed the shawl away. He kissed the tears.

"Ah, Richard, *a rún*, please, you must let me go."

"I will never let you go. You are mine—I love you. Why did you run away, Bridget? Why?"

"The Mistress sees I be with child, and thinks I do be so when first I come. It be best to let them think this; then they will not be angry with you. Please, we cannot marry. They would cast you off. . . ."

"Bridget, we *are* married. In the sight of God you are already my wife. The child within you is my child."

"But this we must not let them know. . . ."

"My brother already knows. And he knows I'm going to marry you. If we have to go away, then we'll go away together. I can make our living. I can do any kind of farm work—and I can build wagons—make furniture—there's nothing I can't do. But come, we can't stand here talking, my horse is hot. And anyway, we have to go back—they're waiting for us."

"Waiting?" Dread was in her eyes.

"Bridget, won't you believe me when I tell you everything will be all right? Won't you trust me?"

"Please—I trust—but of their anger to you I be afraid."

"Don't be. No matter how angry they are, they'll think first of what's right and proper and practical and necessary. My brother won't want to let you go—Virginia needs you. And even if my father disowns me, I'm sure he won't turn me out—he hasn't anyone else to train the colts!"

A smile glimmered through her tears. "Almost you make me believe it so."

"Good. Then come on, so we're home before it starts to rain. I don't want you to get wet—it could be bad for you. You shouldn't have crossed the ford. That cold water . . . Bridget! You're in your bare feet! You could catch your death!"

"Think not so. Till I come to this land I be always bare-foot. Shoes cost much money."

"Well, you never will be again. You will always have shoes, Bridget. And a fine dress to wear on Sundays. And—a necklace of amethysts! Anything you want—anything—I will give you!"

"I want only you, *a chara dhil.*"

"And I you." He kissed her again. "You—and our child. It will be a boy—I know it will be a boy. We'll name him for our fathers."

130

The joy, the beauty, the splendor, the sheer wonder of it came close to putting Richard in a trance. With a great effort, aided by feeling a drop of rain, he brought himself back to the demands of the moment.

"Well . . . Come, Bridget, we have to go home." He led his horse close to a bank. "Put your foot on my hand. Don't be afraid—he won't move until I give the word. There you are." Sliding a leg across, he mounted behind her. "Now, we won't do any more than walk; but just so you don't lose your balance and slip off, I'll keep my arm around you. Ready?"

(11)

At Blue Meadow a crisis existed.

Virginia, waking, had called for Bridget, and Bridget had not come. She had run up and down the hall, searching. Her calls had changed to screams, which reaching to the lower floor had brought her mother from the breakfast room. Of course Bridget was there, her mother had said. But Virginia had caught a strange little note of alarm underneath the assurance.

"She's not! She's not! She's gone!"

"Hush, Virginia. Go back to your room. Bridget is probably in the kitchen. I'll find her and send her to you."

But Jane had not found Bridget. What she had found, instead, in the little closet-bedroom, was Bridget's blue and white maid's dress, the too-tight bodice, the underpetticoat and shift and shoes given her the night she came. Going then to the third floor, she had found the storage closet still locked—as it had to be, since only she had a key. Returning, she too had looked in all the rooms, and had questioned Harriet and Eleanor, Mistress Kershaw, Cook, and the maids. No one had seen Bridget.

By that time Virginia had come downstairs and

was running from room to room, screaming, and the entire household had been thrown into turmoil.

Alarmed for the child, and dismayed by the turn her own perfectly righteous role in the matter had taken, Jane had decided that she had no recourse but to summon her husband or father-in-law. On her way to the front door she had been relieved to hear Vincent nearby, shouting for Richard, and had opened the door just in time to see Richard and his horse go sailing across the paddock fence and tearing down the drive. Quite obviously the madness that possessed the house had somehow spread outside also—or why would Richard be dashing off in that insane manner, and why would Vincent, and his father too, be here instead of in the fields, when earlier nothing had compared in importance with getting the wheat in the ground ahead of the rain?

Sharply she called, "Vincent!"

Both men glanced her way, but neither came. Instead, they exchanged a look between themselves, then continued to stand a moment longer, looking toward the road, whence still came the sound of that crazy galloping. She had to call again before they turned and —with reluctance, it seemed to her—approached the house.

"That girl," Jane greeted them accusingly, the whole deplorable affair being *their* fault, "seems to have disappeared, and Virginia is beside herself!"

"Did you send her away?" Vincent asked.

"I did not send her away. If the stupid creature has gone, it is entirely by her own wish!"

"Did you have words with her about anything that made her think she must leave?"

"I had words with her, yes. Am I not supposed to have words with my own servants?"

"Oh, come, Jane. You found out she's pregnant, didn't you?"

In angry astonishment, Jane stared at him. "*You* knew?"

"I'm a breeder of livestock," Vincent answered with a glint of amusement that did nothing to endear him to his wife. "Where's Virginia?"

"Where, indeed! Have you lost your hearing? And what do you propose to do about her now, pray, if the girl can't be found?"

"Don't worry. Richard's gone after her."

Vincent entered the hall. Virginia, flanked by her imploring but helplessly weeping sisters, had thrown herself down on the stair landing, a pitiful little heap of despair, alternately sobbing and screaming for Bridget. He picked her up, ignoring her struggles to escape and her frantic, "No, no—not you—Bridget!" Seating himself on the steps, he settled her on his lap.

"Stop it now. Bridget will be here in a little while."

"No, she won't! She's gone! Mama sent her away! Mama hates her and sent her away!"

"Your mother doesn't hate her and didn't send her away. Now be quiet, and be sensible, and I'll tell you where she is."

Virginia, though in some danger of strangling over her sobs, became quiet.

"You know the stone you've been touching every day, and the wish you've been making? Well, your wish is about to come true. Bridget has simply gone for a little walk. When she comes back, the prince will be with her."

"A—real—prince?" Virginia whispered, between hiccoughs.

"He may not look like a real prince to you. But

134

don't be disappointed, because as far as Bridget is concerned he is a prince. To you, he may not look much different from—well, for instance, from your Uncle Richard."

"I know." Virginia sounded entirely content. "Uncle Richard said he might be just a very ordinary sort of prince."

"He did, eh?"

"Yes. He said he might even be wearing linsey-woolsey."

"Well, I have an idea that's exactly what he is wearing."

"He said—the only thing was, he has to fall in love with her at first sight."

"I think we can assume he has already done so."

"And then—he said he'd take her away to his father's kingdom. But I won't let him. They have to stay right here."

"They will stay here," Vincent promised. "Wouldn't you like to go outside now, and watch for them?" He set her on her feet and stood up. "Bring your sister's cloak and hood, will you please, Harriet?"

Marcus and Vincent and Virginia did their watching and waiting on the front doorstep. Harriet and Eleanor, forbidden by their mother to go outdoors, hurried upstairs to watch from the windows. Jane neither watched nor waited, but in frigid silence went about her usual things in her usual way—or as nearly as possible. She was furious with Bridget for having brought on this crisis, and even more furious with Vincent, as much for knowing as for having kept the knowledge to himself. Had she listened carefully to the exchange between her husband and daughter, she would have had at least an intimation if not full grasp of the

135

fact that Richard was the one most deserving of her fury.

Through the trees bordering the road at the far corner of the meadow, Vincent caught a glimpse of a gray horse passing.

"Keep watching now. Our prince is almost here."

"Bridget's prince," Virginia corrected, shaking with excitement. "Do you see him, Papa?"

"I saw his horse."

"Galloping?"

"No. Walking."

"Uncle Richard said he'd be galloping."

"Well, after a horse has had a long gallop, he has to have a long walk to cool him out, as even your addle-headed Uncle Richard has sense enough to know."

"Is Bridget with him?"

"Keep watching and you'll see."

Another minute . . . two, three . . . and there they were. At the third floor window Harriet said, "Papa was just pretending, so Virginia would stop crying. It's only Uncle Richard." But Virginia, from her closer vantage point and the innocent, infinite wisdom of her six years, joyfully exclaimed, "Why—the prince *is* Uncle Richard!"

Marcus stepped forward to meet them. As on the evening of Bridget's arrival he had helped her from the chaise, so now he gave the firm support of his hands as she slipped to the ground; and as on that earlier occasion, because fear was in her eyes, he offered the comfort of his arm around her shoulders.

Crying, laughing, reproaching, rejoicing, Virginia ran to the arms that despite all doubt and fear had to enfold her.

"Bridget! Why weren't you here when I woke up?

Why did you go away without telling me? Why are you wearing those awful old clothes? I was so frightened . . . Bridget, I love you, I love you! I'm so glad you're back! And oh, I'm so glad Uncle Richard is the prince!"

"I think it will be well," Marcus said, "if you take the child upstairs now, Bridget, and calm her, so the affairs of the household can return to normal." He turned to Richard. "When you have stabled your horse, Richard, you will find us waiting for you in the library."

"And make sure," Vincent added grimly, "that you don't keep us waiting very long."

It was Jane, not Richard, who kept them waiting. Jane was aloof, professedly indifferent, and extremely busy.

"Why should *my* time be wasted in senseless discussion of what to do about the girl? Unfortunately, thanks to you and your father, our hands are tied by Virginia's irrational attachment. If it weren't for that, she should of course be immediately dismissed and sent back where she came from. Your father's oh-so-generous Cousin Elizabeth is the one who should have to decide what to do with her. After all, if she can't control the low behavior of her own sons . . ."

"Jane, you don't know what you're talking about. Now hold your tongue long enough to come and be told."

"To be told what? I already know as much as I care to know. You and your father created this situation—setting the girl above herself, giving her the opportunity to ingratiate herself with my daughters. There's no use looking to *me* to help you out of it, now that you've discovered she's a strumpet."

"No one's asking for your help—only for your presence. And, damn it, watch what you say. There's nothing wrong with the girl."

"Nothing wrong? Was she raped, then?"

"By God, Jane, another word out of you and you'll be given no consideration in the matter at all! Now put aside whatever you're doing, and come to the library. Richard's in from the barn—you're holding us up!"

Awareness spread through Jane like the creeping ice of a glacier. Richard was in from the barn. Richard was to take part in the discussion of what to do about a pregnant servant girl. Richard had gone tearing off in pursuit of her, and had brought her back. Richard . . . The ice pushed her thoughts ahead of it like the rocks of a moraine.

Marcus, when the door was closed and their privacy assured, said, "Thank you for coming, Jane. We have a grave problem to discuss, something that concerns all of us as a family. So that one discussion may suffice, I felt you should be here to be informed as to the nature of the problem, and to express any opinions you may have as to its solution." He looked from one to the other of his sons. "Since I knew nothing of the matter until half an hour ago, I think the facts should now be openly stated by those who have full and complete knowledge. Richard, you may speak first, if you care to."

In suffering silence, after one look at Jane, Richard stood looking at the floor.

"Do you prefer having your brother speak?"

"Yes, sir."

Briefly and bluntly, Vincent spoke. His words, unsparing of Richard, were equally unsparing of Jane, for he did not choose them with regard to their suitability or unsuitability in a lady's presence, but purely for their

138

plain and open statement of the facts, as requested. They did, however, spare Bridget, whom they labeled a victim; a willing victim, but a victim none the less.

The sparing of Bridget was not lost upon Jane, who though entirely willing to believe the worst of Richard, was unwilling to see Bridget in a merciful light, or to see responsibility shifted from that quarter where earlier she had convinced herself it belonged.

"You are absurdly ingenuous," she said, "if you think the girl had not been used before she came here."

"No." The denial came simultaneously from two directions; in quiet certainty from Marcus; in anguished protest from Richard.

"No," Marcus said again. "Elizabeth sent her to us, Jane, on the assumption—a mistaken assumption, I am grieved to discover—that here with us she would be safe from this very thing. Responsibility for her safety became mine. I failed in that responsibility. Therefore it is all the more incumbent upon me not to fail in this one—my responsibility to deal promptly and justly with the situation that now confronts us."

"Cousin Elizabeth's convenience was well served, Father, by knowledge of your high principles—and of the fact that you, too, have a young son. Undeniably the girl is attractive, and any . . ."

"Rubbish!" Impatiently Vincent cut her off. "Leave Cousin Elizabeth out of it, will you? The girl had *not* been used before she came here. The child is Richard's."

"May I ask how you can possibly know that?"

"I know because *he* knows."

"It comes as a surprise to me," Jane said with a caustic smile, "that Richard is so knowledgeable. I would have thought . . ."

"Oh, for God's sake, Jane! Do you think I haven't

told him a few elementary facts? But if you want it from him . . ." Vincent swung around. "Tell her you know."

Richard, his face burning, met his brother's eyes with silent tortured appeal.

"Tell *me*, then. Speak up!"

"I—know."

In the fireplace a log fell apart, scattering embers. Marcus, filling his pipe, said, "Fetch me a coal, Richard."

The natural tone, the completely natural little act —taking the smoking-tongs from the mantelpiece, picking up an ember, holding it to his father's pipe—steadied and comforted Richard. He felt himself not wholly abominable in his father's sight; in deep disgrace, but not wholly rejected and despised; perhaps not wholly unloved. . . .

"We will say nothing more"—Marcus spoke mildly but firmly—"of what has gone before. Our concern is with what must be done now. Richard, suppose you tell us what you have in mind."

Richard's effort to imitate his father's calm produced a tone of desperate doggedness. "I am going to marry Bridget."

A scornfully incredulous little sound from Jane greeted the announcement; but Marcus asked, "Are you planning to do so whether or not you have my consent?"

"Father—I'm sorry—yes."

"Then is my consent immaterial to you?"

"No. I want your consent. And I want to marry her. But I thought . . ."

"Continue. What did you think?"

"I thought you would say I must marry her, whether I wanted to or not."

"I take that as a compliment, Richard. And you thought correctly. That is what I say."

"*Father!*" Jane's incredulousness passed the point of being contained in a small wordless sound. "You can't be serious!"

"Indeed I am serious, Jane. My son has behaved in a shameful manner, unworthy of his name. There is no possible way he can redeem himself, now, except by giving his name to the young woman he has violated, and to the child she will bear."

"But the girl is a servant!"

"He did not take that into consideration at the time, and cannot do so now. He must marry her. And I will say that although my displeasure with his conduct is great, it is tempered somewhat by his willingness to meet his obligation properly and honorably, no matter what it may cost him."

"Cost *him!* What of the cost to *us?* The shame? The disgrace? It is preposterous to talk of his marrying the girl. Nothing could be more *dis*honorable, and nothing so totally unnecessary. She can be provided for. Not that she should be. You spoke of dealing 'justly.' In justice she should be sent packing at once—and Richard should be flogged!"

"That would be a poor way of dealing with the situation, Jane. Even if it were a just way—and it is not—it would by no means be a final way. I spoke of Richard's willingness to meet his obligation. I should have used a stronger word, for there is another factor here, you see. Richard, would you care to name that factor?"

Name it—to Jane? No, Richard would not care to. Again he stood mute, and Vincent said, "There is a little thing called love."

"*Love!*" Jane's scorn made the word sound loathsome. "For a servant girl? You are mad—all of you! Oh, I can understand Richard's giving way to his animal passions —he has never been disciplined—he has always been indulged, permitted to follow every foolish whim that enters his head. But *you*. You are men of sense. Of *good* sense, I would have said, up to now. How can you even have such a thought, let alone entertain it for one minute? He is a Stafford, a gentleman—no, let me amend that—the *son* of a gentleman. He cannot marry a servant. We would all be disgraced!"

"Perhaps so," Marcus agreed, "to some extent. But I think you will find that here in the Colonies that particular disgrace is not of such magnitude as in England. Names and good breeding count for less, over here, than material wealth and the power wealth gives to anyone able to acquire it, regardless of the means by which it is acquired, and regardless of birth."

"*I* am not regardless of birth! Do you expect me to live in this house," Jane asked, white with fury, "on a basis of equality with a servant—an illiterate peasant— a lowborn nobody—perhaps herself a hedgerow brat? And do you expect that of my daughters?"

"That is one of the aspects we are here to discuss, Jane. I believe Vincent has a solution you will find acceptable."

"They will live in the gatehouse," Vincent said.

"Will they, indeed! So that's why you have been so dilatory about finding a tenant. You have plotted and connived with your brother. And while permitting me to remain in ignorance of the girl's low character, you have set her up as a companion for my daughters!"

"The girl's character is good. So, for that matter, is Richard's. They're young, they fell in love, and things got out of hand, that's all."

"You defend them!"

"If that's defending them—yes. Come down off your pedestal, Jane. These things happen. They have happened before, and they will happen again. What we have to do is make the best of it. Do what's sensible. Do what's right."

"And you think *this* is right? For whom? Richard? You would have him make a base marriage in preference to one whereby he would acquire a fortune?"

"It's not a matter of what we prefer. The thing is *done*. Can't you get that through your head? He loves the girl, he's had an affair with her, he wants to marry her, and—as you've already been told—he must marry her."

"And forever shame us before our neighbors? We will be laughed at, reviled, and utterly ostracized!"

"What our neighbors think of us," Marcus spoke again in his mild firm way, "is less important than what we think of ourselves. The Staffords do not cast off their own. Bridget is with child, and that child is a Stafford."

"Can you mean by that—the equal of *my* children?"

"Richard is my son, Jane. As my sons are equal in my sight, so will their children be. But, on your behalf, knowing how you would feel, Vincent has proposed that Richard and his wife occupy the gate cottage instead of sharing this house with you. That proposal is satisfactory to me—and to Richard, I am sure. So, if you will try to view the matter objectively, my dear, I think you will find it not too hard to reconcile yourself to the arrangement."

The coldness of Jane's anger had become physical coldness, through and through her. She was shaking with it, and had to fight to keep her voice steady and her words clear.

"I find it impossible, Father, to reconcile myself to

having my servant become my sister-in-law. As to residing in the cottage—they will not be under lock and key, will they? No. They will remain in daily contact with the rest of us, they will come to this house, they will continue to insinuate themselves into my daughters' lives, winning their affections and alienating them from me. . . ."

"*Jane.*" Partly in protest, partly in compassion, Richard took a quick step forward. On a table beside him lay a Bible. Placing his hand on it, he said, "I swear to you, on this Book, that neither Bridget nor I nor our children will ever enter this house except as servants . . ."

"*. . . as long as you or any of your daughters are here.*"

The qualifying addition was Vincent's. They looked at each other.

"Say it!"

Richard said it.

Meeting Jane's eyes, he saw the anger and scorn, for these were uppermost; but there was something else, almost a look of shock. Abruptly she turned and left the room.

A strange heavy silence fell on the three who remained. Richard didn't know the cause. Wasn't everything all right? Wasn't Jane satisfied, or at least silenced? Weren't his father and brother, though displeased with him, in accord as to what must be done?

The silence became painful. "Father . . ."

"You are impetuous, Richard." His father smiled, yet sadness was in his voice. "Your oath will haunt all of us, I am afraid, for many years to come."

"But wasn't that what Jane wanted? Wasn't her greatest objection to our being equals? Now she can look on us only as servants. . . ."

144

"Yes. Well, I thank God your brother is quick-thinking."

"*I* will thank God," Vincent said, "if the men finished with the wheat ahead of this rain. It's coming down hard. And if we've settled things here, there's work to be done at the barn."

"Yes. Richard will be along in a moment."

When Vincent was gone, again there was silence, again painful.

"Isn't there something you wish to ask me, Richard?"

"Yes, Father. I . . ."

Marcus waited, but silence closed on Richard like a trap.

"Do you wish me to tell Bridget?"

"Yes. Please—yes."

"And would you like me to send her down to the cottage, in a little while, so you can tell her also?"

"Yes." Richard's joy was agony.

"Very well, I will send her to the cottage. Now, is that all?"

Tears blurred Richard's sight of his father's face. He wanted to beg forgiveness. And wanted to go close, to feel the forgiveness in a touch, not merely hear it in words. When he was younger, his father often put an arm around him, held him close; and still did, sometimes, seeing no reason why it should be thought unmanly for a father and son to show affection in that way. But not now. Perhaps never again . . .

"Father, I'm sorry I did wrong, sorry I've displeased and disappointed you. Thank you for not being angry—for being kind—and most of all, for being my father. Please forgive me . . ."

The longed-for touch was given. More than a touch —a warm embrace, forgiving, loving, healing, exalting.

Richard's spirits lifted as if borne heavenward on great springing columns of fire.

"Father, I promise you—my sons will be worthy of their name!"

"I know they will be, Richard."

The fires leaped higher. Life was beautiful, life was good, life went on forever, across the years, across the centuries, time without end.

Richard ran to the barn through wind-driven looping silver sheets of rain. He did not go alone. All the future sons and daughters of Blue Meadow ran with him.

Part II

(1)

Through 1775 the rebellion in the Colonies affected the lives of the Staffords and their neighbors principally as something to talk about. They were conservative, distrustful of change, and most were Loyalists. They felt neither the need nor the desire to take part in the making of history, if such it was. True, there was the Militia, which every free and able-bodied male was more or less legally required to join; but enforcement was lax, since the usefulness of the Militia had long ago receded with the ever-westward receding of the frontier; in any case its purpose was defense of home territory, and Massachusetts was far away. The Congress, in September, assumed responsibility for a Continental Army and appointed General George Washington to command it. Few in the Westbridge and Willowfield area had any disposition to offer a year's service. Farmers had better uses for their time. Who would plant and harvest the crops if they or their sons were sent off to help the embattled New Englanders? No, the independence seekers would have to manage their own affairs; and so, for that matter, would King George.

Apart from the Staffords' loss of their Patriot gate-house tenant, life at and around Blue Meadow went on as usual, untouched by conflict between the Colonies and the Crown. Even Richard Stafford's marriage, itself in revolutionary defiance of long-established rule, produced little or no disruption of the ordinary and orderly routine of daily living. Blue Meadow routine was broken that winter by only one event, and that of a purely social nature.

Five years before, a week-long Yuletide party was given by the Edward Findlays in honor of their cousins, the Staffords, who had recently moved into the big new house at Blue Meadow. Marcus and thirteen-year-old Richard, making the move, had only to walk up the drive from the gatehouse, where they had lived while the big house was being built; but Vincent and Jane and their three small daughters had endured and—thankfully—survived the rigors of a long sea voyage, exchanging the refinements of manor life in England for the crudities and discomforts of life in what was still (in Jane's eyes, at least) a veritable wilderness. It was chiefly on Jane's account, then, that the party was given, to demonstrate that even in the "wilderness" of Willow-field the social graces could be maintained.

There was feasting and drinking and good conversation by day, and dancing every night to the music of violins, violoncello, flute, and harpsichord. Most of the guests were local country gentlemen, their wives, and such of their young sons and daughters as had attained sufficient maturity to conduct themselves as ladies and gentlemen, twelve years (Margaret Findlay's age at the time) being considered within that range; but some came greater distances, and a few came all the way from Philadelphia. Those who had far to travel

150

arrived well ahead of time, against the chance of the
roads being closed by snow; and as deep snow did come
with the coming of the new year, they remained long
after the festivities were over—two of them, indeed,
until the winter was over.

The Findlays' party established a precedent. The
following year a similar one was given (but lasting only
three days, and only for the local gentry, who would
not be too long stranded in the event of bad weather)
by the Spensers, and the year after that, by the Staffords.
A pattern thus being set, the gala Yuletide celebration
then circled back to the Findlays, then again to the
Spensers, and in the year 1775 should, in accordance
with the pattern, once more be held at Blue Meadow.

Jane was bitterly opposed. No one would come,
she declared, for the Staffords were everlastingly disgraced by Richard's marriage, and the gentlefolk of
Willowfield would avoid Blue Meadow as they would
a house of pestilence. It would be useless to issue invitations that would all be declined "with regret" or
ignored altogether. Far better simply to withdraw into
the shell that was all they had left of former dignity and
honor.

But Marcus said no, the invitations would be sent.
He did not feel that his dignity, much less his honor,
had suffered by Richard's marriage. If others thought
so, then it was their right to attend or not attend as they
saw fit. He would see to all the necessary preparations,
if Jane did not wish to give her attention to that of
which she disapproved. He had already, as early as the
first of October, engaged the musicians. Ample supplies
of food and wine and brandies were of course on hand.
And the Findlays would (as the three families had done
on the previous occasions) share their servants, so that

151

the needs of a houseful of guests could properly be met; that the Spensers would be equally cooperative remained in doubt.

The invitations were therefore sent; were in fact delivered exactly as three years ago—by Richard, riding from farm to farm. Jane, seeing this as flagrant shamelessness, fully expected them to be disdainfully thrown to the ground, and seemed more suspicious than relieved when told that none received this treatment.

"What did you say," she demanded of Richard, "when you gave them the notes?"

"I said, 'My father sends his respects, sir.'"

"What did *they* say?"

"They said, 'Thank you, Richard.'"

"That could not have been *all* they said."

"Well, two or three asked, 'How are things at Blue Meadow?'"

"And what did you answer?"

"I answered, 'Fine, sir.'"

"'Fine,' indeed! Did they look at you with utter contempt, as you deserve?"

"No, I don't think so." Richard pushed his hair back from his forehead, trying to remember exactly how his father's friends had looked at him. He had found the looks somewhat embarrassing, but hadn't thought very much about what they revealed, for he had quite a number of calls to make and Vincent had told him not to dawdle. "I think—with curiosity."

"Do you dare to imagine," Jane asked witheringly, "that any gentleman would permit himself to be curious about your despicable conduct?"

Suitably withered, Richard offered no reply; but Vincent, with that glint of amusement which his wife always took as a personal affront, commented that there were few things a gentleman was likely to be more curious about than another gentleman's affair with a chambermaid.

None of the invitations was formally answered; but as no answer was requested or expected, this merely left the matter open and indeterminate. It was known only that the Findlays would attend.

Edward Findlay and Marcus, first cousins, had always been close, not only in blood relationship and friendship, but in temperament, in mode of living, in their likes and dislikes, their opinions on almost any subject, and their ethics. Edward, visiting the Colonies to inspect a two-thousand-acre tract purchased sight unseen some years before, had been so impressed by the beauty of the rolling hills, the purity of the streams, the magnificence of the forests, and the fertility of the farm lands, that he decided he wished to live there; and had persuaded first Marcus and then their friends, the Spensers, to share his purchase, each taking six hundred acres, he retaining the rest. Additionally, he had designed and superintended the building of their houses. Marcus and Richard had lived with the Findlays while the barn and cottage were under construction at Blue Meadow, and a brother-sister relationship had quite naturally developed between Richard and Margaret, then eleven and ten years old. It was their fathers' hope that the relationship would later develop into a still closer one. Indeed, the marriage of Margaret and Richard was taken for granted.

The Findlays, therefore, though deeply shocked, were more saddened than horrified to learn of the happenings at Blue Meadow. In confidence Marcus told his cousin the full story, leaving to his discretion how much would be told other members of the family. As a result of certain merciful omissions in the retelling, Margaret learned only that Richard had most indiscreetly been familiar with a servant girl, that the girl was with child, and that his father had compelled him to marry her. Thus being spared the bitter knowledge that Richard actually loved and wanted to marry the girl, actually preferred a girl of mean birth to herself, Margaret saw him as a sacrifice to his father's principles. She could overlook the "familiarity"—young men would be young men. She could grieve for Richard, thinking him too severely punished for a youthful indiscretion. She could —and did—grieve for herself, because she loved him and had looked forward to the day when she would be his wife. Had she been told the full truth, pride would not have let her grieve. As it was, her regard for Richard suffered no diminution, but was increased; and the bitterness she felt was directed solely toward his stern and iron-willed father. If she glimpsed any incongruity here, having previously held the opinion that her Cousin Marcus was one of the gentlest and kindest of men, it may have been that she deliberately blinded herself to what she glimpsed. Early in December she departed for Philadelphia to spend the winter with friends.

The feelings of the Spensers were not known. They received the news second hand from Edward Findlay, the same condensed version he had given his own family. He had the impression that they were numbed by shock, perhaps because they also had a marriageable daughter who looked with favor upon Richard; as to what their feelings would be when the shock wore off, he could only speculate.

To Cordelia Spenser, eighteen, the removal of Richard from the limited list of eligible young men was a blow, though not so great a blow as it was to Margaret Findlay. It had always seemed almost a foregone conclusion that the Findlays would snare Richard.

154

Cordelia's one advantage lay in being much prettier than Margaret, who really was not pretty at all, but quite plain, with a boyish look well in harmony with her all-too-frequently boyish behavior. Also, Margaret knew nothing of feminine wiles, or if she did, scorned to make use of them. Cordelia, on the other hand, was well schooled in femininity (and not in Latin and Greek, as Margaret was). The girls were friends, and intended to remain so, no matter which way the cards fell. Neither could ever have dreamed that Richard Stafford as a matter of choice had passed them both over in favor of a penniless and lowborn Irish girl—a chambermaid in his father's house! The thought did cross Cordelia's mind, *I wonder if she's pretty.* But, like Margaret, she thought, *Poor Richard!* and wondered how Mr. Marcus Stafford could be so cruel.

Meeting at church, the Spensers and Staffords exchanged their usual greetings and made their usual inquiries into the state of one another's health. Constraint in the Spensers' manner was attributed by Jane to coldness and disgust; by Marcus, simply to embarrassment. A similar constraint was in the manner of others also, whose disapproval quite naturally was great. They slid glances at Richard, but in the presence of the family no reference was made to his disgraceful marriage. To Edward Findlay someone remarked that at least the Staffords had not the effrontery to bring the girl with them to Sunday services; but his reply—that she was a Roman Catholic—seemed to indicate that were this not so, they could expect to see her at Richard's side. It was noted further that Richard appeared not in the least chastened, and that neither his father nor his brother gave any sign of holding him in low regard.

The scandal kept tongues busy for a month; but

by December its edges had worn down somewhat; and as parties were not so frequent that anyone could choose to miss what had become Willowfield's main social event of the year, all the invited guests turned up, with the single exception of Margaret Findlay.

As Richard had sensed and as Vincent well understood, curiosity took precedence over shock and disapproval. What, the guests were wondering, would the Staffords now do about Richard's wife? And what would they themselves do if she dared make an appearance among them as a social equal? Would any of them walk out? Would *all*? The uncertainty added a lively little fillip to the occasion.

But Richard's wife did not appear among them. No one caught so much as a glimpse of her the first two days; and had Cordelia Spenser's curiosity not outrun everyone else's, the Willowfield gentry might have continued to assume that Edward Findlay's abbreviated account comprised the full story.

Richard they saw. Richard was there to take their horses and pleasure wagons to the barn. Richard, in his usual homespun farm clothes, was in and out of the house, carrying firewood to the drawing room, dining room, library, and bedrooms. As dusk approached, Richard went about with a taper in a long brass holder, lighting a hundred candles. None of this was surprising, for they remembered that three years ago he had performed these same menial chores, and they all knew that both brothers worked in the fields with the hired hands and bondmen—the Staffords maintaining that physical labor did not make a man any less a gentleman provided he was a gentleman in the first place. But in the evening, when the ladies in silk or satin or velvet gowns, and the gentlemen scarcely less ornate in their finest coats and breeches, brocade waistcoats, flashing silver buckles on their garters and their shoes, descended the wide curving stairs and assembled in the hall, and the dancing began, Richard was not there.

To other young ladies besides Cordelia Spenser this was a sore disappointment, for Richard was by far the best dancer they knew, as light and quick and graceful as themselves, whether in the minuet or the lively country dances. One might think, the girls said, that Mr. Stafford would not be *so* unkind, or so thoughtless of the pleasure of his guests as to deny them Richard's attendance at the dance. After all, no matter what Richard had done or whom he had married, he was still a Stafford, was he not? It was only his wife who was not socially acceptable. Richard himself was not only acceptable but downright necessary; half the fun of the dance was lost without him.

Cordelia, prodded by her friends, at last had the boldness to inquire. "Mr. Stafford, isn't Richard going to dance with us?"

"No, my dear. Richard is taking care of his nieces. They are rather too young, you see, to share in festivities of this sort, so they were promised festivities of their own—the entire three days with Richard and Bridget"—Marcus spoke the two names as if they naturally and properly belonged together—"at the cottage." Aware that others standing near were listening, he went on: "Chiefly with Bridget, I should say, as we must of course depend on Richard to do a great many other things as well, while the rest of us are here enjoying ourselves."

How easy it was, he thought as he moved among his guests, to speak true words yet make them serve to cover and conceal a deeper truth; words that gave no indication of the sadness or the pain. . . .

The day before yesterday, the Eve of Christmas,

Richard had brought pine and hemlock branches from the woods, had decked the hall and drawing room with wreaths and garlands of the fragrant boughs tied with bright ribbons of scarlet and gold. Richard had brought in the Yule log, a great five-foot length of beech, and had laid it, with kindling and smaller logs underneath, ready for lighting. But Richard was not here to dance beneath the garlands he had hung, nor had he seen the Yule log burn. They had gathered around it as always, Jane had played the harpsichord, and dutifully the children had tried to raise their voices in the old carols, but the singing had turned to tears. For they all too well remembered—even Jane too well remembered—how in other years Richard had led the singing; how he had introduced to them, singing alone, the beautiful new carols, "Joy to the World," and "Hark, the Herald Angels Sing"; how his clear young voice had brought to them the joy and triumph of the angels' proclamation.

Your oath will haunt us, Richard. . . .

The haunting had begun almost at once, and painfully, the day of the marriage, when going to his room to get his clothes and his few other personal possessions, Richard started up the stairs and then, remembering, stopped on the landing. For a moment he stood there, looking up, one hand on the smooth wide banister rail. How often in younger days, though forbidden by Jane, had he slid down that rail? Turning with a quick smile —but Marcus could not summon a smile in answer—he came down from the landing and went through the narrow part of the hall to the servants' stairs at the back, and so to his room—no, to the room that had been his, chosen because from the west and north windows he could see more of Blue Meadow than from any other room in the house.

Outside it was easier, for outside nothing was different. The work went on as usual—the tending of the livestock, the corn harvest, the splitting of chestnut logs for fence rails and of beech and hickory and white oak for firewood; and on the barn floor the flailing of the summer grains. In the fields, in the woods, in the barn, Richard was Richard, a Stafford, not a servant.

A new girl was found for the upstairs work; Bridget continued only with her duties as nursemaid, coming to the house before Virginia wakened and not leaving until she slept again at night. Bridget prepared early-morning and late-evening meals for Richard and herself at the cottage. Her midday meal was with the children. Richard made do with breakfast leftovers or cold meat or bread and cheese, alone in the cottage kitchen.

The Staffords, though far from happy with the vacancy thus created at their own table, adjusted themselves as best they could. But Cook was outraged. Unaware that Richard was denied his rightful place not by the family but by himself, she gave Jane a generous piece of her mind.

Cook, a self-respecting middle-class German woman, did not consider herself a servant. Cookery was an art, she an artist, and she *obliged* the Staffords with her services. She addressed Jane as *"Gnädige Frau"* purely as a formality; and accepted the appellation "Cook" as in no way derogatory but as a tribute to her skills, hearing in it always a suitable note of respect, and often, from one member of the family, a teasing note of affection—even when she laid her broom on that young *Dummkopf* for muddying her kitchen floor.

"Gott in Himmel!" she exclaimed when told by Jane that only four would henceforth be served in the dining room at midday. "Is the young gentleman then all day to work with no food in his stomach from rising to sleeping?"

"Certainly not. He is eating at the gatehouse."

"And who to have ready what he eats, when he comes hungry from the fields and needing hot food and drink?"

Jane, thinking to mollify her, made the mistake of suggesting, "If you have no objection, quite possibly he would be willing to have his noon meal here with the others."

"Be willing, would he? You tell me to feed the Master's son in the kitchen? Why not throw scraps to him on the ground, as dogs are fed!"

In excitement or wrath, Cook's English, given strong German pronunciation and interspersed with German phrases, became largely unintelligible, and the rest of her tirade was clear only in the emotions manifested. Jane wisely chose to say nothing more, for if one word led to another, where would they be without Cook? But Marcus, when told of the incident, felt that in fairness to everyone the situation should be explained.

It was not, he told Cook, that any of them wished Richard to absent himself from their table. Richard had chosen to do so. He felt he could spare them and at the same time be loyal to his wife by not asking that she be accepted in the house at their level, but by relegating himself to hers; and had so sworn. This had not been required of him, and indeed was regretted by all of them. But, "He is very young," Marcus said, "and does not always think before he acts—or speaks."

"There's many a young gentleman takes a poor servant girl to bed, *mein Herr*, and few that would take her to wife. He is a good boy, your son."

Smiling, Marcus thanked her. "You think, then, that Richard was willing to meet his obligation?"

Dryly Cook answered, "I think had you not *made* him marry the girl, he would be absent from more

160

than your dinner table, and she with him; for so it is with young ones when the fire is in them."

"You have been with us five years," Marcus said, again with a smile. "I suppose it should not surprise me that in that time you have come to know and understand us. Tell me: Do you approve of my son's marriage?"

As dryly as before, she answered, "The girl will have strong healthy children, *mein Herr.*"

No more was said; no more was needed. An intelligent woman, Marcus thought.

Richard continued to eat his noon meal alone in the cottage, but he no longer had to make do with breakfast leftovers. Waiting for him in a bake kettle or on a warming shelf in front of the fire was a good hot dinner, carried down each day by Cook herself—and if the others were kept waiting, let them wait! A young boy, still growing, and doing the work of a man, had to be well fed. And—*mein Gott!*—who knew what outlandish Irish cookery *that* one might be feeding him!

Well, it would all become easier as time went on, Marcus told himself. After the first of the year Bridget would no longer come to the house every day. Relieved of her duties, she would not be their servant but a housewife in her own right, and that alone would make it easier.

Virginia, now in better health than ever before in her six years, accepted the prospective change with surprising grace, after her first protesting "*Why?*" was bluntly answered by her father, "Because Bridget is going to have a baby."

Harriet and Eleanor, who possessed vague knowledge of three babies that had come to their mother but had not lived, perhaps had also some vague knowledge of where they came from. Virginia had none.

"Like ours, that Uncle Richard made cradles for?"

161

"No, not like yours. A real baby. Alive."

Virginia did have very limited knowledge of real babies. One time when they visited the Spensers there was another visitor, with a baby. She had seen it asleep in a beautiful quilted basket.

"Is somebody going to bring it to the cottage, in a basket?"

"It will come to the cottage, yes."

"Are they going to give it to Bridget to keep?"

"Yes, it will be Bridget's own baby, to keep."

Virginia had no difficulty understanding that Bridget would of course want to be right there waiting for it, or finding nobody home, whoever brought it might take it away again.

Eagerly she asked, "Will it be a princess?"

But her father answered, "We are counting on a prince."

Yes, it would be easier, Marcus thought again, when Bridget could give all her attention to making the cottage a place of warmth and comfort, a home; when Richard would no longer sit down to his midday meal in lonely isolation; when they would live as any other young married couple, normally, completely, and—God willing—happily. Much easier, even though Richard had shut himself off from dining at the family table, or dancing beneath the pine boughs he had hung, or watching the beech log burn on Christmas Eve.

Virginia had made no hysterical demands that night; had not screamed, "I want Uncle Richard!" or "I want Bridget!" and had tried not to cry, for she had promised Richard to be "good," when he explained that Bridget must go to the cottage and lie down and rest. She had simply stood there with bowed head, drawing deep sobbing breaths while tears ran down her cheeks and dripped on the bodice of her beautiful new red velvet Christmas dress.

Helplessly Jane said, "*Virginia.*" And then, to Vincent, "Are you just going to sit there and watch her cry?"

"I can make her stop," he answered, "but you might not approve of the means."

"Oh, don't be absurd. *Any* means."

Reaching a hand to the child and drawing her close to his chair, Vincent said, "Now listen, Virginia. You know we're having a party, and that it will last three days? Well, if all our guests come, we may need your room. So why don't you suggest to your mother that it would be helpful to us if you and your sisters were to spend those three days at the cottage with Richard and Bridget?"

"Mama, Mama—may we?"

"Yes, if you wish."

The answer brought all three little girls to envelop their mother with hugs and shower her with kisses—something Marcus had never seen them do.

Strange, he thought, beautifully strange how love once planted sends its shoots in all directions, to flower like fruit trees in the spring. . . .

(2)

Richard went outside at midnight.

He had gone late to bed, for the girls had stayed up until ten, an hour that would have appalled their mother. The excitement of a whole day at the cottage, helping Bridget make bread and biscuits and honey cakes, then sitting before the kitchen fire in the evening, listening to his stories of enchanted castles and beautiful princesses and knights in shining armor, and then going to bed, all three together in a strange bed in a strange room warmed by a black iron stove instead of a carefully covered hearth fire, had them wide awake, and for a long while they lay whispering and laughing and clinging to the joys of the day.

In the kitchen was a bed that folded into the wall when not in use. Richard pulled it down, and when the bedding and pillows were placed, Bridget gratefully yielded to his insistence that she lie down at once. Six months, now, the child had been growing within her, and after a long day on her feet she was very tired. In less than five minutes she was asleep. Richard waited until no more sounds came from the front room, then quietly went in to put another chunk of wood in the Franklin stove. As quietly, he tended the fire in the great chimney place in the kitchen, and then took off his waistcoat and shoes and breeches, and slipped into bed. Beside him Bridget stirred and murmured his name but did not waken. He turned himself toward her, wanting to take her in his arms; but not wanting to disturb her, contented himself simply with her nearness.

But he couldn't sleep. He listened to her soft breathing, and to the whisper of steam still coming from the teakettle over the banked fire, and to the little creaking sounds as the mantel boards and floorboards near the hearth gave up their warmth, and presently to sounds from outside—not loud but recurring—the sound a horse would make kicking or striking the planks of a stall partition.

The barn was full of visitors' horses. One might be out of its stall. Or down and unable to get up. Or having an attack of colic. He slipped out of bed as quietly as he had slipped in, put on his clothes, took a lantern, and went outside.

Nothing was wrong at the barn. The sound was only one of the horses pawing in its efforts to reach across the partition to a little hay dropped in the feeding alley. He removed the hay, and after a careful look around went out again, closed and latched the door. But instead of crossing the barnyard to the cottage, he walked over to the carriage drive.

Under the stars Blue Meadow lay cold and silent, the hard ground silvered by frost. He looked toward the house. All the windows glowed with soft golden light—the candles he had lighted. No, those would have burned down long before now, and been replaced. His father hadn't wanted him there, trimming or replacing candles after the dancing started, though he had offered. His father had said no, that would be too hard. He meant—because the other time, three years ago, he had been there dancing, not trimming candles. But which of them did his father mean it would be hard for?

Almost he could believe he heard the music. He didn't, of course; all the windows and doors were closed against the winter night. But he heard it in his mind—lovely lilting music—the high thin tones of the violins, the deeper fuller tones of the cello, and the sweet gay piping of the flutes that could sometimes sound like a human voice and sometimes like the songs of birds.

He would like to hear it. He had really never heard enough music. There was never enough time and there were few opportunities—only on special occasions such as this, or at church, or when Jane once in a while played the harpsichord. Music, whether the holy music of hymns, or the bright secular music of the dance, or the tunes of old songs and ballads that he often sang while working—no matter what kind, music gave him warm and beautiful feelings.

He pictured the dancers up there in the hall, himself among them, and the polished oak floor reflecting the lights from the two great chandeliers, each holding forty candles. The hall would smell of pine and hemlock, mixed with the flower scents used by the ladies, and with just a trace of tobacco smoke drifting from the library where three or four of the older gentlemen would retire to enjoy their pipes while the young ones danced. There would be wines, amber-colored and ruby, and fruit brandies for those who liked something a bit headier.

All the boys would be vying with one another to win Cordelia Spenser as a partner, for she was the prettiest of the girls, and the liveliest, and the best dancer. He liked to dance with Cordelia, though sometimes he felt rather embarrassed when the others stopped, and formed a circle around them, clapping hands in time with the music while he and Cordelia went on dancing alone.

It seemed strange to be standing outside in the dark, looking at the house, instead of being inside, dancing. Not sad, exactly; just strange. Or, if sad, not so much because of being shut off from the music and the gaiety, as of being shut off from an earlier part of his own life. As if the Richard Stafford of last year and the Richard Stafford of this had suddenly become two separate persons. It was like the sudden and illogical happenings or transitions that occur in dreams; except that in a dream nothing ever seemed illogical, whereas in real life such things were confusing.

He wondered what his father and brother were doing, whom they were talking to, what they were talking about. The rebellion, very likely, and whether or not the Colonies really would declare their independence and really would fight for it. Or about farming, and crops, and horses, and other things that had to do with their own lives. He wondered if they were wondering about *him;* if it seemed strange to them, too, that he wasn't there in the hall, dancing; and if it seemed sad. When his father said, "That would be too hard," had he really meant sad? Perhaps it would have been easier—for them—if they had been angry and had sent him away, putting him out of their lives, having nothing more to do with him, forgetting him. Could he have endured that? The thought chilled his soul.

From where he stood, there on the drive, he saw the North Star above the center of the housetop. Always that seemed to him exactly the right place for it—

167

the fixed star, the hub of the great wheel of heaven, the beacon to guide by on land or sea. There it was, where it belonged, fixed forever right over the house at Blue Meadow.

But there were millions of stars. To the northwest were five that looked like the letter M. Overhead was one that flashed so brilliantly it seemed to move. And there was a cluster of tiny ones, the Pleiades. He could count only six, though he had been told they were the seven daughters of—he couldn't remember of whom—transformed into stars, according to an ancient legend. He had often wished he knew the names of all the stars. His father had books that told about them, but there was too much else to be done, he had never had time to read the books. He did know the names of two or three constellations. Turning, he looked for Orion—no, he didn't have to look for it, it couldn't be missed—the Great Hunter striding across the south. And at the heels of the Hunter, the Dog Star, the biggest and brightest of all stars in the sky, its piercing light now directly over the cottage, over his own rooftop, like the star that long ago shone down on Bethlehem. . . .

He was shivering; he had stood too long in the cold. Quickly he let himself into the warm kitchen. Before extinguishing his lantern he looked in on the three children, then undressed a second time, and a second time slipped into bed.

Bridget was lying on her right side, her back to him; but drowsily aware of his coming, she turned her head. He hadn't wanted to wake her, yet he wanted her awake; wanted her to know he was there; wanted to hear her soft voice welcome him. Outside in the winter dark were all the millions of stars; but here in this quiet room was his love. . . .

"Richard, you be cold."

He had forgotten how chilled he was. He should have kept a little space between them, should not have let his body touch hers.

"You come from outside?"

"Yes. I heard a noise at the barn, but everything's all right. I'm sorry I woke you. Am I too close? Am I making you cold?"

"Not so. Do you come closer, then I will make you warm."

The invitation was not one he could resist. He put his arm around her, fitting himself to the sweet curve of her back.

"Bridget, I saw a bright star shining over our house. But not so bright as the one that shines inside. You are my star. I love you, Bridget. Say you love me."

"That be well known to you, *a rún*."

"Yes, but I want to hear you say it."

"I love you."

"Forever?"

"For so many forevers as there be stars in the sky."

His arm tightened around her. "All right, now I'll let you go back to sleep."

They were quiet. He had to let her sleep, for her own good and the baby's. And he had to make himself think only of loving her, not of wanting her; for he had a long time to wait.

"Richard, the party . . . ?"

"It's still going on. They'll dance until two or three o'clock, and then sleep the whole morning away."

"You saw them dancing?"

"No, but I saw the lights. Every window."

Again they were quiet. But under his arm he felt

169

her drawing short convulsive breaths, as if . . . He touched her cheek and found it wet with tears. "Bridget, why are you crying?"

"Because you should be there. You should be dancing . . ."

"No, I shouldn't. I have to be up at daybreak." He spoke with exaggerated reasonableness, to make her laugh. "How could I get up at daybreak if I were dancing until three?"

She didn't laugh. "Richard, you give up too much for me. Your father's house be closed to you. . . ."

"It isn't. *This* is my father's house. And this is where I want to be. With you."

But she whispered again, "You give up too much. . . ."

"No. Not anything really important. Not anything one-tenth—one-thousandth—as important as you. You and . . . Bridget, when I saw the star shining over this house, do you know what I thought? I thought it was there to lead me, as the Great Star of the East led the Wise Men . . . The *other* wise men," he added, kissing her shoulder. "Now go to sleep."

"Richard"—so low and soft the voice, so awe-inspiring the words—"the child moves."

"Moves?" He scarcely dared believe she meant . . . "*Now?*"

"Now, but this be not the first." She guided his hand. "Feel."

And under his hand he felt it—a pushing and thumping, vigorous, impatient, almost incredible, certainly unnerving. He had of course many times seen a foal move in a mare, or a calf in a cow. But . . . A baby, in a *woman?*

Alarmed, he asked, "Does it hurt you?"

Her gentle laughter reassured him. "Not so."

"But he feels as if he's kicking!"

"He be turning, I think. Soon he will be still."

Long after Bridget drifted off to sleep, Richard lay awake. The miracle was too stupendous; his senses reeled under the impact.

His child.

Candlelight and music and dancing . . . cold winter fields . . . blazing winter stars . . . What were these by comparison?

He had touched the secret and wonder and glory of life. All the past and all the future were in that touch; all things known and unknown; all the beauties and truths and mysteries of earth and heaven. His hand had felt the stirring of life in the womb, the new beginning, the resurrection, the eternal recurrence, the immortality sprung from the first seed thousands of years ago.

As it was in the beginning, is now, and ever shall be . . .

Richard did not drift off to sleep, as Bridget had. He was whirled off on a great starry wheel that spun three times around the universe before plummeting into the purple velvet dark.

(3)

The Christmas Party was two-thirds over, only one afternoon and evening left, and Cordelia Spenser was piqued by curiosity.

There was more to the situation at Blue Meadow, she felt sure, than had been told. And more than met the eye; much more. Specifically, Richard Stafford's wife had not met the eye of a single one of the Staffords' guests. Nor even been mentioned, as far as Cordelia knew, beyond that one time in answer to her question about Richard's dancing with them. But that was of course understandable, since the Staffords themselves would naturally be reluctant to mention her, and the guests would naturally be too polite.

It was not the invisibility or the unmentionability of Richard's wife that excited her curiosity. It was Richard. The afternoon before, she and most of the other guests had caught glimpses of Richard, but rarely anything more than glimpses. Indeed, he had been so much here, there, and everywhere that afternoon, doing so many things in so many places at the same time, that although nearly everyone saw him, no one—not even members of the family—ever knew where he was but only where he had been an instant before.

"Richard has wings on his heels," Cordelia heard Mr. Marcus Stafford explain when a puzzled guest commented on the phenomenon of these flashing appearances and disappearances.

Wings? It seemed very strange to Cordelia that a boy who was in disgrace, who was now—or so she surmised—banished from the house except when needed to perform servants' chores, who in all probability had already been legally barred from inheriting any of the family fortune, should be going about with wings on his heels. Somehow that suggested not only lightness of foot but lightness of heart as well. How could Richard, under the circumstances, be light of heart?

But she heard him singing. That was yesterday, at noon, after the last of the stayabeds had finally straggled downstairs. She had been down for an hour, but went back for her embroidery bag, to have something with which to occupy herself until the others finished eating, when more interesting diversions would be in order. Knowing that the voice she heard singing, *"Lavender's blue, diddle diddle, lavender's green,"* was Richard's, she went to the door of her room just in time to see him carry an armload of firewood into a room at the western end of the hall. When he reappeared a moment later, she called, "Richard!" He looked in her direction, but with no sign of recognition immediately vanished again. She hurried down the hall; but, as it turned out, he hadn't gone into another room but into a narrow passage leading to the back stairs. From below, his voice floated lightly up to her. *"Down in the vale, diddle diddle, where flowers grow . . ."* Then another voice, harshly: *"Dummkopf!* It is here first! You think my fire burns without wood?" Then his again, laughing:

173

"Dear Cook, kind Cook, honored Cook, for you I reserve the best, in good time . . . *And the birds sing, diddle diddle, all in a row.*"

Well, Cordelia thought, if he was disgraced, banished, disinherited, and otherwise being made to suffer for his sins, no one would know it. A more joyous penitent could scarcely be imagined.

On the afternoon of the third day, she decided that if her curiosity was to be satisfied, there was no substitute for taking direct steps to satisfy it, impertinent as that might be.

An opportunity came when the older ladies were gathered in the drawing room, the older gentlemen in the library, and the young of both sexes, agreeing that the cold bright outside air would be refreshing, went walking on the hill. From this jaunt Cordelia excused herself on the pretext that she had a slight headache and preferred to take a short nap, to be ready for the night's dancing. She did not, in truth, prefer anything of the sort. What she preferred was a short walk alone, in the opposite direction.

From an upstairs window she watched until her friends were well on their way, then put on her cloak, and taking a box of imported sugar candy that she had intended to leave for her hostess but now had a better use for, descended the stairs, unobtrusively slipped through the hall, and went outside.

No one was in sight. She had more than half expected to find Richard flitting around in one of his varied and apparently limitless activities, but was just as well pleased not to, for Richard's presence was not essential to her mission and indeed might interfere with it. As she passed the barn she heard voices and the sound of flails, but the big threshing-floor doors were closed; she saw no one and presumably no one saw her. She went on to the gatehouse. Ordinarily she would go to the front door of a house, not the back; but as the back was nearer, and as the kitchen was the likeliest place for Richard's wife to be, she turned in upon reaching the gravel path to the back door, approached, and knocked.

The door was opened by Harriet Stafford, who said a surprised, "Oh!" and then nothing.

Cordelia laughed. "Don't you know me, Harriet?"

"Why yes, Cordelia; but we weren't expecting . . ."

"I brought you a box of candies. Your grandfather told me you three were here, so I thought I'd better run out to see you, since I wouldn't be seeing you at the house. May I come in?"

"Yes, of course." Harriet politely stepped back, opening the door wider. "But . . ."

"But you're just a visitor too, aren't you? Well, perhaps the *lady* of the house will invite me in."

Cordelia was already in, choosing to take the invitation for granted; and looking over Harriet's head, her eyes were already on the lady of the house.

Bridget and the three children had been sitting in a half circle before the fire, knitting. Closer to the fire a roast of beef hanging from a clock jack rotated slowly, dripping savory juices. Other fragrances—of apples and spices and fresh-baked cookies—mingled with that of the meat. The kitchen was scrupulously clean and tidy, shining copper pans hung from the mantel, the teakettle was singing, an oval rug made of many-colored braided scraps of cloth brightened the floor.

Of all these things Cordelia was aware, but only

as background. The two girls turned on their cricket stools; but Bridget stood up, looking surprised, uncertain, and . . .

Oh, la! Cordelia thought. So that's how it is! She's beautiful; utterly, perfectly beautiful. The contrasts . . . That jet black hair and gardenia skin, the heaven-blue eyes and those half-inch-long black lashes . . . My faith! Richard Stafford probably started being familiar with her the day she came!

Harriet said, "Bridget, this is Miss Cordelia Spenser."

The murmured reply, *"Go mbeannuighidh Dia dhuit,"* was as surprising to Cordelia for the soft pleasing quality of the voice as for the foreignness of the words.

"That's Irish," Harriet helpfully informed her. "That's the way Bridget's people greet each other. It means 'God bless you.'"

Cordelia's surprise doubled. *"You* understand *Irish,* Harriet?"

"Only a few things like that. Bridget's teaching us."

"And we're teaching her to read English," Eleanor said.

"And to write," said Virginia.

"Well! It sounds as if you have a school down here. But you haven't hold me—Bridget is your *Aunt* Bridget, isn't she?"

"She is Princess Bridget," Virginia said firmly. "We thought she was just a servant when she first came. But she wasn't, really. She was under a spell, you see."

Cordelia in some bewilderment looked at Bridget, who, with a smile of tenderness for the child and of embarrassment for herself, explained, "It be told them for amusement, but the little one has the mind made up to think it true. Will you not be taking off your cloak,

176

please, in the warm room? And will you not please sit at table with the young ladies and have a cup of tea?"

"And oat cakes with honey," Eleanor said eagerly. "May we, Bridget? May we have the oat cakes?"

"They be not so fine cakes for fine company. . . ."

"Oh, yes, they are. Please. Cordelia will like them."

"Bridget makes all sorts of delicious things we never heard of," Harriet said. "Champ, and *Brothchán Buidhe* . . ."

"And potato scones, and boxty-in-the-pan . . ."

"And egg collops, and haggerty . . ."

"And apple puddeny-pie!" Virginia finished in triumph.

Divested of her cloak Cordelia sat down, still feeling bewildered. Bridget was under a spell, Virginia had said. Were they *all* under a spell? The three girls . . . She knew them as mousey little things, seldom having a word to say, moving only at their mother's direction as if controlled by strings. Now they were chattering, laughing, fairly bubbling and bouncing as they moved about. Had they, too, sprouted wings on their heels?

Bridget put a plate of thin crisp golden-brown oat cakes on the table, a pot of honey, cups and saucers, sugar and milk. But she did not sit with Cordelia and the children. After pouring their tea she busied herself basting the roast with the drippings caught in a pan beneath it on the hearth, and then returned to her chair near the fire and took up her knitting.

Harriet and Eleanor asked about the party. How many guests were there? Who was in their room? And had the dancing gone on all night? Cordelia answered their questions rather briefly, for she was burning to ask one of her own.

"Tell me more about the spell. How was it broken?"

"By the prince." Virginia was more than willing to

177

tell the story. "We wished on the magic stone Uncle Richard gave us, for the prince to come. He'd marry Bridget, and then she'd be a princess again."

"And the prince came?"

"Well, actually he was right here all the time; but we didn't know that, until the magic worked."

"I see. And the prince was . . ."

"Uncle Richard, of course!"

Cordelia looked at Bridget, who kept her head bent over her knitting. "Did your Uncle Richard know all along that he was the prince who would break the spell?"

"I don't know if he was absolutely sure, but he told us afterward he *hoped* all along he was the right one. Because he did fall in love with her, you see, the very first minute—when he went to Westbridge to bring her here—and that was exactly what the prince had to do. And he told us, to start with, that the prince didn't have to be a *crown* prince, or be dressed in fine clothes, or riding a pure white horse. He said he might be riding just a plain gray horse—and that's what he *was* riding, when Bridget ran away and he went galloping after her to find her and bring her back."

Again Cordelia glanced toward the fire. "Why did Bridget run away?"

"Oh, don't you know? Because the prince—Uncle Richard—wanted to marry her, and she was afraid everybody would be terribly angry with him, because they all thought she was just a servant. She didn't know Papa knew about the magic."

"Your Papa knew?"

"Oh, yes. Ever since last summer when I was so sick. I had to have the magic stone, so I could touch it every day. Papa went up to the playroom to get it for

178

me, and he asked Harriet what the magic was, and she told him."

"Was your Papa glad the magic worked?"

"Heavens, yes! He likes Bridget. He gave her a wedding present that made her so happy she *cried*."

Harriet interposed a correction. "Papa didn't give it to Bridget, Virginia. He gave it to her father. What he did," Harriet explained, "was to have his solicitor in London put money in what they call a trust. Bridget's father will receive the interest—five pounds every month—for the rest of his life. After that, the money in the trust will be divided among his children."

"Bridget's father was the last High King of Ireland," Virginia said happily. "He had to flee from the Sasanachs, and now he lives with the fairies in a beautiful enchanted palace inside a hill. It's lighted by thousands of sparkling little lamps, and the furniture is made of pure gold, and their dishes and wine glasses and things are cut out of rubies and emeralds and diamonds!"

Cordelia, sorting through this intriguing mixture of fact and fantasy, found that only one or two points needed clarification.

"Was your grandfather pleased when the magic worked and the prince turned out to be your Uncle Richard?"

"Well, I don't believe Grandpapa knew about the magic. But when he knew Uncle Richard and Bridget loved each other and wanted to be married, why, of course that was what he wanted them to do."

Well! Cordelia thought. *Well.* So Mr. Marcus Stafford *made* Richard marry her, did he? Poor, poor Richard!

"So then they were married," Virginia went on,

"and Grandpapa said they could have this house, because Mama . . ."

Harriet said, "*Virginia*," in a warning tone, but Virginia cheerfully ignored her.

". . . doesn't believe in magic. Mama says Bridget is still a servant. But she's not—she's a princess. And *Papa* says when Bridget's baby comes, it will be a prince!"

Very interesting. Oh, very! Mr. Vincent Stafford had no son. But if Richard had, *that son would be a prince*. Richard had not been disinherited. Far from it. His brother was willing to let Blue Meadow and all the rest of the Stafford fortune pass eventually to Richard's oldest son, *even if the child of a servant girl*.

Well, *that* would be something to tell around. Her mother wouldn't even be in a pet about her coming down here, when she passed *that* information along. That and . . .

How much of the story could she tell? Could she let people know Richard Stafford preferred a servant girl to *her*? To Margaret Findlay? She could treat it as a joke; but could Margaret?

Well, she'd have to think about it. Oh, yes, she'd think about it! Falling in love at first sight . . . a wishing stone . . . the girl running away . . . Richard bringing her back . . . Why, it was a romance! And a baby coming (another glance, but Bridget wore a large loose-fitting apron that did not reveal how soon), a baby that was to have full rights as a Stafford . . .

Anyway, Meg Findlay was in Philadelphia and wouldn't be home until spring. By that time everybody would have found something else to talk about, and certainly Meg herself would never ask any questions about Richard or his wife—she was too proud to let anyone know she cared a tuppence.

Cordelia chatted a few minutes longer with the girls, remembered to tell them her brother Geordie sent his regards, thanked Bridget quite graciously and not at all patronizingly for the tea, and took her departure —wondering how she could keep the story to herself even long enough to decide whom she wanted to tell it to first.

(4)

The month of March was wretchedly cold and stormy. A few mild days in the second week held forth the tantalizing promise of spring, but these were followed by the heaviest snow of the winter, and then by freezing rains and continuing blustery winds. Blue Meadow hugged its fires; but as supplies of wood ran low, there were those who had the restocking to do in order that others might do the hugging.

Richard's workday could not be extended; it already included all the hours of light. Nor could time consumed in frequent hurried trips to the cottage to make sure Bridget was all right be subtracted from the work that had to be done; rather, it had to be made up by working just that much harder and faster. He went to bed bone weary and at once to sleep, yet slept lightly, any restlessness on Bridget's part bringing him wide awake.

There was one afternoon when Bridget felt sure her travail had begun, and Richard went flying to the house to fetch Cook, who would tend her; but the pains subsided and then ceased entirely, and Cook said it was only that the child was "settling," but that any time now the true labor could be expected.

It was very reassuring to know they could depend on Cook. There was in fact no one else to depend on, the nearest midwife being at Westbridge; and though Bridget said that at home many times a woman had her baby quite alone, and many times did her housework right up to the very moment of its coming, and in but a few hours was back at work again, Richard could not see it as so offhand an event. He remembered that when Jane's children were born there was always a doctor or midwife in attendance, and a nurse who stayed for weeks afterward; and that one of the times when a stillborn child was delivered, Jane herself had been very close to death.

On the other hand, he knew that in nature the bearing of young was usually a very simple matter (though always the miracle of it filled him with awe), and that only once in a while did a mare or cow or ewe need assistance. He had several times watched Vincent render that assistance, and twice had done so himself; but more often all that was required of him was simply to be on hand to make sure mouth and nostrils were immediately cleared of the membrane so the new little creature could breathe, or by rubbing and slapping to stimulate it into drawing its first breath; or, when the weather was cold, to rub it dry with handfuls of straw so it did not become chilled, if the dam herself did not lick it dry. But the difference, of course, the very great difference was that this was human birth; and, even greater, that it was Bridget, his beloved, from whom the new life would come.

At one o'clock in the morning, on the thirty-first day of March, Bridget lay stiffly quiet, wondering if the pain in her back could mean that the time was on her. Often her back ached, through the day as well as at night, for the weight of the child pulled on the muscles; and often she had to lie down to ease herself. This, which had begun soon after she went to bed, seemed the same ache, yet not altogether the same. It came and went. In between, she dozed off; but then it came again, waking her, each time more severe, and each time spreading, until it began to seem not only in the small of her back but clear through her. Yet it did not seem as she thought the pains of childbirth would be. Not wanting to wake Richard—he was so tired, and this might well be like the other time when the signs were false—she made herself keep very still.

An icy rain was falling. She listened to the hard sweeping sound of it, and to the pebbly sound of sleet against the window glass, and to the wind tearing at the branches of the pine trees that sheltered the little house. How could she ask Richard to go out in that cold rain and fierce wind, or Cook to come, perhaps for nothing? She would wait a while longer, on the chance that the pain would stop. And even if the baby was indeed coming, very likely it would not come before morning. She had known women, her own sister and others, to be in labor many hours, a whole day or more, before the baby at last came. Especially was it that way with a first one.

The pain didn't stop; instead, its recurrences were much closer together, always with less and less time in between. Then came one of such violence that she found herself bearing down, seeking relief from the pain but only making it worse, so that she had to set her teeth against crying out. She realized, then, that she had no choice whether to wait or not to wait; no control over what her body must do. Her womb of itself had chosen to expel the baby, which even then was pushing through the portals.

The pain came again . . . "Richard! Richard!"

Instantly awake but momentarily dazed by that agonized cry, Richard put out a hand to her and felt her nightdress clammy with sweat. "Bridget! Are you . . . ?"

Another pain seized her. She bunched the bed clothes against her mouth to keep from screaming. When it eased she gasped, "The child comes!"

Richard fell out of bed in haste and panic.

"I'll get Cook!"

"No, no—stay—there be not time. Do not go. Help me, Richard. It comes now. . . ."

Richard stood paralyzed by shock.

Now. The baby was coming now, and no one here, no one to do what must be done, no one but . . .

How could *he?* He was only a boy—how could she depend on him to help her? What did he know about helping a woman have a baby, or caring for the baby when it came? He knew only about animals. That wasn't enough; and even if it were, he could never have the courage. Not even the courage to witness her suffering, let alone . . .

"Richard, it comes. . . !"

Panic would have sent him running for Cook; but strangely, instead of yielding to panic he became calm. She needed him. Bridget, his wife, whom he loved, was suffering and needed him. No one else was there to help her, the responsibility was his. Somehow the responsibility itself would give him the knowledge, the competence, the courage. What must be done, he would do.

He gave her his hand until the pain ebbed and she

lay quiet again. He leaned down and kissed the wet curls on her forehead.

"Do not leave me, Richard. Please, please do not leave me."

"No, Bridget, I'll stay. I'll help you. It will be all right," he promised. "I know what to do."

While he was bringing candles, all the candles they had and the whale-oil lamp too, little remembered things swarmed through his mind. Things Vince had told him . . . "It's harder for women . . . They suffer more . . . Normally the head comes first . . ." He remembered Vince speaking of how vital it was for the woman not to surrender to exhaustion but to keep trying to push the baby out; and of various small aids, such as something to hold on to, and a folded piece of cloth to bite on, because sometimes she loosened or broke her teeth—Jane did—clenching them too hard against the pain. And then there were the things he knew to do when helping an animal: how to ease the bulging forehead through, if the front legs and muzzle had not sufficiently opened the way; how to pull, to hasten the birth, each time the dam herself was straining; how to tie and cut the cord, if necessary; and, of course, how to make sure the infant creature immediately drew air into its lungs, for unless it did, it would not live.

He could wonder, afterward, how it was that when the paralysis of shock left him, that strange strong calm came to take its place. Only God knew where it came from, but there it was. He couldn't stop to marvel over it; he simply accepted it and put it to use. Later, he would be appalled to think that he had been so calm when Bridget was in agony.

How long the birth took he could not have said, for the minutes fused and blended, unmarked by anything except the advance of that pushing head. His hands were steady and sure, deft and gentle, obeying his will. His voice soothed and encouraged.

"There now, there now, my darling . . . Try once more . . . It will be soon, now, very soon . . . Just once more . . ."

And there it was. There was the tiny slippery new thing, delivered into the world, out of the dark into the light, separated from its mother by his hand and dependent now on him . . . He gave it a smart slap on the buttocks, felt it make a convulsive move, heard it draw a gasping breath, then another, and another . . . In triumph he lifted it up for Bridget to see, and from it came a thin wailing cry.

"Greetings to you, beloved, from our son!"

Minutes later, wrapped in a square of clean soft linsey-woolsey, the baby lay in the curve of her arm.

"So beautiful," she whispered, "so beautiful . . . Richard, *a rún*, so much I love you, so much I love our son . . ."

Tired and spent, the pain gone, deep peace in and around her, Bridget closed her eyes, yielding to a sweet drowsiness on which she seemed to float as on a cloud. She would rest for a while; she would sleep.

It was not yet over, but Richard's part was done. Now he ran for Cook.

Their coats, his and Cook's, his boots and her clogs, Richard placed near the fire to dry; and placed himself there also, sitting down because his legs felt weak, and counting on the cheerful blaze to put an end to his shivering—though that might take some time, for the coldness was inside him, a reaction to the incredible, impossible thing he had done, and the heat of the fire did not reach it.

187

From the front room came voices—chiefly Cook's, but now and then Bridget's soft murmur—the words indistinct, seeming to come from a vast distance. He didn't try to understand the words; it was enough just to hear the voices. He was out of it now, unneeded, excluded, thankfully knowing his wife and baby were safe, wholly safe, in Cook's care. In a minute he would be able to relax and be calm again, and then he would stop shivering.

But ten minutes later he was still shivering.

Cook came into the kitchen. Quickly he stood up, for she was carrying the small bundle in the linsey-woolsey blanket, and he thought there was something she wanted him to do or get for her. But holding the bundle out to him she said, *"Deine Arme, Dummkopf! Setzt!"* and explained that he was to sit there and hold the *kleines Kind,* as its mother feared it would not like being put at once alone in its cradle, and there were many things to be done, the young *Frau* properly cared for, and much cleaning and changing since he had not the sense to protect the bed she lay on but took no more care than if it were straw in a stable! But no wonder, for what did a *Knabe* know of such things? Certainly it was only by God's mercy that mother and child lived, such misfortune as was theirs in having none but the likes of him to do for them! But, for all the harsh scolding, her eyes looked on him with kindness, and she smiled as she laid his son in his arms.

At first he could do nothing but sit there holding the bundle as he would hold something so fragile that the mere act of breathing might shatter it; but then—and to his surprise he found he had stopped shivering, perhaps because of that great need to exercise the utmost care in protection and preservation of that which his arms held—cautiously with one finger he pushed the edges of the blanket aside so he could look down on the small puckered face. Bridget had used the word *beautiful.* No doubt all mothers thought their babies beautiful; but he was in complete agreement. He had never seen so beautiful, so perfect a baby. Nor ever one so new. No longer as new, though, as when he first saw it. Memory of that moment made him weak with fright. How had he dared? And memory of Bridget's suffering made him sick with horror. But he remembered the triumph, too—the first breath, the first cry of the son God had delivered into his hands. Belatedly, as he sat looking into that flower face, he said a prayer of thanks.

Marcus Brian Stafford. They would call him Brian. Bridget would like that; and then, too, it would avoid the confusion of two Marcuses. There had never been a Brian Stafford. The Staffords were Norman English; mixed with Saxon from time to time, but mainly Norman, clear back to the days of William the Conqueror. If there had ever been any admixture of Irish blood, he didn't know about it; though his father said if you went back far enough, the Gauls of France and the Celts of Ireland were the same. So, in his son, two lines of the same sound base stock were brought together again. And that was good; very good.

Everything was good. . . .

Faint gray light was just beginning to touch the east window when Cook left. Bridget was sleeping. Brian in his cradle—the smooth white pine cradle Richard had made during the long evenings of winter —slept close beside her, within reach of her hand. They would sleep for hours, Cook said. He was not to disturb them, and she would come back when her affairs at the house were in order.

Richard, irresolute, stood looking in rapture at his

two sleeping loves; put wood on the fires; came back to look again, torn between his longing to stay beside them and his duty to go out and start his morning work.

He had asked Cook to tell his father and brother as soon as they came downstairs. "*Ja*," she had answered stonily, "it is not of so much importance that they could wish to be told except at their convenience." It might, therefore, be another hour before they knew; and even then—would they come at once?

But Cook, before taking time to stir and tend her own kitchen fire, or even to remove her clogs, went clumping upstairs to rap imperiously on bedroom doors and proclaim the tidings.

"*Mein Herr!* You have a fine strong grandson!" And, "*Mein Herr!* Your brother's child is born!"

She was waiting for them in the hall when they came down. Marcus started to thank her for her middle-of-the-night attendance upon Bridget, but she cut him short.

"*Nein.* She thought it would not be so quick, and did not wake the boy to come for me in time. I do only what comes after. If so the child's life was in the hands that received it, *mein Herr*, then you have your son to thank, not me!"

Richard, still torn between the need to go and the desire to stay, had got as far as putting on his coat and boots when they came.

Joyfully he carried the cradle with its sleeping occupant into the kitchen. They expressed great pleasure; and told him, besides, that he was not to come out but to stay here with his wife and child, at least for the next twenty-four hours, since here his first duty lay. But all the while, though their pleasure was every bit as great as he had hoped it would be, their eyes seemed on him more than on the baby. In his father's eyes he could plainly read satisfaction and thankfulness. In Vincent's . . . These, too, but what else?

Vincent seemed to be appraising him, measuring him, looking at him in a new way. What was different —or added—in that look?

"So you've grown up." If the words held approval, it was somewhat counteracted by the next ones. "And about time!"

Richard, with an abashed smile, said nothing, still trying to read the new thing in his brother's eyes.

"Well, what is it?" Vincent demanded. "Haven't I said all the proper things? Haven't I congratulated you on providing an heir to the Stafford crown? What more do you want me to say?"

"Nothing, Vince. I was only . . . You keep looking at me . . ."

"And can't you decide *how* I'm looking at you?"

"No."

"With respect, Richie."

(5)

By the middle of April the ground dried enough for plowing, the wheat and rye and barley quickened, grass began coming lush and green in the pastures, two foals were dropped, cows freshened, and Blue Meadow was deep in the spring work; but over everything was a faint cloud of uneasiness, for the armed rebellion was growing stronger and coming nearer.

During the winter there had been many news accounts of the siege of Boston by the Continental Army and the Militia. On the seventeenth of March, the British and the Tories who had assisted them evacuated that city. Immediately afterward, General Washington began moving a large part of his army to New York, he himself arriving on the thirteenth of April. It appeared that a major engagement there against the British forces was certain.

New York, too, was far away, but not so far as Boston. Blue Meadow could no longer feel itself completely remote, apart, and safe from a conflict not of its choosing and not to its liking. Still, the immediate demands of each day left little time for worrying, and even less as spring passed into summer and the demands increased. But in July, when the Congress declared "That these United Colonies are, and of Right ought to be Free and Independent States," that declaration grievously affected Blue Meadow, for it was the cause of serious bodily injury to Marcus Stafford.

He and Edward Findlay had ridden to Philadelphia, Edward having certain legal matters to attend to, Marcus going along chiefly to provide companionship on the ride, but partly to visit Cousin Elizabeth Peirson, who in reply to a note informing her that her quondam servant was now the mother of his first grandson, had written to say that she knew not whether he was thanking or reproaching her, and to beg him to pay her a visit so that she might be told the full story.

They were handsomely entertained by Elizabeth for several days. On the fifth of July they read a printed copy of the Declaration of Independence, and on the eighth heard the bell in the State House tower ringing to proclaim the news to the world. Early in the morning of the ninth they set out for home.

The Declaration was still being celebrated. A group of drunken young roisterers shouting "Liberty!" and "Death to Tories!" and making a sudden great din by beating sticks against the bottoms of tin pans and kettles, frightened a team of horses into lunging off in a runaway at the moment Marcus and Edward were passing. The wagon lurched toward them, the hub of a rear wheel caught Marcus's horse a glancing blow on the hock, he lost his footing and went down. Marcus, in the fall, managed to keep clear of the horse and to keep hold of the bridle reins, and counted himself lucky in escaping with no more than a bad jolt and doubtless a bruise or two. He had landed on his back, and at the moment of impact had felt an excruciating pain, presumably from striking his spine on a stone; but this was succeeded by numbness, and beyond feeling so shaken and unsteady that he needed assistance to get to his feet and remount his horse, there seemed no reason for not continuing the ride home.

It developed, however, that he could not proceed faster than a walk, as the numbness impaired his balance. Curiously, he could not feel the stirrups under his feet. Reaching the Westbridge inn at two in the afternoon, quite fatigued, he decided it would be well to stop and rest. He had to be helped from his horse. On the ground, his legs would not support him. He was assisted inside, and Edward summoned the village apothecary, who knew something of doctoring. The apothecary strongly advised against riding any farther that day, and indeed against riding at all, as it was his opinion that one of the bones of the spine had been fractured. The paralysis was perhaps due to pressure on the spinal cord by the broken bone. Marcus should lie down at once and not attempt to go home that day. If he insisted on going home the next day, then he should be transported lying flat in a wagon and not astride a horse.

The advice seemed sound and Marcus followed it. He would take a room at the inn for the night. Edward would go on to Blue Meadow, would explain the nature of the accident and its temporary effects, and would instruct Richard to come in the morning with one of the farm wagons.

Richard, whose imagination was of the untrammeled and wide-ranging kind, was instantly and exceedingly alarmed, even though the carefully worded message stressed the "temporary" nature of the "semi-paralysis" resulting from the fall. Additionally alarming was the fact that Edward was going to return to Westbridge that same evening. To that, Richard could attach only one meaning: his cousin was very deeply concerned, and that meant his father was very seriously injured.

Expressing his fears to Vincent in the hope of having them allayed by some explanation he himself was unable to think of, he succeeded only in having them increased, for Vincent had the same fears; not as immoderate, not as discomposing, yet much the same. Richard wanted to go at once; but Vincent said no, he should wait until morning as instructed, for it would be senseless to spend the night in Westbridge when he was needed here.

After hastily doing his morning chores, Richard made preparations to set out. In the wagon, over straw packed a foot thick, he placed the soft flock mattress from his own bed, a clean linen sheet, and pillows. He thought these preparations might be viewed as extreme to the point of absurdity; but Vincent merely took a long look at the wagon, then a long look at him, said it was going to be a hot day, and handed him a wooden bucket containing a jug of cider packed all around in sawdust.

Controlling his impulse to hurry, for if he tired his horses they would need to rest before starting back and he would get his father home no sooner, he reached Westbridge at half past seven.

Mr. Findlay had already left, the innkeeper told him, to fetch a doctor from Philadelphia. Mr. Stafford was ready and waiting, and here were two stout fellows to carry him out to the wagon. *Carry* him out? Those chilling words confirmed Richard's fears; but he found his father smiling and in good spirits, and pleased that he had arrived so promptly.

"This would not have happened to you, Richard.

But I hope Edward told you it was a very minor accident, and that I'll be back on my feet in a day or two."

"Yes, that's what he told us."

"You should have believed him, my dear boy; then you would have no reason to wear so worried a look."

The two "stout fellows," making a chair of their locked hands, bore Marcus outside and with great care settled him in the wagon. Lying back on the excellent bed that awaited him there, he gratefully said, "You were indeed thoughtful of my comfort, Richard. A king could not travel more royally than this."

Richard tied his father's horse to the tail of the wagon, and slowly began the long drive home.

During the first hour they talked. Marcus told of the events in Philadelphia—the Declaration, the crowds, the ringing of the great bell—and of the latest news from New York, and of his pleasant visit with Elizabeth, who had sent gifts, a gold pin for Bridget and a little Swiss musical box for Brian—these were in the pocket of his coat and fortunately had not been damaged when he fell. Richard told of the events at home—the hay was in, the barley was cut, and they were well along with the wheat; Virginia was riding her pony as expertly as if she had been riding all her life; and yesterday Brian sat erect without being held, for a full minute before leaning too far forward and losing his balance.

But during the second hour Marcus became quiet; and though Richard guided the team so the wagon wheels were always on the smoothest part of the road, even the smoothest parts were rough, and he knew the jolting was painful in spite of the straw and the mattress. The sun was now halfway up the sky, mercilessly bright and hot. In a shady place they stopped for a few minutes to refresh themselves with the cool cider. Before going on, Richard removed his work frock, fastening it across the wagon as a canopy. Slowly they came to Willowfield, turned down the long hill, crossed the ford, turned west again, and at last were home.

Now it was Marcus Stafford's two sons who made a chair of their hands and carried him into the house and upstairs. He was very tired, and in more pain than he would admit, though they were not deceived. They helped him undress, then drew the window curtains to darken the room and left him; because for the next few hours he wanted only to sleep, he told them, having slept poorly at the inn. They were not to worry about him, but to proceed as if this unlucky interruption had not taken place; and later, if he needed further assistance, he would send word out to them.

So they went on with the day's work; but not as if nothing had happened; for there was a shadow over the house and the fields, and they worked in that shadow.

And that night, looking at his son, Richard thought again of the circling, the great wheel of life in which beginning and end are one. This time the thought did not bring that vaulting sense of immortality, but a feeling of deep sadness. Tears came burning to his eyes, and he bowed his head over the sleeping child to hide them.

Bridget dropped to her knees beside his chair. "Richard, you be afraid for your father?"

He couldn't answer; couldn't let his fear take shape in words.

"Tomorrow your cousin brings the doctor. After the doctor comes, he will be better."

Wanting her to think he accepted this message of hope, he made himself say, "Yes, he'll get better. But . . . He shouldn't have been hurt. *He* never hurt anyone, never in all his life. . . ."

"Ah, sure not, such a kind gentleman. And you be like him, Richard. I think it must be great happiness to him, a son so much the same."

Richard tried to draw comfort from thinking that he was, in some ways, like his father. For if he was, and if in turn his son was, then no matter what . . . But he said, "No, I only look like him. I'm not the same. No one could be. He is great and good and kind and wise. And I . . . No, I'm not like him, Bridget."

Tenderly she answered, "I think there be no difference except that you be young."

He let his thoughts dwell on that difference. His father was fifty-eight, more than three times as old as he. He tried to think what it would be like to be fifty-eight, to have lived that long, to have seen so much come and go. Why, he would be a grandfather long before he was that old. Perhaps even a great-grandfather. And some men lived far past their three score years and ten. In England he had known an old man, ninety-five, who remembered when Charles the Second was king. If he lived that long . . . But he could not picture himself an old man. He could not picture himself as old as his father or even as old as Vince. Perhaps no man ever really changed in his own sight. Perhaps no matter how long he lived, he would still be *this* self, this same Richard of this moment. Did his father feel that way too? Was his father at fifty-eight the same Marcus Stafford who long ago loved and married the vicar's daughter? And had he gone on loving her these past twelve years, just the same?

"Bridget, if we have a daughter—sometime—may we name her Lavinia? That was my mother's name. I'd like my father to know . . ."

"It be a lovely name, Richard."

"He used to call her Vinnie. She was . . ."

What did he remember of his mother? Someone gentle and warm and laughing and sweet-smelling. Someone with soft red-gold hair that he liked to touch. Someone who told him the names of the flowers in the garden, and took him driving in a wicker pony cart, and sometimes sat on the floor and played games with him, and sometimes as a special treat at tea gave him little square cakes covered on all sides with frosting. It was Norrie who took care of him—the dressing and undressing and putting to bed—until he was old enough to do for himself; but he remembered that his mother always came in to hear his prayers and to kiss him good-night, and that after she became ill and couldn't come, he was allowed to go to her instead, until she became too ill.

"She was . . . I think when she was young she must have been like you, Bridget. Because I think my father loved her very much, and—I think we would love the same kind of person."

There it was again—the sameness. And the wheel; the endless circling. You lived and had children and grew old and died, yet still lived in your children, just as the seed grew into the golden wheat which in turn became the seed, over and over and over again. *That which hath been is that which shall be* . . . Was the sole purpose of life simply to perpetuate itself? A little time under the sun and the stars, a little time to sow and to harvest, to love, to know joy and grief, and then . . . *Our longest sun sets at right descensions and makes but winter arches.* . . . From light to darkness, from darkness to light . . . *Man solemnizes nativities and deaths with equal luster.* . . . Why? Because, as with the wheat, each was end and beginning together? And as part of life was it every man's lot to rejoice in his son and weep for his father?

"Richard, *a rún,* it be late."

"Yes, I'm coming, Bridget."

He took a last look outside. The big house, the barn, the fields, all were dark and silent; but somewhere to the west a dog was barking, an angry note in the sound. Their own dogs, a Scotch collie and a Gordon setter, trotted briskly down the drive to determine whether or not the barking merited their participation. More and more strangers were passing through, that summer; ragged fellows, deserting militiamen cutting across from the Lancaster road on their way to their homes farther south. Well, if anyone came by, Duff and Duke would keep them at a distance. Nevertheless he settled the door latch firmly and pulled the latch string in.

This was his hearth and home. Here he was husband, father, guardian, protector. But this was also the gatehouse, and that made him guardian of his father's house as well. The weight of the double responsibility, pressing heavily, kept him listening until the barking stopped and the night was still.

Then, in the warm dark, seeking comfort, he took his wife in his arms. For this, too, was part of life . . .

The paralysis persisted. In the beginning, any move caused Marcus intense pain just above the injury, and there was a great ugly bruise that would be a long time disappearing. Later, as healing took place, he was able to sit up. Twice daily Vincent or Richard massaged his legs to maintain circulation, and together lifted him up and supported him while he tried to will himself to stand or take a step. But his legs remained useless.

Richard, working secretly at night in the cottage kitchen, fashioned a chair on wheels. In it his father could propel himself from room to room anywhere on the first floor of the house, and even outdoors by means of a gently sloping ramp laid from the front doorstep to the drive. The convenience of the wheeled chair let him come to the training field and to the barn, and to the terrace or to the front lawn where in the shade of the beech he spent many afternoons with his small grandson close at hand—for Richard also made a little portable wooden pen in which Brian could sit or sleep or creep or, by the end of September, pull himself up by grasping the smooth round bars and stand triumphantly on his own two sturdy legs.

So, with the necessary adjustments, life at Blue Meadow went on; somewhat harder for everyone, and still under the shadow that had not lifted since that day in July; but in other ways much the same, the affairs of the farm well managed by Vincent, and of the household by Jane; and Richard in his customary role as man-of-all-work, gathering up the various loose ends.

In this role, since he was the one who took wheat and corn to be ground, or logs to the sawmill to be made into boards, or was dispatched on sundry errands to Westbridge or other nearby places, Richard was frequently the bringer of the latest reports on the fighting. Previously he had never paid much attention. His world—everything that touched him, everything that had meaning, everything that mattered—lay within the boundaries of Blue Meadow. But now he listened, storing unfamiliar names in his mind—Gowanus Road, Flatbush Pass, Kip's Bay, Harlem Heights—and carrying the news home to his father. General Washington's army was badly defeated on Long Island and in New York. The Militia was deserting, not by ones and twos but by fifties and hundreds, sometimes a whole regiment. General Howe was now occupying New York. Everyone was saying it would soon be over . . . He was glad to bring these tidings, for this was what his father hoped for—that it would soon be over. War was senseless and wicked, his father said. Men should settle their differences by peaceable means, not by gunfire and bayonets and wanton destruction.

And then, too, as a bearer of news, on rainy days or on days too chilly for his father to sit outside, Richard could, without being directly summoned and yet without breaking his oath, enter the house, for the bearing of news was as much a servant's function as a son's. He could bring a Philadelphia paper, or tell what he had heard. He could not, of course, stay more than a few minutes, unless needed to perform some other service; and could not, as a servant, sit with his father by the library fire, unless—"I find the print hard on my eyes, Richard. Sit down and read it aloud to me, will you, please?" Other little excuses, too, his father sometimes invented to keep him there: questions about the farm work—though Vincent kept him fully informed; a discussion of what colts to sell in the spring—though that was not a matter to be decided in the fall; or searching the shelves for a mislaid book; or swinging a certain hinged shelf forward, to take from or replace in the wall safe hidden behind it some article of special value kept there.

Patiently Marcus accepted his misfortune and kept up an appearance of hopefulness and good cheer, speaking of being on his feet by Christmas. He spent a good part of each day reading, and at other times did not want for entertainment and companionship—Harriet learned to play chess with him, Edward Findlay was a daily visitor, and frequently in the evenings Vincent wheeled him down the drive to spend an hour at the cottage. Yet he knew, and they knew, that his condition was deteriorating. He developed a troublesome cough, experienced difficulty in breathing, and could sleep only when well propped up on pillows. Bodily disorders of one sort or another had to be expected, he told them, when an active man was suddenly rendered inactive; the heart, for example, could sometimes be as adversely affected by cessation of normal activity as by overexertion. But all this, he was careful to say, would correct itself in time.

Richard, on his nineteenth birthday, was given Red Earl and four mares of his own choice, a gift that greatly pleased yet secretly distressed him. Some weeks later, his father had a visitor, brought from Philadelphia by Edward. When the visitor left, Richard was summoned to the house and told that under the terms of his father's will he would annually receive twenty per cent of the produce of the farm during his brother's lifetime, and that upon his brother's death the entire estate would pass to him, or if he should predecease his brother, then to his oldest son.

Stunned, he protested, "But Vince could still . . ."

"Yes," his father agreed, "if at some future time he were to make a second marriage. But your brother feels that you are the rightful heir, because"—he smiled —"while you live, I live, Richard."

There were no words to say in answer. Even had there been, Richard could not have spoken them; pain closed his throat.

Presently his father said, "Do not grieve, Richard. I find great comfort in that thought, and you will too. You are a man, now. Whatever comes, you will meet it with strength and courage and dignity and fortitude. And with recognition of the fact that although death comes to all of us, we are not on this earth merely *to fecchen fyr and rennen hoom ayeyn*. We are here to

203

build, each of us, for those who come after. I expect you to be a Master Builder, Richard."

"Father, if I build, it can be only on the foundations you have laid. . . ."

"Thank you. No higher tribute can be paid a father by a son."

Richard dreamed, that night, that all the Blue Meadow fires went out, no tinderbox would strike a spark, and he went to the Findlays for live coals. Running back, all along the road he met ragged shivering men, one after another, each begging him for just one coal to start a little fire. *A small fire sufficeth for life*, their pleading voices reminded him. By the time he reached home, all but one of the few coals left in the pan had turned to ash; but that single glowing coal his son Brian plucked out and put to the tinder, and soon in every chimneyplace the fires were again burning.

(6)

On a cold gray Sunday afternoon in January,
Richard went alone to the woods. An inch of snow had
fallen in the night and more was to come; against the
dark boles of the trees he saw flakes as fine as mist
starting to drift down. The air was still, the woods were
shrouded in silence.

He walked on down to the clearing. The day he
first saw Blue Meadow, this had been a small natural
clearing; but as it was a level place, convenient for the
barking and hewing of logs that would be dragged
down as timbers for the framing of the barn, they had
cleared a larger space around it. By eye he knew the
approximate dimensions, but now he stepped them off—
thirty-four by sixty-two paces. Beyond its southern side
a heavily wooded slope dropped to the creek a quarter
of a mile away. On its eastern edge was a rocky bank
from which a good spring flowed. He stood for many
minutes looking at that broad open place and the dense
screen of trees around it, while plans took shape in his
mind.

His mood was somber. If bitterness was in it, there

was no more than a trace, for bitterness was alien to him; but there was a deep resolve not to let Blue Meadow be robbed by those who had robbed him of his father. *Liberty.* Men who talked of it most made sure of doing so from a place of safety—the Congress had fled to Baltimore. Was liberty a state to be desired if it must be won at the expense of other men's lives?

Up to now he had taken little interest in the war for independence, beyond picking up news to tell his father. The war was part of the outside world. He had no time to think about what was going on in the outside world; there was more than enough going on right here to occupy all his thoughts and all his time. But that outside world had destroyed his father, and conceivably could destroy them all. Whether or not he wanted to, he had to think about it now.

General Washington's retreat from New York had been through the Jerseys, with the British in unhurried but steady pursuit. There had been the battles of Trenton and Princeton; but farmers could find little comfort in American victories, for their goods were subject to seizure by both armies, no matter which way the tides of battle ran. The British at least paid in hard money; who knew what Continental paper or promises were worth?

The hard fact was that warring armies had come within fifty miles of Blue Meadow, and might come much closer. Foraging parties would take their horses and cattle, their stores of grain and hay, their wagons, their foodstuffs; and they themselves could be left without enough for subsistence. There were reports, also, of indiscriminate looting; and of burning, for what one side couldn't transport was set afire to prevent it from falling into the hands of the other. That was war; senseless and wicked, as his father had said; and brutally indifferent to the rights of those who asked only to be let alone.

He had spoken to Vincent of the foraging and the danger of losing everything they had except the land itself.

"We'll do as others do," Vincent said. "Hide all we can."

Where? Vincent said he didn't know. They would decide that when the time came. There was no immediate need to worry, as the armies were comfortably distant, General Washington's in winter quarters at Morristown, New Jersey, General Howe's in New York, and there would be no more fighting that winter.

"But people are saying that General Howe's next move will be to divide the Colonies by taking Philadelphia. And if that happens, the fighting will be very close to us, Vince."

"In the spring," Vincent said.

"But spring will soon be here. . . ."

"Well, *you* think about it, Richie. I haven't time."

Richard was thinking about it now, while the snow-mist became thicker, the flakes larger, a white curtain closing around him. The soundless fall of the snow deadened all sound of anything else. Engrossed in his thoughts, he did not hear a horse coming along the trail behind him until it was only a length or two away. Turning, he saw that the rider was Margaret Findlay.

"Why, Richard!" Perhaps because surprised she did not sound aloof—though she had been very aloof ever since her return from Philadelphia the preceding spring. "I didn't see you—you were so still you merged with the trees."

His own surprise was twofold: at her unexpected

207

appearance in his snow-wrapped solitude, and at the friendliness of her tone. Smiling, he said, "That's one of my Indian tricks. How are you, Meg?"

"Quite well, thank you."

He thought she would now give him a cool little nod and ride on. That was all he had had from her these nine months past—a cool nod or at most a cool "Good-morning" when they met at church. It troubled him, for they had been friends since childhood and he had hoped to keep that friendship; but Jane said his marriage was an insufferable and unforgivable affront to Margaret, and so far every indication had been that Jane was right.

The curtain of the snow was between them. He saw the flakes gathering on her hood and on the skirts of her riding habit. He could not see her face clearly, shadowed as it was by the hood and obscured by the falling snow; but in her voice—halting and husky, not smooth and cool—he heard the Margaret of earlier times.

"Richard, I'm so very sorry about your father. I wanted to tell you—at the cemetery—but I knew how hard it was for you, and that anything I might say would only make it harder—even though you were so calm and strong. I did admire you for that—for being so strong—because I know how you always felt about your father."

Strong? He wondered if he should try to explain that the strength given him that day was his father's strength; that he had felt it pass into him, and had accepted it as a waiting courier accepts a message from the hand of another whose course has been run. No, because in a way it seemed self-glorification—this feeling that he *was* his father. It couldn't be explained.

"You think better of me than I deserve, Meg. Things have to be faced, that's all."

"But not everyone can face things. Not—losing someone you love. Some people break down, and some build defenses. But you do neither. You simply accept. That's what I mean by being strong—that acceptance—and going right on. Even my father . . ."

He waited, but she was silent. "What about your father?"

"Richard, he's not himself. He has become old—so very old. He isn't interested in anything—doesn't do anything—just sits looking at—nothing. Your father was his dearest friend. . . ."

In compassion Richard's thoughts went to Edward Findlay, whom he held in affectionate regard and never addressed as "Cousin Edward," which seemed distant, but always as "Uncle Ed," which seemed close. Edward had shared the anxiety of those last weeks, and the bedside watch of those last hours; but long before his father died, Richard had seen the change in his cousin. There was no Christmas party that year. It was the Findlays' turn, but even though in a sense an obligation, something Willowfield counted on, Edward had not the heart for it. Music and dancing, when across the fields at Blue Meadow the friend of all his years was wasting away? No, there could be no party.

Remembering his cousin's face, gray and cold, empty, all feeling locked away, that morning two weeks ago in the churchyard, Richard searched for words of comfort. "When spring comes, he'll be different, Meg. When there are things to do. When he can be out more. Winter is always hard on older people."

"Last winter wasn't hard on him," Margaret said. "He never cared how cold it was. Now he's cold even beside a roaring fire. And I don't think he says twenty words from morning to night. Nothing Mother and I can think of to talk about is of any interest to him. My brother might be able to help, but he's away at school. Mr. Spenser drops in now and then, but he might as well not, for all the good it does."

"I'm sorry, Meg. I didn't realize . . ."

"Oh, please. I'm the one who should apologize. It's detestable of me to worry you with our troubles, when you . . ."

"I'll tell Vince," Richard promised. "He'll come over. They'll have things to talk about."

"No, Richard. You and your brother have so much to do, and more than enough trouble of your own."

"We've been sharing this particular trouble all along," he reminded her. "I don't see how we could stop even if we wanted to. And as a matter of fact"—he sent a glance around the clearing—"there's something Vince may want to discuss with him. That is"—his eyes came back to her with a smile—"if he considers it worthy of discussion and not just one of my unbridled flights of fancy. So I can't say for sure, but—perhaps this evening, if that's convenient for your father?"

"You are very kind, Richard."

"And you are very lovely, Meg, all dusted with snow, that way."

"Thank you. That is very kind, too. Well, I'd better go."

"Meg"—he put a hand on the bridle rein—"you aren't still angry with me?"

"What an absurd question. I never was angry with you."

"Jane said you would never forgive me."

"Jane can hardly speak for *me*, Richard."

"Then are we still friends?"

"Well, we're *cousins*, certainly."

Though this wasn't quite the answer he wanted,

it held a teasing note that let him ask, "Meg—sometime—won't you stop at the cottage?"

"To meet your wife and child?" Coolness replaced the teasing note. "You surely know I am not an inquisitive person."

He stepped back. "It's been good to see you, Meg. Be careful at the foot of the hill—there's a patch of ice under the snow."

"Oh, *Richard.*" She sounded vexed, contrite, and despairing. "I didn't mean to hurt your feelings. But you're so . . . How *can* you ask that of me when . . . Oh, very well." She gathered up her reins. "*Some*time I will come."

Early that evening when a visitor was announced to the Findlays, to their surprise the announcement was not, "Mr. Vincent Stafford to see you, Master," but, "Mr. Richard Stafford."

Richard was apologetic. "I'm sorry to disappoint you, Uncle Ed, after leading you to expect Vince."

But his cousin said, "Come in, come in, Richard. It is not a disappointment but a great pleasure. Have a chair, here, close to the fire. You must be chilled from your ride."

Margaret and her mother, after an exchange of greetings, moved to withdraw but were persuaded to remain by Richard's protests that he did not wish to disturb them, that the matter he had come to discuss concerned all of them, and couldn't he just draw up another chair?

He explained that the reason Vince hadn't come was that he and Jane had visitors of their own who rode out from Westbridge that morning and were staying the night because of the weather. (He did not add that

211

Vince had still another reason: "Seeing you will do him more good than seeing me, Richie.")

Edward asked, "Is it still snowing?"

"No, but there's a wind blowing up drifts. We may find ourselves snowbound by morning."

"Then you must not let us keep you too long, as we will be inclined to do. There are places where drifts close the road very quickly. We won't want you to risk getting into difficulties on your way home."

"I'll be all right, sir."

"Yes." Edward looked long and searchingly into the face of his cousin's son—the face so like the one so well remembered. "You will be all right, Richard. You have proved that in many ways. I think all of us will come to lean on you, as time goes by."

Not understanding how any of them, let alone all, could ever lean on him, and feeling somewhat embarrassed by what seemed an unduly extravagant compliment though unquestionably offered in sincerity, Richard pushed the forward-hanging lock of hair back from his forehead.

"Well, if the leaning is from opposite sides, that's one way of being supported. And I need support—that's what I've come for. I'd like your opinion and advice on something, Uncle Ed."

"I have never known a man," Edward replied, smiling (*the first time in a month,* his wife noted gratefully), "who didn't enjoy giving his opinion and advice, sought or unsought. What's weighing on your mind, Richard?"

"Foraging, sir. I heard a number of reports last month, and some of the places were less than twenty miles from here. It may come closer, when things open up again, and I think we should be prepared."

"To conceal our livestock and provisions, do you mean?"

"Yes. Not everything, because unless we have enough on hand to satisfy the foragers, we would be in greater danger of looting and burning. But the more valuable of our animals, and hay and grain for them, and adequate provisions for ourselves—these I think we should hide, or be prepared to hide."

"For ourselves that won't be too difficult," Edward conceded. "But horses and cattle are much harder to hide than smoked meats and sacks of flour and things of that sort."

"Uncle Ed, you know the clearing in our woods? Well, I want to fence it, and build log shelters there for our horses and cattle. And for storage, in advance, of enough to feed a given number for a given time—say at least two months. Then, if we hear of raiding parties coming anywhere near, we can immediately move our stock. Yours can be moved directly through the woods without being seen by anyone. The Spensers would have only to cross the road."

Richard detailed his plans. To begin with, he would build a good tight shed for storage. They would pack the hay into bales, to conserve space. For the livestock he would build shelters facing south. The sides would be of notched logs, the roofs would be shingled. In good weather the doors could remain open, permitting free access to the clearing. Water was readily available; he would run the spring through a chestnut trough just inside the fence. The clearing could be enlarged, and divided if necessary or desirable to separate the animals. There was no likelihood of anyone's searching so far into the deep woods from the south or west or north; but as a search might be made from the Blue Meadow

213

fields on the east, he would fell a few trees so their tops would effectively screen the trails.

Edward nodded approval as he listened. "An excellent idea, Richard, but entailing a great amount of work. You will need help, and the undertaking requires secrecy. Whom can you trust not to reveal what you're doing?"

"I can do most of the work myself, sir. But we can trust our redemptioners—Gideon and Tom. I should say our former redemptioners. They each had another year, but Father said their agreements should be canceled and they should be given their terminal gifts. Vince did that, but they want to stay. So now he's paying them, and he's buying two hundred acres east of us to divide between them when they marry and set up for themselves. There's no question of their loyalty to Vince. About the others I'm not sure. That's one reason why I want to start immediately. Through the winter nothing will be thought of my working in the woods; later, it might arouse curiosity."

"You must not work alone when felling trees, Richard."

"They will be fairly small trees, sir. But Vince said the same thing. He also said the idea was worth thinking about, but he wouldn't give his consent until we had your opinion. And he said that even though these will be very simple structures, I have the instincts of a cabinetmaker, not a carpenter, and there's a difference between dollhouses and stock sheds."

They laughed; all of them, even Edward.

Richard went on: "He said I'd need supervision by someone who knows something about building. So naturally we thought . . . Well, who knows more about it than the architect who designed and built these houses? I hope it's not insulting to ask an architect's

214

advice on log sheds; but Vince said if you could spare a little time to superintend, he might be persuaded to approve the project."

Margaret's hands were tight on the edges of the book she wasn't reading. Her mother's knitting needles were still. Edward Findlay sat looking into the fire. At nothing? At the past? At a transparent effort to secure his interested participation in the future?

Still looking into the fire, he asked, "And how about you, Richard? Do you feel that you need my advice or help, or supervision by anyone to build temporary shelters for horses and cattle?"

"Uncle Ed, if my father were here, *he* would supervise."

Edward raised his eyes; more than the light of the fire was in them. "Had you needed time to invent that answer, Richard, I would be less impressed. Very well. I'll be only too glad to give you all the help I can. When do you propose to start?"

"Tomorrow, if . . . Do you think you could ride over tomorrow to look at the site and do a little preliminary planning? If the snow doesn't drift too much, and if it's not too cold?"

"Snow and cold will not stop me. Will nine o'clock be too early?"

"Nine o'clock will be fine, sir."

(7)

It was not inquisitiveness, nor old friendship, nor even gratitude to Richard for the minor miracle he had wrought in restoring her father, that led Margaret at last to the cottage. Rather, the visit was a test of her own courage.

She loved Richard. *She* had thought to be his wife; *she* to be the mother of his son. But he had chosen another. Not in reasonableness and sobriety, as he might have chosen Cordelia Spenser or some other girl of good family in preference to herself. No, he had let his heart make his choice, and in reckless disregard of all that was sober and reasonable, had chosen a servant girl.

Cordelia had not spared her the full story. Cordelia could no more keep from telling the full story than dry leaves could keep from swirling in the wind. But long before hearing all about the "spell" and the "magic stone," Margaret knew her father had spared her. Because she knew Richard. Perhaps that was why there had never existed in her mind any question as to whether she could or could not forgive him. Such a question would have been paradoxical. Forgiveness would require that she forgive him for being Richard; and it was for being Richard that she loved him.

By accepting her father's presentation of the matter —that Richard in an unfortunate moment had simply behaved as young men do sometimes behave, and had then been compelled to marry the girl—Margaret was able at first to reject the thought that under no ordinary circumstances would Richard ever have behaved so, and that the circumstances therefore must have been extraordinary to the extreme. But to reject the thought was merely to banish it from the surface, not from the deep inner recesses of her mind. Consequently, Cordelia's story came as no surprise.

Margaret had never seen Richard's wife, not even at a distance; but from her father she knew the conditions of Marcus Stafford's will, and nothing could more conclusively establish that the girl must indeed have something to recommend her, for he would never otherwise have been willing to let his estate pass eventually to Richard's firstborn son. Whether or not the stigma of the mother's lowly origin would also pass to the son was an open question.

Edward Findlay said not. The times were changing, he said, and in twenty years it would not matter that Brian Stafford was the son of a servant girl. It might, on the contrary, be to his advantage, for the revolution here in the Colonies had begun long ago; the war for independence was only one manifestation of that revolution. Did not the Declaration itself set forth that all men are created equal? The Staffords, it could be argued, had simply been in advance of Mr. Thomas Jefferson, espousing that democratic principle in the espousal of a gentleman's son and a chambermaid.

Margaret was not prepared to espouse the principle. In her opinion Mr. Jefferson's statement was sheer rhetoric, the more absurd the more one sought to examine it in the light of reason. To ignore class lines, in marriage or anything else, could lead only to degeneration and chaos. Still, she was willing to concede that every rule should have just enough flexibility to permit an occasional exception when warranted. That did not mean she considered Richard's marriage a warrantable exception; it meant only that in fairness she must admit the possibility of its being so. But she did not go to the cottage to satisfy herself as to the existence or non-existence of that possibility. She went because she recognized or at least suspected that her aloofness was a form of cowardice; and pride would not let her be cowardly.

She scorned to go as Cordelia had gone, uninvited and impertinently prying. Nor could she take Richard's plea to "stop some time" as a proper invitation. Therefore, having ridden over to the clearing one afternoon to see how the shelters were progressing, she told Richard that if he cared to ascertain a convenient time, and would so inform her, she would be pleased to call upon his wife.

As anticipated, he eagerly replied, "Go down now, Meg."

But she said, "I will *not* go down now. I will go only upon invitation from your wife, specific as to the day and hour."

Her father, upon his return home that same day, told her, "Mrs. Richard Stafford requests the pleasure of your company tomorrow afternoon at three."

"Oh?" Margaret was not surprised, but neither was she incautious. "Is that authentic, or did Richard presume to fix the time?"

"Richard obtained the invitation from his wife, as

you requested. He interrupted his work to go down and do so."

As this was precisely what she had supposed Richard would do, there was still no element of surprise. "How very flattering."

"He did not mean it as flattery, Margaret. He values your friendship and is deeply grateful for your kindness. So am I."

"I am not being kind, Papa. But if I were, why should *you* be grateful to me for calling on Richard's wife?"

"Because I am indebted to Richard. Your act of good will helps me discharge my debt."

"My 'act of good will,' as you call it, is an act solely in my own interest; solely to prove to myself that I am capable of acting in good will."

He smiled. "Whatever your reason, a benefit accrues to all of us. And though you may have a need to prove something to yourself, you have no need to prove it to me. I am proud of you."

"Proud of a Findlay for soliciting an invitation to have afternoon tea with a servant girl?"

"Proud of you for having the courage and the courtesy to meet Richard's wife at your own level, Margaret."

"Well, I hope you will still be proud, after tomorrow. I'm far from sure I can conduct myself in a manner deserving of your pride. An act of apparent kindness can be deceptive—in truth a screen for a thousand subtle cruelties."

"You will not be cruel."

"I shall try not to be, for Richard's sake. But you can scarcely expect me to have kindly feelings toward his wife."

"I expect you to be unable to have any but kindly feelings. I have met her several times, you see."

"Jane Stafford's feelings are not kindly, Papa; yet she lost nothing through Richard's marriage."

This was the nearest Margaret had ever come to speaking of her own loss. She had wept in the privacy of her room; in public she had worn a mask of unconcern, which, though perhaps deceiving no one, had effectively turned sympathy aside. Having now said this much, she avoided her father's eyes, knowing they would be sad and troubled, as his voice was.

"Margaret, my dear . . ."

Quickly she said, "Not that *I* lost anything. One cannot lose what one never had. It was just . . . Well, knowing how you and Cousin Marcus felt, I suppose I assumed that Richard and I . . ." Not trusting her voice, she left the rest unsaid.

"That was our hope, yes. But fathers cannot with certainty plan the lives of their sons and daughters, and perhaps should not presume to try. There are too many unknown quantities . . ."

"Yes," Margaret agreed, "including those 'unalienable Rights' we're hearing so much about—'Life, Liberty, and the pursuit of Happiness.' One might almost imagine," she added wryly, "that Richard had a hand in composing that document. Well, I do not begrudge them their happiness. And I shall pursue my own, in my own way."

"Of course you will, my dear." Relief was in his voice. "You are only eighteen. You will meet other young men."

Now she met his eyes. "Doubtless I will. Many others, to whom one hundred thousand pounds will make me very attractive, though nature did not make me so. But I shall not find *them* attractive. No"—she spoke lightly—"you're going to have a spinster daughter on your hands. But don't worry—I shall go about performing good works to justify my existence. Papa, do you know what I would like to do? I would like to teach. I would like to open a school in Willowfield."

She watched surprise and pleasure replace the sadness.

"That would be splendid! A day school, do you mean?"

"At first. Later, perhaps a boarding school for girls. But to start with, just a school for the local children. It isn't right that children whose parents haven't the means to send them away, or to engage tutors or governesses, have no opportunity to receive even a rudimentary education."

"Why, Margaret, I believe *you* are a revolutionist!"

"Perhaps I am," she admitted, laughing, "in that one respect. But so are you. If you weren't, then I—a mere female—would not be qualified. Do you think a small piece of the land you bought for the church could be spared for a school?"

"That will be a perfect location, yes. Immediately after dinner we'll start sketching plans for a building!"

Under a south wind and a bright March sun, the winter's accumulated snows were melting when Margaret set out for Blue Meadow. In low places the road was a morass of slush and mud; elsewhere, bright runnels filled the ruts and cascaded through the gutters. Keeping her horse to a walk, she picked her way carefully; and where there was no choice but to splash straight through, she gathered up the skirts of her riding habit in a manner that Jane Stafford might well have called hoydenish. A lady's riding habit was a most decorous garment; and certainly no lady would ever ride along a public road with her skirts immodestly bunched above her knees.

Margaret, grinning at her own impropriety, reflected upon the circumstances that justified it. Had she been riding over to see Cordelia, she wouldn't have cared a farthing about the condition of her clothes (and indeed would very likely have been riding astride, wearing her brother's boots and breeches). Why, then, did she take such care not to present herself mud-spattered and bedraggled when calling on Richard Stafford's wife? Because what Cordelia would see merely as typical indecorum, Richard's wife might see as contempt. But why not show contempt? Why her velvet riding habit and plumed hat instead of corduroy or deerskin—the wholly practical attire in which she used to go galloping over the countryside with Richard? The answer was that she went as one lady formally calling upon another; and formal calls were not made in informal attire.

The carriage drive at Blue Meadow had been turned into a streambed by the melting snow. There was a hitching post at the cottage, but as a small torrent surrounded it, Margaret rode on up the drive, ruefully wishing she had brought along a pair of clogs.

Vincent Stafford came from the barn to meet her, saying with an unusually warm and welcoming smile, "Don't dismount here, Margaret. I'll walk down with you and bring your horse back."

"Oh, that would be kind, but really I don't want to put you to the trouble."

"It is no trouble. But if it were, you are not putting me to it. I was requested to watch for you and perform this small service. And I will add"—they started down the drive—"that for all he is apt to accomplish this afternoon on his sheds, Richard might as well have remained here to perform the service himself. You have him walking on air, Margaret."

"Richard is easily transported; but do you mean there are times when he does actually have his feet on the ground?"

"Somewhat to my surprise, yes. Quite firmly."

"He's working so hard," Margaret said. "I certainly can't hope the armies come close, yet I hate to think of all that time and effort wasted if they don't."

"Richie will be glad if it turns out that he's been wasting his time and efforts. And if his sheds aren't needed, we'll have a year's supply of firewood. Well, here we are."

Six broad flagstones of dark gray slate, clean and dry, made low steps to the front door of the cottage.

"I was asked to introduce you, Margaret, unless you prefer to handle that yourself."

"Oh. I hadn't expected . . . But that would be more strictly polite, wouldn't it? Yes, please, Vincent, if you will."

"And what time would you like your horse back here at the door?"

"Oh, I'll come to the barn. Wet feet won't matter then."

"No, Margaret. Your hostess would be distressed to see you walk from her house through water above your ankles. What time?"

"Well, then—an hour."

After tying her horse to the hitching post, Vincent escorted her to the door, raised the iron knocker, rapped twice——but before the second rap the latch was lifted. With grave formality he said, "Bridget, I would like you to meet Miss Margaret Findlay. Margaret—Mrs. Richard Stafford."

I've done it all wrong, was Margaret's first thought

in that first moment of looking into the face of the girl in the doorway. I should have done as Richard asked me to, just dropped in . . .

Politely she said, "How do you do?"

Politely Bridget said, "It be a great honor, Miss Findlay, that you visit. Please come in."

She may consider it an honor, Margaret thought, but certainly not a pleasure. She didn't want me to come—she sent the invitation only to please Richard. She thinks I hate and despise her. If this is an ordeal for me, it's a hundred times worse for her. . . .

"Oh, tut!" Margaret turned with a sudden grin. "Vincent, would you mind going through that little ritual again? But please just say, 'Bridget, this is Meg. Meg, this is Bridget.' "

Vincent complied.

Margaret said, "Well, I've been an inexcusably long time about it, Bridget, but I'm glad to be here at last."

And Bridget, smiling through quick tears, answered, *"Céad míle fáilte.* I be glad you come, Miss"—with an effort she caught and corrected herself—"Meg."

"I take it," Vincent said, "that you girls have no further need of my good offices?"

"No, but thank you very much. And Vincent—if it won't inconvenience you—may I change that to an hour and a half?"

Margaret had not been in the cottage for a number of years. She remembered this as a very pleasant room, beautifully furnished, and was surprised to find it almost as she remembered. Surely that was the treasured mahogany and satinwood desk Cousin Marcus brought along from England? Drawing off her gloves she paused to say, "How lovely the room looks, Bridget. So very nearly the same as it was the year Richard and his father lived here."

224

"It be so," Bridget answered. "At Christmastime, when the Master knew he was not to live, he gave these things to Richard, so it would be the same."

Slowly Margaret pulled off her other glove. "That must have made Richard both sad and happy."

"Yes. Sad, then; now happy." With reverence Bridget touched the desk. "This and the chair—also the chair there beside you—and upstairs the bed and chest of drawers and other things—these were in the Master's own bedroom. Richard has great love of these things." Timidly she asked, "Will you sit down, please? And may I take the gloves, and perhaps, if you would wish, the hat and coat?"

"Oh, I'll just put them here"—Margaret tossed the gloves on a windowsill—"and this ridiculous thing, too." The plumed hat followed.

Margaret wore no cap, having rebelled against the custom. Her straight brown hair was drawn back and braided, the braid then coiled and pinned at the nape of her neck. To adorn that plainness with any sort of frill or furbelow would in her opinion be worse than useless. If you were plain, the best thing was to be perfectly honest about it. Frills were for those who had the least need of them; those already endowed with beauty; those like Bridget . . .

Bridget was wearing a white lawn cap with a lavender ribbon drawn in and out through its ruffled edging. Bridget was wearing a low-necked lavender dress of fine muslin, and a dainty white apron trimmed with lace. And Bridget was wearing a necklace of amethysts.

These were the amethysts—Margaret had heard all about them—that Richard found there at Blue Meadow. Vincent had had them cut and polished and set by a jeweler in Philadelphia, and then had given the neck-

lace to Richard to give to Bridget on the first an-
niversary of their marriage.

Margaret herself never wore jewelry, nor any but
high-necked gowns. She was much in the sun and
wind, whereby her face was browned (disgracefully so,
according to general opinion), and of course the dividing line between brown and white had to be covered.
Bridget had not that problem. Bridget . . .

Oh, God, Margaret asked herself, how could he
help losing his heart and head the minute he laid eyes
on her? And she fits. She doesn't need a dust cloth in
her hand to belong in this room. She belongs here this
way, doing exactly what she'll be doing a few minutes
from now, pouring tea from a Dresden pot into ex-
quisitely fragile flowered Dresden cups, the set that belonged to Richard's mother, or I miss my guess. . . .

And I? Where do I belong? Anywhere?—except on
a horse, tearing around *over hill, over dale, through
bush, through brier, over park, over pale, through flood,
through fire?* Look at me. My mannish coat and neck-
cloth, my weathered freckled face, my long-legged
stride, my tomboy ways . . . And I came here as a
lady?

"Bridget, you're exactly as I knew you must be. I
knew—because it simply wasn't believable any other
way."

With folded hands, and still by no means at ease,
Bridget sat facing her guest. If there was a suitable
answer, her look showed that she did not know what
it was.

"And the curious thing is," Margaret went on, "that
I *wanted* to think you were this way—someone so ut-
terly lovely that I'd have no trouble understanding
Richard's regard for you."

Color rose in Bridget's cheeks. "You be too kind."

"Not at all. It was pure logic. I had to put a reasonable explanation to it because—well, I hate not being able to understand things. And it would be incredibly stupid of me not to understand Richard, when I've known him all my life."

"Richard speaks of you many times," Bridget said. "Of such good friends as the two of you have always been. And the three young ladies, they also speak of you. It be Miss Virginia's dream that one day she will ride the horses as her Cousin Margaret rides."

Margaret grinned. "Jane will have something to say about that. But I wouldn't be surprised to see Virginia have her way—she's turned into a strong-willed little thing. And the picture of health, besides. I understand it was you who accomplished that, Bridget."

"Not so. I take care of her till she be well. But it was the Master who made her well. When he promised her a pony—that quick she began to mend, you would not believe."

"The only thing I would find hard to believe is that Jane was consulted about that promise. She's always been so fearful for those children, she scarcely lets them breathe."

"Yes, the Mistress was much worried at first; but now I think it be happiness to her to see Miss Virginia so well and strong."

"*Bridget.* You must stop saying 'the Master' and 'the Mistress' and 'Miss' Virginia. They're *Vincent* and *Jane,* and the girls are your nieces!"

Bridget looked down at her hands. "It be not easy to make such change."

"Well, easy or hard, you have to do it. You're Richard's wife!"

"But at the house I be a servant. . . ."

"Nonsense. I know about that. But not entering

the house except *as* a servant doesn't mean you are one, any more than Richard is. It's entirely obvious, Bridget, that you were a servant only because you were poor. And being poor is a misfortune, but it's not a measure of what a person really *is*. Richard saw that at once. And his father saw it. And Vincent saw it. Jane may see it too, in time. It's a great pity Richard so rashly and needlessly swore as he did. But"—quickly—"don't *you* worry about that—it wasn't your fault. And anyway, I know he was happy coming back here; because I remember he felt rather bad about leaving this little house. He helped build it, you know, carrying stones and whittling out the treenails—the wooden pegs that hold the beams together. He made almost all of them. Did he never tell you?"

"No, this he does not tell me. But in the lintel above the kitchen door—when first we came he showed me his initials cut in the wood, and told how he did this when no one was by to see, and how the house was almost finished before one day his father looked up and saw them there."

"Oh, yes, and I remember Cousin Marcus saying, 'You have put your mark upon time, Richard. Future generations will not forget you.'"

Tenderly Bridget said, "Richard thinks much of the future. Sometimes he speaks beyond my understanding —that it be all one, the future and the past. This he says, too—that as the sun goes from the place of its rising to the place of its setting, and then again to its rising—so it be with the generations of men—the father giving life to the son, and the son again to the father, so there be no end."

"Richard is a curious combination of science and mysticism," Margaret commented; and added with a grin, "Mothers and daughters have a place in there too, if I am not mistaken. Bridget, am I going to meet your son?"

"Much I wish you to. He be sleeping, but soon he wakes. Please, I bring the tea now, if you will excuse me. I think then he wakes, hearing me in the kitchen."

Waiting, Margaret listened to their voices.

"A-mah, A-mah, tea!"

"A *Bhriain,* now you shall have your tea. But a guest be in our house, and you will come say good day to her, and then you will sit and have your tea with us as a gentleman. Here be your cup. Do you carry it, now, in your own hands."

Brian preceded his mother into the front room, he carrying a pewter cup, she the Dresden tea set on a silver tray. Bare feet planted wide apart under a bright blue petticoat, he stood gazing solemnly at the stranger who came as a guest to their house.

And Margaret thought: *A Stafford. Yes, of course, a Stafford.* Deep within her she felt pain—*Richard's son, but not mine*—and then a diffuse sadness spreading away from the pain, as ripples spread on water when a stone is dropped in a pool. But smiling she said, "The curls are Bridget's but the face is Richard's. And how straight he stands! So young, but so self-reliant, and so strong!"

"He be strong, yes. When he has two years, Richard says he will make for him a little wooden fork to pile the hay, and then they will work in the fields together."

"But you'll never let Richard take him away from you at only two years."

"Please, I will wish Richard to have him always close. They be father and son. And"—Bridget looked down, pouring tea into the flowered cups—"another little one comes in the summer, to be here with me."

"That must make you very happy, Bridget. And Richard, too."

229

"Yes. Many times each day I say 'Buidheachas le Dia' for such happiness. It be so much more than I deserve—that I be mother of Richard's children, he a gentleman and I a servant."

Sharply Margaret said, "No. You must stop thinking of it that way. You are exactly the right wife for Richard, the right mother for his children. You are warm and loving and gentle and good. *Naturally* so, just as you are naturally beautiful. That you were a servant doesn't matter. You are a person of instinctive refinement, and that counts for more than any amount of acquired refinement."

Bridget, her hand trembling, poured a little tea into Brian's cup, which she then filled with milk. Taking him on her lap, she held the cup for him to drink. Her eyes, meeting Margaret's, were full of tears.

"I know well you be Richard's friend. And I think —Meg—you be my friend also, even though you be the fine lady, and I . . ."

"Don't dare say it again," Margaret warned, "or you'll have me shouting at you like a fishwife! Bridget, don't you understand? The only important thing is what we are, ourselves, not what our positions are in an artificially divided society. Haven't you heard? *We hold these truths to be self-evident: that all men are created equal; that they are endowed by their Creator with certain unalienable Rights . . .*"

An hour later, riding home, Margaret tried to put her thoughts in order; but she found her mind filled with a hodgepodge of pictures, impressions, half-thoughts, non-thoughts, recollections, which, together with intruding emotions, made clear thinking impossible.

Richard's wife, Richard's son . . . Amethysts . . . The little house with *R G S* cut in the back-door lintel . . . The place of the sun's rising . . . Tea cakes . .

She had eaten three of those delicious things; Sunday cakes, Bridget called them. She had sat on the floor, building and rebuilding a tower of wooden blocks for Brian to knock down. She had promised to ride over two afternoons each week to teach Bridget to read and write and do simple arithmetic; the girls hadn't been doing a very good job, and Richard hadn't time. She had promised to bring Bridget the shoulder harp (and wasn't it an Irish harp?) that she herself had never learned to play. She had said that as soon as the road was passable, Richard must drive Bridget and Brian over to have tea with the Findlays—*all* the Findlays. She had said . . .

How could she remember all she said? How could she explain what came over her? How could she clarify her thoughts?

Only one thought was clear and sharp and final.

The die is cast. Papa was right. I am a revolutionist.

(8)

It was a quiet spring.

By the end of March, Richard's livestock shelters were ready and waiting, the clearing was fenced, the storage shed was filled with hay taken from the big mows in the barn and hauled up by night.

In April, most of the young stock was sold. A buyer came to Westbridge, and word was quickly passed around that he was paying good prices for horses, cattle, sheep, and swine. As payment was in British gold or Spanish silver, it was of course known that he was a representative of the Crown, though not openly identified as such. For two weeks all roads to Westbridge came alive with the desired animals, singly and in droves. From Blue Meadow went all but the very best of the three-year-old Thoroughbreds and some of the two-year-olds; yearling bull calves and heifers; gilts and young barrows; and the money received for them went into the safe behind the swinging bookshelf in the library.

To be hidden if the need arose were the oxen, the milk cows, heifers of breeding age, and at least one

young bull; most of the sheep and hogs; the Thoroughbred brood mares, the work mares, the individual favor-
ites, and the remaining two- and three-year-olds. The
yearling colts and fillies, of no use to either army, would
be turned out to pasture. A few meat animals would
remain at the barn, as would two light work geldings.
Red Earl also would remain, Richard being confident
that no one would attempt to put a hand on him, intol-
erant as he was of strangers.

April passed and the breath of May was over the
land. Fruit trees blossomed, grass sprang up, checked
rows of Indian corn unfurled their green banners. Each
day at Blue Meadow was patterned on the one before—
orderly, busy, productive, peaceful. Reports came of
fighting in Connecticut and the west; but General Washington still tarried in winter quarters at Morristown,
General Howe in New York, and except for skirmishes
between rival foraging parties there was no word of any
renewal of hostilities that would directly affect south-
eastern Pennsylvania.

"Two months of good weather," Vincent said, "and
they're still sitting on their tails. What do you make
of it, Richie?"

"I think each is waiting for the other to make the
first move."

"To Philadelphia? But there's nothing to stop the
Continentals from moving down."

"No, but if they do, General Howe may move north
instead."

"Do you think there's any chance that the whole
thing will end in a stalemate?"

"No. I think a move will be made before long."

Through May, Richard continued his preparations
in expectation of that move. There were three rooms on
the second floor of the cottage, one of them not furn-

ished. Working at night, he built a partition closing off a portion of that room, the opening a removable panel so artfully made that even on close scrutiny it could not be detected. Here supplies of wheat flour and corn meal, sugar and salt, tea and coffee, could be—and well in advance were—concealed. Similarly, in the cellar he made a secret storage place for potatoes and other root crops, fruits, cheeses and butter, crocks of lard, salted meats, smoked hams and bacon, cider and wines. And at the house he fitted false bottoms in chests and false backs in cupboards for the concealment of silverware and other things of relatively small size but substantial value, which looters would be quick to seize.

Jane disapproved. "Anyone will know things are hidden. The place will be torn apart until everything is found."

"No," Vincent answered, "I think not. Richard's plan is to leave enough readily available to satisfy the searchers."

"*Richard's plan.* What have we come to, pray, that Richard now does our planning?"

"Well, speaking for myself, what I have come to is recognition of the fact that Richard has reached maturity."

"At nineteen?"

"To be exact, at eighteen. Don't you think he passed a rather severe test?"

"If you're referring to delivery of the child, that only proves he is rash enough to attempt anything, and that the girl had an easy time."

Vincent shrugged and would have dropped the subject; but Jane said, "All this planning for something that in all probability will never happen. I'm sure no one else is taking such elaborate precautions, when there's no indication at all that either army will come within a hundred miles of here."

"Perhaps no one else has quite so strong a motive. Our neighbors have only themselves and their own possessions to think of."

"And what has Richard to think of?"

"His father, and everything that was his father's."

"I fail to see the distinction, since everything will be his."

"He isn't doing it for himself, Jane. He's doing it for Blue Meadow. And that means everyone here."

"Oh, yes, I suppose so. But he is so extreme. It amazes me that you let yourself be influenced by his wild imaginings."

"I sometimes wonder if the word isn't prescience."

"You credit him with ability to foresee the future?"

"I credit him with good sound judgment. Sometimes intuitive rather than the product of pure reasoning, but nonetheless sound. And yes, I think Richie has somewhat better perception of the future than most of us have."

At the end of May, General Washington's army moved twenty miles south, and through June there were various and often conflicting accounts of maneuvers in New Jersey, but no word of any major engagement. Disturbingly, however, it was reported that the British, retreating to Amboy, burned all houses and barns along their way.

Haymaking at Blue Meadow took an altered form that summer. In the hope that an empty barn was less likely to be set afire than a full one, only a portion of the hay was put in the mows; the rest was stacked outside in ricks, well apart from the buildings, so that if put to the torch only the hay itself would be lost. And in July, when the wheat was ready for harvest, it was at first decided to leave it shocked in the field indefinitely; but then, upon hearing that the British army had been entirely withdrawn from New Jersey, to Staten Island, that decision was reversed and the wheat was hauled to the barn and stored as usual.

Worry lost some of its edge during those bright hot days of July. The outside world in which men were bent on killing one another, and on plundering, or destroying whatever lay in their path, receded just a little from the borders of Blue Meadow. With a lighter heart Richard could swing his scythe through the golden wheat, and watch the corn grow tall, and take his little son to the fields with him, and look eagerly forward to the birth of his second child.

With regard to that event there was no need, as on the first occasion, that his work be interrupted by repeated trips to the cottage to assure himself that Bridget was all right. Margaret appointed herself a daily companion as the time drew near, coming every morning and staying until evening.

The neighborhood had come to look with mixed feelings upon Edward Findlay's daughter, as it had upon Marcus Stafford's son, and for much the same reason—her flouting of the rules of social custom in ignoring the barriers between herself and a servant girl. There were raised eyebrows and disparaging comments in some quarters; in others, hearty endorsement, especially by those who had watched the breaking of ground near the church for a school, and had learned that their children were to have the opportunity to be educated by none other than Miss Margaret Findlay herself, and altogether free of charge—though voluntary contribution would be accepted from any who could afford it. The villagers, some of whom had come to the Colonies as bond servants, saw Bridget as one of their own, and took vicarious satisfaction in her marriage to a gentleman's son and her friendship with a gentleman's daughter. And they did not look askance at Margaret, as the gentlefolk did, for her unaffected and independent ways; on the contrary, they admired her.

As things then stood, in midsummer, Margaret's friendship was still the only indication that the better families—the rich landowners around Willowfield— might eventually close their eyes to the barriers. Richard had not, up to that time, driven Bridget over to have Sunday afternoon tea with the Findlays. He couldn't plead the press of work, not on a Sunday afternoon, and was reluctant to offer the true explanation; but Margaret guessed.

"I know exactly why. You're thinking that if my parents received Bridget, the Spensers would do the same, and then others would—and where would that leave Jane?"

"Yes," he admitted. "It wouldn't be fair."

"You weren't fair to yourself, Richard, when you made that oath. Nor to Bridget. Nor to your children."

"I know, but there's nothing I can do about it now. I made it; I can't retract it. And if we were received in other houses when we aren't—and can't be— received here, it would put Jane in a very uncomfortable position, would make her appear in the wrong, when she had every right to feel the way she did."

"You are too generous. Your father and brother were willing—what right had Jane to stand in the way?"

"She didn't stand in the way; but it was a very hard thing for her to accept, and . . ."

"And you thought this would make it easier. Well, perhaps it did, at the time; but unfortunately it locked a door that she might someday have been willing to open."

"Yes. They saw that at once—Vince and my father. I didn't. But even if I had, the words were already said."

"Do you think Jane's feelings will ever change?"

"Vince thinks so."

"And does he think you should turn down *our* acceptance of Bridget because you made it impossible for Jane to accept her even if her feelings do change?"

"I haven't asked him, Meg. No, I think he would tell me to go ahead. But at the same time, I think he would feel it wouldn't be fair to Jane. And he would want me to be fair."

"Yes, it's a rather ticklish situation. And if in all this time, almost two years, she still hasn't made the slightest move, hasn't once gone to the cottage to see Bridget, hasn't even sent baby clothes or anything like that—I suppose it will be a long while before she does make any such move."

"Vince thinks she would, if she weren't so proud and stubborn."

"Well, then there's hope," Margaret said, smiling. "*I* was proud and stubborn—and just see how things turned out!"

It was Margaret who summoned Cook one sultry afternoon, and then hurried to the field to tell Richard the baby was coming. He had Brian with him, and staying well behind the flashing scythes of the reapers, was tying the wheat into sheaves with twisted ropes of straw. Later, all the sheaves would be gathered into shocks; but for the present he was merely setting four together, propped one against another, at twenty-foot intervals. These were Brian's "homes," a succession of them being necessary because twenty feet was the utmost distance he would tolerate between his father and himself, and so kept abandoning one and demanding another—"Home, Rish—make home!"

Though not needed this time, and though Bridget, wanting to spare him, had asked that he not come to the room, Richard wanted to be close, within call, only seconds away. But he paused to look anxiously at the sky. Clouds were piled in the west, there would be a thunderstorm before the afternoon was over. The cut wheat should be tied and shocked. . . . Vincent was waving him toward the house. Gratefully he accepted the dismissal and turned away.

"Now don't worry," Margaret said in sympathy. "Bridget isn't the least bit worried—just *happy*. And she asked me to tell you—please take Brian into the meadow while you're waiting, so he can watch the minnows."

Staying within a hundred feet of the cottage, Richard and Brian explored the meadow world of grass and daisies and dragonflies, and in clear pools watched the silver darting minnows. Where the brook ran broad and shallow over a bed of smooth flat glittering stones, they went wading. And Richard tried not to worry, tried not to remember, not to think of Bridget's suffering then or now, but only of his little son's joy in the bright running water.

Margaret was calling. He scooped Brian out of the water and set off at a run, forgetting his shoes.

"Eighteen years between the two of you," she greeted him, laughing, "but it doesn't show. Everything's fine. Let me have Brian—we'll go get your shoes."

Richard went into the kitchen. Cook was there, poking up a blaze around a bundle of rags she had laid on the fire.

"Cook, may I . . . now. . . ?"

"*Gott in Himmel!* Is it not your own house, and your own *Frau,* and your own *kleines Mädchen?* Go, *mein Herr.*" She put exaggerated emphasis on the polite term of address—the first time she had ever called him anything but *Dummkopf.* "They wait for you."

In his father's big four-poster bed—theirs now—Bridget lay, pale and tired, smiling. A white lace shawl, Margaret's gift, was around her shoulders. A blue ribbon held the black curls away from her face. So lovely she looked, so lovely . . .

"Bridget . . ." He kissed her.

"Richard, *a rún,* see."

Now he saw the baby, there in the shelter of her arm.

"It be Lavinia. . . ."

His vision blurred as he looked at them. Mother and child. His wife, his daughter. And he remembered . . . He had been able to tell his father there was to be another child. If a boy it would be Vincent, he had promised; if a girl, Lavinia. He heard his father's voice . . . "Thank you, Richard, I will tell her . . ."

"Richard, you be glad?"

He knelt beside the bed. "Very glad. Bridget, now I have two of you."

Tenderly she touched his cheek. As she so often did. As she had done that first day in the woods. All his life he would feel her hand touching his cheek.

"*A mhíle ghrádh,* I be so sleepy. Will you stay now, while I sleep?"

"Right here. I'll stay right here beside you."

"I so much like you to be close, Richard."

"I'll always be close. We'll always be together, Bridget. Always."

At the house, Virginia came running with the news. "Mama! Bridget has a baby girl! Lavinia! She's so tiny and so beautiful and so . . . Mama, what's wrong? Are you sick?"

Her mother was on a couch in the sitting room. Not sewing or knitting, but lying down. At five o'clock in the afternoon Virginia had *never* found her mother lying down. Her mother was always busy, either doing something herself or watching the servants do things —not lying down, pressing one hand tight against her side.

"I'm all right, dear. Just resting."

"Does something hurt you?"

"Yes, but it will pass. Bridget has another baby, you say?"

"Yes! It came just a little while ago. Bridget's asleep, but Uncle Richard let me tiptoe upstairs to see the baby. I was the very first to see it—except Uncle Richard and Bridget and Cook and Cousin Margaret!"

"Where is your father?"

"Shocking the wheat. There's a storm coming—it's black as night. Hear the thunder? It's going to be a fierce storm!"

"Well, go get yourself ready for tea, Virginia."

Jane listened to the racing footsteps through the hall and up the stairs. *That child. I should call her back and make her go up again like a lady. . . .* But what was the use? And did it really matter? Long ago she had conceded that Vincent was right—better a healthy happy child than the pale sickly wraith of a "little lady." Let them have their way—Vincent, Richard, Margaret Findlay, and that girl. Let them make of Virginia what they would. Perhaps it was all for the best, everything that had happened. Who could say?

So Richard was a father again. Only nineteen, and twice a father.

Upstairs was a chest full of children's clothes. Some had scarcely been worn—she had made or bought

241

or been given so many things. Perhaps some time she would look them over, and anything suitable . . . There were quilted petticoats, and jackets and hoods of the finest wool, and stockings, and soft leather shoes. When winter came the little boy would need warm clothes, for no doubt Richard would take him outside, in defiance of everything sensible. Well, she would see.

The storm was close. Rushing ahead of the wind, thunderclouds darkened the sky and the room. There was a flash of lightning and a long roll of thunder.

Cautiously Jane sat up, still pressing a hand to her side, low. Yes, that was better; lying down at once was the thing to do; the bulge was gone. But last fall the doctor had warned her that there would come a time when it wouldn't go. It was still reducible, he had said; but when no longer reducible, if it became strangulated, only a surgical operation could save her life. She hadn't told Vincent. There had been enough to worry about last fall. This was her personal problem, and she would deal with her personal problems—as long as she could—in her own way.

Rising stiffly, she went to make sure no doors or windows were open to the rain.

The month of July ended with a mystery. The entire British fleet of more than two hundred sixty warships and transports sailed from Sandy Hook on the twenty-third, bound for—who knew where? On the thirtieth it was sighted off the Delaware Capes. Then it was gone. Where? To the Chesapeake? To Charleston? Back to New York and the Hudson? Over and over the question was asked; but no one—not even General Washington and certainly not the Continental Congress—knew the answer.

242

(9)

An old man with a knapsack on his back came walking along the road from Willowfield.

It was a Sunday morning, the last day of August. The road was dusty, the sun was high and hot, a faint breeze stirring the leaves in the very tops of the trees could barely be felt near the ground. When the old man reached the carriage drive at Blue Meadow he stopped and stood there, leaning on his walking stick, looking in.

Bridget and the dogs saw him at the same time.

"When you're here alone," Richard had told her, "if any stranger comes by, go inside and latch the doors."

She was alone at the cottage that morning, she and the baby; and none but the Mistress, who was not feeling well, and Cook, at the house. Richard had gone to the woods to feed the horses and cattle now hidden there, taking Brian with him. All the others were at church.

But . . . An old man? Under a tricorn hat his silver hair hung loose, touching his shoulders. And though his clothes were shabby from long wear, they were the clothes of a gentleman. Fearful that if he raised his stick to ward off the dogs they might attack, she called them; but in a friendly and unafraid manner he held out his hand, and after only a moment of circling and barking they approached him, tails awag.

This Richard had said too: "Unless it's someone Duff and Duke know and accept."

She did not think the dogs knew this old man, but plainly they accepted him. And the day was so hot, if he had walked far he must be thirsty and tired. How could she not invite him to come sit in the shade and rest, and refresh himself with food and drink?

He did not wait to be invited. Coming in the drive —and a firm, free step he had despite his years—he swept off his hat and greeted her, bowing as a courtier to a queen.

"May the day smile upon you, O Daughter of the Morning!"

Laughing, for her surprise was not so great as her delight, Bridget returned the greeting. "May the road rise with you, Grandfather, and may the wind be always at your back."

The old man's eyes, almost black, were deepset but very bright and piercing; nor was his smile the less glowing for being all but toothless.

"A Gaelic blessing," he exclaimed, "spoken in a soft Gaelic voice such as I could not have hoped to hear except on that fair isle westward of England! Tell me, Daughter. Have I the good fortune to meet one lately come from the holy land of Ireland?"

"Whether the land be holy," Bridget answered, "and whether your fortune be good, I cannot say. But it be so—not much more than three years past did I come from Ireland."

"From what part, Daughter?"

"Near Ballyshannon, in Donegal."

"I know it well. Was not Michael O'Clery, the Chief of the Four Masters who compiled the Annals of the Kingdom of Ireland, born at Ballyshannon? Two hundred years ago," the old man said, "of a family of hereditary scholars. What is your name, Daughter?"

"Bridget Gallagher it was; but now I be Bridget Stafford."

"Stafford? A Gallagher of Donegal married an Englishman?"

Bridget laughed. "Such an Englishman I think any poor Irish girl would be pleased and proud to marry—he a gentleman's son and myself then a servant in his father's house."

"This young man must be as rich, Daughter, as you are fair; for the price of wisdom is above rubies."

"You speak kind words, Grandfather. Will you not now come sit for a time, and let me fetch you a cool drink?"

"Greatly tempted am I to do so. And a cup of buttermilk, if you have it, would surpass the nectar of the gods."

"Buttermilk I have. Will you come inside, please, or will you like better to sit here on the bench in the shade?"

"The bench looks very comfortable, my child, and I would be reluctant to trade this leafy bower for a roof." He sat down with a grateful sigh. "It is good to take one's ease on a summer day."

When Bridget returned with the buttermilk, he had removed his knapsack and was taking from it an assortment of articles—an oval palette, several very fine brushes, and a number of small paintpots and vials—

placing them on the bench beside him. Also a square of thin wood; but after letting his eyes rest thoughtfully on her for a moment, he laid that aside and took out a small disk of some substance creamy-white and very smooth.

"Ivory," he said. "Only ivory will do."

Surprised, Bridget asked, "You be an artist?"

"Let us say, Daughter, that long years ago, when dreaming the dreams of youth, I fancied myself an artist. Now I am a painter. To avoid being excessively burdened as I travel about, I confine myself to miniatures. In this way I attempt to repay the many kindnesses of those whom I meet in the course of my travels. With your permission, I will now to the best of my ability copy your face upon this bit of ivory."

"But there be nothing to pay me for. The buttermilk is not . . ."

"Buttermilk? Oh, yes. That will indeed be refreshing." He drained the cup. "Thank you, Daughter. Now, if you will sit there at the end of the bench, turning your head this way . . . Or if there are other things to which you must give your attention, by all means do so. I have an excellent memory, upon which you are already indelibly printed; still, there is no substitute for the living model."

After making a few quick sketches on the wooden square, the old man mixed small dabs of color upon his palette, and then with infinitely delicate touches of the brush, began to paint.

Several times Bridget went inside, to tend her meat turning on the jack, or to see if the baby still slept. Between these trips she sat quiet, watching his hands. Very thin they were, and with that fine papery skin of the old; but very steady, very dexterous. The thought came to her that when Richard was old his hands would be like that; for Richard too was an artist, not with paints but with wood, and many times she had marveled at his skill in carving with tools as fine as this old man's brushes.

Thinking of Richard she glanced toward the drive, and at that moment he came within her sight, riding slowly past the barnyard, Brian in front of him on the saddle. As always when she saw him such great gladness filled her . . .

"Ah, that's beautiful," the old man said, not turning to follow her gaze but keeping his eyes intent upon her face. "That is what I must catch, that exquisite joy."

When he applied himself again to his painting, she rose and lifted Brian down from the saddle. Richard gave her a questioning look, but she laid a finger to her lips, and without speaking he turned away and rode back to put his horse in the stable. She sat down again. Brian, leaning against her knee, stared in grave and wondering silence.

The miniature was finished by the time Richard returned. Carefully the old man laid it on the bench, cleaned his palette and brushes, put his paints away, and buckled his knapsack. Only then did he relax, looking very weary, as if the intense concentration had drawn deeply upon his strength; and only then did he appear to notice that he and Bridget were no longer alone.

Richard smiled and said, "Good day, sir."

Weariness did not rob those deepset black eyes of their piercing look, on which Richard felt himself impaled.

"Good day, young man, good day. I have no doubt your name is Stafford, and this young woman lately

247

come from the Land of Saints and Scholars is your wife. I have taken the liberty of putting upon this ivory medallion a most inadequate and imperfect representation of her lovely face. Here, my dear boy." Picking up the disk he laid it on Richard's palm. "To yourself it is a mere trifle, the original being before you; but preserve it for the children of your children's children, that they may rejoice in having among their ancestors one of Beauty's Daughters."

"Thank you." Richard looked long at the painting. Inadequate? Imperfect? That delicate, delightful portrait? That tiny but faithful likeness of his beloved? "It's beautiful, sir. It's . . . You are a great artist. You must let me . . ."

"Do not speak of pay," the old man said. "It is a gift in exchange for a gift—my poor talents for the pleasure of meeting on this lonely road one so fair and kind."

"Have you walked far, sir?"

"Far? Ten thousand miles and back, twice over, through the years. In England, Scotland, Wales, and Ireland I have walked, and in France and Italy and Spain, and in the mountains of Switzerland, and the deserts of Egypt. Here in the Colonies I have walked from Boston to Charleston, thence north again to Philadelphia. And now . . . Well, now wherever the roads take me, in the direction of the setting sun."

"But this morning. Have you come far this morning?"

"Not far at all. From the small village of Westbridge."

"You came to Westbridge from Philadelphia?"

"Quite so. Three days I walked the road from Philadelphia. I am never in a hurry, you see. One misses the best of life when one hurries."

"Sir"—Richard looked again at the miniature—"will

you excuse me while I put this in a safe place, and then will you tell me any news you have heard along the way, of the armies?"

"Oh, the armies. Yes, the armies are moving about. Very unfortunate. War is a great blunder, you know. A great waste. But yes, I can tell you of the armies."

Bridget went into the cottage to take care of Lavinia, now awake; Richard to put his treasure in a safe place. When he came back he sat on the bench, taking Brian on his knee, and listened to the old man's account of General Washington's army marching through Philadelphia just one week before.

"A fine brave sight it was, indeed. Easily fifteen thousand men stepping briskly along to the fifes and drums. Some were rather poorly attired, but all bore their arms in soldierly fashion, and jauntily wore sprigs of green leaves in their hats. And the General himself—a splendid figure, riding at the head, the young Marquis de Lafayette beside him, and the mounted staff following. They came down Front Street and up Chestnut, foot soldiers, artillery, light horse. It took them more than two hours to pass by."

"We heard they are now camped near Wilmington," Richard said.

"That is correct. About—let me see—little more than fifteen miles from here, as I estimate the distance. I hope their proximity will not spell misfortune for you and your neighbors, here in this peaceful valley."

"But General Washington will advance farther south, won't he, to meet the British?"

"Advance? No, he is most certainly waiting to meet them at his present location. He does not wish to give them opportunity to move between himself and Philadelphia."

"But the British are still very far away, aren't they?

We were told that the fleet came up the Chesapeake Bay. Isn't that a hundred miles or more south of the Delaware?"

"By sea, yes. But they have disembarked at the Elk."

"That's what we heard. But I thought . . . the Chesapeake being so much farther south . . ."

"My dear boy! Have you never seen a map of the Colonies?"

Richard never had. His education, such as it was, had included the geography of Europe and Asia, but not America. He knew which Colonies were north of Blue Meadow and which were south. He knew, vaguely, that the Chesapeake Bay, its mouth far down at Cape Charles, Virginia, made a great indentation in the coast, dividing eastern Maryland and extending—how far north? He had no idea. And place-names were only names—he had never seen any of the places, except Philadelphia.

"Bring me a board." The old man rummaged in his knapsack for a stick of charcoal. "I will show you. I will draw a map."

Richard brought a smooth clean board, and in fascination matching his son's, watched the strokes of the charcoal pencil.

There was the curve of the Atlantic coast, from the New England states to the Florida peninsula. There was Boston, Long Island, Manhattan Island, the Hudson River. There was the Delaware, the Delaware Capes, the Bay, Wilmington, Chester, Philadelphia. There was Cape Charles, there the Chesapeake, and there the Elk River. There was the Lancaster road, there the road to Baltimore.

"And here, my boy—here is the village of Westbridge, where I slept last night. Here is the Brandywine River, its east branch and its west, both of which I crossed at the fords this morning. Here they join, flowing on to Wilmington. And here"—the pencil made a heavy circle—"is the spot where I sit at this moment, under your trees, beside your cottage, drawing this map for you."

Richard had felt dismay upon seeing those first swift strokes that outlined the Chesapeake. Now he felt a sharpening of all his senses, an alertness and readiness; and deep thankfulness for not having remained in ignorance.

"Then General Howe's army is closer to us right now than it would be if it were in Philadelphia."

"Precisely. And you can see—a march up the Baltimore Road will bring that army very close to you —within five or six miles. But it is not my intention to alarm you. I think, in fact, you have less to fear from the British than from the Patriot army."

"The British looted and burned in New Jersey," Richard said.

"So they did. But in retreat through an inhospitable country. They will have little reason for such action here. This is Tory country."

"Sir, we are neither for nor against either side."

"That is prudent; but it will behoove you to be as cooperative as possible with the British."

"You are not a citizen of the Colonies, sir?"

"No, I am a citizen of the world. A wanderer without ties. But I have seen wars, and have seen the innocent suffer, often just such innocents as that one upon your knee. My sympathies are never with the makers of war, but always with the victims."

"Do you think the Colonies will win their independence?"

"Yes, I think they will, in time. A volunteer army fighting on its own ground, for a cause, does not easily yield. The British are vastly superior in numbers and

251

in the tools of war; but their mercenaries have no cause except the pay that goes into their pockets; and the British soldier no cause but the greed of the Crown. Here, the cause is freedom. I am not certain just what that word means—it is one with which men often delude as well as inflame themselves—but it is a grand-sounding word, and through the ages men have been willing to die for the sound of it—for the grand dream. Then, too, the Patriot army has an inspiring leader, a man of high integrity, of true nobility in both presence and purpose. And for such a leader, men are willing to die."

"There is much criticism of General Washington, sir."

"Very true. He is not as experienced in military affairs as General Howe. He has made costly mistakes. He will continue to make mistakes. But in the end he will triumph."

"Yet you advised me . . . "

"In your present circumstances, my dear young man. The British will move north in a day or two. You will be almost directly in their path. They will perhaps be checked, briefly, somewhere along the way, but they will not be stopped. They will occupy Philadelphia. Therefore the way of wisdom, though you are neutral, is to receive them courteously and helpfully when they call on you, as undoubtedly they will. I have every reason to think you will find them equally courteous, for their officers are gentlemen, and one gentleman recognizes another."

Richard smiled. "Blue Meadow will receive them courteously, sir."

The week after the old man's visit was a time of waiting. It was learned that on September second the

British began a northward movement, and on the third, after some scattered fighting, were encamped in northern Delaware near Iron Hill. There they remained, reconnoitering, foraging, and bringing up provisions from the fleet. Also in Delaware, but farther to the northeast, were the Continentals, awaiting the next move.

Willowfield's "scout" was twelve-year-old Geordie Spenser, who each day rode south to the Delaware line, picking up news, as well as surveying the surrounding country from every hilltop, looking for clouds of dust or other signs of an advancing army. But the week passed without incident, and with no incursion of the British forces into Pennsylvania.

Blue Meadow, its preparations already made, most of its livestock already hidden, had little to do but wait. There was some inconvenience—the fall plowing was delayed, because to bring the work horses or oxen down to the fields would be to lose them, should a raiding party suddenly appear; but apart from that, the affairs of the farm went on as usual. Except that Jane was ill.

Jane, for undisclosed reasons—simply that she felt unwell—had kept to her bed the previous Sunday. After that, she was up and about during the early part of the week, but near the end again felt unwell, spent most of Friday in bed, and on Saturday was forbidden by Vincent to get up at all, for it had become apparent that she was gravely ill. By Saturday evening she was obliged to admit to him the nature of her trouble—an abdominal hernia—and also to admit that it was interfering with her bodily processes, that if not already strangulated it shortly would be, and that there was no help for it except by surgery.

Calmly she said, "And that is of course out of the

question. Even if you could take me to the city—and you can't, with the war at our doorstep—it would be useless, as there is not one chance in a thousand that I could survive the operation. But please don't worry—it matters very little."

He stared at her. "My God, Jane! Are you out of your mind? Do you think I'll just stand by and do nothing? Just let you die?"

"There is nothing you can do."

"The devil you say! There's a hospital in Philadelphia. I'll take you to the hospital!"

"You can't. You can't be away from here. The children . . ."

"Richard will look out for the children."

"No. We can't depend on Richard—he's only a boy. There could be fighting right here. . . ."

"Jane, we can't stop to think about their damned fighting. We can't even stop to think whether or not you can stand the trip. You *must* stand it. We'll start at daybreak."

"Vincent, please, I'm telling you it doesn't matter."

"It matters to me, damn it! You're my wife!"

A strange thing happened then. Jane began to cry. In all the years of their marriage he had never seen Jane cry. And a strange feeling came over him. In part it was pity, in part embarrassment; but the rest was something he couldn't put a name to, though the thought, *Richie could*, told him what it was.

Awkwardly he patted her hand, and even more awkwardly leaned down and kissed her. He couldn't remember when last he had kissed her, certainly not in years, and certainly she had never wanted him to; but now he felt her fingers tighten on his hand, and that pressure seemed a wordless answer to whatever it was he told her wordlessly with his kiss.

Her hair, loosened, was soft around her face; pale gold, like the children's hair. He drew a strand of it through his fingers.

"Wasn't it Portia," he asked, "whose sunny locks lay on her temples like a golden fleece?"

"Vincent, how do you possibly remember that, when you haven't opened a book in years?"

"Why, dear wife, there was a time when I opened books, chiefly to find just such appropriate phrases. There was a time, you see, when the son of the vicar's daughter, not daring to approach you, worshipped from afar. In yours he saw the face that launched a thousand ships and burned the topless towers of Ilium."

"But I never dreamed . . . and you never told me . . ."

"My God, no! I'd have felt a perfect fool!"

She laughed, though it hurt to laugh. "Don't you now?"

"Yes. Damnably so. But I have to make you understand why we're starting for Philadelphia at daybreak—and to hell with their stinking war!" He patted her hand again. "Lie quiet now, Jane. Try to sleep. You'll need all your strength for tomorrow. It will be a hard trip, but you have to make it."

Richard was at the barn, covering his chaise with wheat sheaves, when Vincent came to tell him. Stunned with horror, he repeated, "An operation?"

"Yes, and it has to be immediate. I've been told there's a very fine surgeon at the hospital—studied at Edinburgh—very skilled, very quick."

"But—how can she stand it?"

Grimly Vincent answered, "She has to stand it. They give opium or something of that sort to dull awareness of the pain. She has a strong will—and courage. She'll stand it."

"You'll want this." Richard started to uncover the chaise.

"No, I'll take a wagon. Fix it the way you did the other time, Richie."

The other time . . . They were silent, each thinking—and knowing the other was thinking—of what that other time led to, and of that same wagon on its way to the churchyard, on that cold January day, slowly, they walking beside it, one on each side. . . .

"I'll take old Sam and Harry," Vincent said. "There's a ten to one chance of losing them, but not before I get there—no one's going to seize a team and wagon carrying a sick woman. But that will leave only your stud-horse in the barn. If you think you'd better bring two others down, just be sure you don't bring any of your own. Understand? And Jane will feel easier if she knows you're close to the girls at night. She told me to ask you—either have them at the cottage, or you and your family sleep in Nurse's old room. I don't know how long I'll be gone. A few days, a week—it depends on how things turn out. You'll be in full charge of everything here—the outside work, the men, the house, the girls—everything. So square your shoulders, Richie. It's a big load, but you can carry it. You know that, don't you?"

"I only know—I'll do my best, Vince."

"Good. Then I have nothing to worry about except Jane."

Dawn was no more than a narrow gray edging between earth and sky when Richard stood watching the wagon disappear into the dark tunnel of the roadside trees. Stars were shining; the day, when it came, would be fair. Beyond a field bordering the road on the south was the creek, its waters dammed for the race that turned the big wheel at the mill; he could hear the sliding rush of water over the spillway of the dam.

He turned to look in that direction. Somewhere beyond the familiar fields and hills, beyond Willow-field, beyond other fields and hills and villages, danger lay. For some, danger of shot and shell and bayonet; for others, though taking no part, danger of rapine and burning.

And here lay Blue Meadow, if not squarely in the path of an advancing army, yet so close there was little chance it would remain untouched. Here were its fields and crops, its barns and houses, its livestock, its people —and upon him responsibility for its safety. "Do whatever you think best, Richie, about anything, as the need arises." Vincent's parting words. Not "Do this," or "Do that," not orders to follow, not the carrying out of someone else's decisions, his father's or brother's, as in the past. No, the decisions must be his. And not a boy's decisions; a man's.

When had he changed from being a boy? When his son was born? When his father died? Or had it been a gradual change, unmarked by any single event, un-timed by any single moment? Almost a year ago his father had said, "You are a man, now." How had he known? How did Vince know? And he himself—why did the thought of being master at Blue Meadow until his brother's return not fill him with a sense of inade-quacy or with dismay? Why did it not seem an unfair and frightening and intolerable burden? Why did he feel no impulse to run from it, to reject a responsibility greater than any his years had prepared him for? Per-haps something else had prepared him? Perhaps simply being a Stafford, his father's son?

257

The stars were fading as the gray spread up the sky. He could see the thick white low-lying mists that shrouded the meadow.

Nothing would happen today, some instinct told him. The hours would pass quietly and undisturbed, as Sunday hours should always pass. But tomorrow? And all the tomorrows, until the threat was lifted and the land at peace again?

Turning, he walked up the drive.

The burden was not too great. He would know how to meet the tomorrows—it was bred in him to know.

While you live, I live, Richard. . . .

(10)

Somewhere south of Willowfield, smoke was rising.

Richard had been able to determine from the hill that its origin was several miles away. But an ordinary field or brush fire would not send up those billowing clouds; it had to be a house or barn. Uneasily he watched the smoke drift closer, borne on a light southeast wind.

On Monday, Geordie Spenser, scouting the roads, had picked up the information that the whole British army was on the move northward; on Tuesday, that General Washington had withdrawn his forces to Chad's Ford on the Brandywine. On Wednesday he was forbidden by his father to go any farther than Willowfield. Passing Blue Meadow, he stopped to complain bitterly of the restriction; but Richard, though not without sympathetic understanding of the call of high adventure, advised against going even that far.

"There's a double risk, Geordie. Both sides may be foraging over the same ground. You'll lose your horse if you're caught. But there's a much greater danger than that—the danger of being caught in the middle, in cross fire."

"As if I wouldn't see them before they'd see me," Geordie scoffed. "And as if I'd be caught on Toby! Why, you told me yourself—*any* of Red Earl's get is faster than anything they'd be riding. The British, anyway. All of theirs that didn't die on shipboard were *half* dead by the time the fleet got up the Bay!"

"Yes, but that's the reason why they're desperate for horses, and scouring the country for them. If I were you, I'd put Toby back in the clearing and go on foot."

"But you're riding *that* one, right here in the open, in plain sight from the road."

"I'm prepared to offer this one as tribute. You don't want to offer Toby, do you?"

"No, of course not. And I'm not going to. They'll never catch *me!*"

"Well, keep your eyes open, and be careful."

Geordie went trotting off toward Willowfield, and Richard went on schooling the big bay Thoroughbred colt—one of the replacements he had selected to have at the barn in case anyone came. The other was a three-year-old filly. Though Vincent's instruction not to bring down any of his own had let him thankfully exclude Sea Mist, his selection had primarily been made on the basis of reasons other than ownership or personal feeling. Three of the heavy Flanders mares were his, and the light driving mare, Gretchen (the four given him on his nineteenth birthday); these he excluded because Blue Meadow needed its work teams, and because Gretchen would not long remain serviceable under daily use. The bay colt stood sixteen hands; the filly, fifteen. Both were strong and sound, well-muscled, fast, surefooted over any terrain, and of spirited but

tractable disposition. Foragers having the good fortune
to acquire these two, he reasoned, should be satisfied;
perhaps so well satisfied that they would not inquire
too closely as to the whereabouts of others, even if
suspecting that others were hidden; and would not—
perhaps—loot or burn.

He was looking again at that gray spreading cloud
when he caught the sound of hoofs and saw Geordie
come streaking past the meadow. For a moment the
barn hid him, then he was pounding up the drive.

"Redcoats! At the mill! They're after me!"

"Cut across behind the house," Richard instantly
directed, "and head straight for the woods. They won't
see you."

Geordie obeyed. Richard turned back to the training field and was putting the colt through neat and
nonchalant figure eights when the pursuers arrived.

There were ten of them, resplendent in scarlet
coats, white breeches, black boots, and plumed hel-
mets; but they were mounted on a sorrier and more
emaciated lot of horses than Richard had ever seen.
They surrounded him, right hands on their sword hilts,
faces grim.

Pleasantly he said, "Good morning."

One of them moved closer. "Major Halleck of the
Seventeenth Light Dragoons! Where's the boy on the
gray?"

"He isn't here, sir."

"Well, he didn't go on up the road—there's a clear
view for another half mile. He must have come in
here!"

"He did, but he went on through. If you wish to
search for him . . . "

"Where do those cart tracks go?"

"Up to the woods, then down the other side of the hill and out to another road—a more northerly road to Westbridge."

"Then I suppose he's got away. Where's the owner of this place?"

"This is Blue Meadow Farm, sir. It's owned by the trustees of my father's estate."

"Who's in charge?"

"At the moment, I am."

"Very well. We want horses. As a start"—a gleam of pleasure lighted Major Halleck's eyes—"we'll take that one."

Richard smiled. "I thought you would like him, sir. He's well up to your weight, and I've been giving him a few days of intensive training, to have him ready for you."

This drew first a look of surprise and perplexity, then a faint answering smile. "I take it you've been expecting us."

"Yes. We heard you were moving north."

"We were obliged to burn a barn this morning." The information was offered with heavy significance. "I hope we won't have to burn yours."

"I hope you won't, sir."

"We'll want more than one horse."

"We have another very good one in the barn."

"What have you over there?" Major Halleck pointed to the meadow.

"Nothing but yearlings."

"This is a breeding farm? Where are your mares?"

"We sold most of our stock in the spring, sir. For British gold," Richard added.

"You are farsighted. And you've hidden the rest?"

"Sir, this one was hidden. We didn't know who

262

would visit us first. But when we heard you were starting north . . ."

"It is gratifying," Major Halleck said with good-natured irony, "to run into someone so thoughtful of us. Well, let's see what you have in the barn."

With Richard at its head, the brilliant procession left the training field. Looking toward the house, he saw the girls watching from a window. The men—two on the barn floor, two in the wagon shed across the drive—stood staring. Brian came running, pursued by Bridget, who caught and lifted him in her arms, holding him safe —though not at so great a distance that he could not drink his fill of the amazing magnificence of his father's visitors.

Richard and Major Halleck and two of his party dismounted. To one of the men in the wagon shed—one of the former bondmen, who could be trusted to do and say precisely the right thing—Richard called, "Come bring the filly out, will you, please, Gideon?"

Again there was that gleam of pleasure as Major Halleck's eyes went over the sleek mahogany coat, the sloping shoulders, the strong hindquarters, the good clean legs. "Splendid! She'll do—oh, by God, yes, she'll do." His attention was distracted by shrill repeated sounds within the barn. "What else have you in there?"

"Only their sire. And he'd be of no use to you, sir."

"*Any* horse is of use to us. Have him brought out. Here"—to one of the dragoons—"take this one. And you, fellow"—to Gideon—"bring him out!"

As a gesture of respect Gideon took off his hat, but made no move to obey. In polite but firm refusal he said, "Begging your pardon, General, I'll not put a hand on that horse for all the King's gold. Nor will you, I'm thinking, nor any of your men."

If Major Halleck was on the point of demanding why not, the need was to some extent obviated by recognition of the unmistakable challenging scream of a stallion ready for a fight to the death against invaders of territory exclusively his own.

Richard said, "It will be better if you come in, sir. He is resentful of your horses—he will kill any gelding. And he's unfriendly toward almost everyone, especially strangers."

The big box stall was well barred; otherwise Major Halleck would not have gone close; for with ears flattened the Earl lunged at him, wheeled away, screamed, reared and struck, and lunged again.

"My God! How does anyone handle him? Who *does* handle him?"

"I do, sir. We're friends—we grew up together."

"Well, I can see you're right—he'd be more trouble than use to us. If I weren't sure he would also be more trouble than use to our enemies, I'd have to put a bullet in his head. And damned if I'd want to." Major Halleck glanced around. "A fine big barn you have here. And nothing more in it, you say?"

"Down at the other end, a young bull and his freemartin twin, sir. We kept those two to butcher later on; but you're welcome to them. Then there are three sheep in the meadow, and a dozen chickens in the hen house. And we have an old sow, but she weighs above forty stone and would die of the exertion and the heat if you try to drive her, I'm afraid."

"More than likely. What's above?"

"Only the grains to be threshed this winter. No hay —we stacked our hay outside in ricks this year."

"You have wagons?"

"One very heavy farm wagon. If your horses can

264

pull it, I think we can put together some harness for them."

"Where are your work animals?"

"Sir, my brother's wife became ill—he had to take her to Philadelphia. He took our team of work geldings and our light wagon."

"How many live here?"

Richard made a quick calculation. "Fifteen."

"I suppose it takes a good bit to feed fifteen people."

"Yes, it does, sir."

"Well, we won't ask for any of your food supplies, beyond the live meat. We're loading flour and meal at the mill down below here. But we want hay, so show me where your ricks are. And—well, damn it, I'm sorry— we'll have to burn what we can't take. In the fields, of course. We won't touch your barns or houses. How much farther to the next farm?"

"About one mile. But . . . All of us on this road sold most of our livestock in the spring. I doubt that you would find enough on the next two places to be worth your time."

Major Halleck smiled. "You take good care of your friends. Better than they take of you. We wouldn't have come beyond the mill if we hadn't spotted that boy."

"Boys are inquisitive," Richard said. "He was setting out to investigate the smoke. I was inquisitive too, but I only went up on the hill. It looked as if it might be near Kennett Square."

"It is. We reached Kennett Square early this morning, by the Nottingham Road."

"You mean—you and your men?"

"I mean General Howe's army."

Richard's heart lurched. "His whole army?"

"Most of it. But rest easy—we'll not visit you again,

not in the immediate future. We're on our way to Philadelphia."

"Sir, I'm sure you already know that General Washington is at Chad's Ford on the Brandywine, where the
Nottingham Road—the road from Baltimore—crosses?"

"Yes. He will not be there long."

The dragoons were gone.

Smoke drifting across the fields and woods from the
burning hay ricks brought the Spensers and Findlays in
alarm to Blue Meadow.

"Thank God," Edward said. "When I saw the smoke
I thought . . ."

"No, they were very reasonable, Uncle Ed. The
officer in charge had to burn the ricks; but he spared
one—over there behind the trees—he thought it might
escape notice if anyone else comes, and we would need
it. He seemed very pleased with what we had here for
him, and he was—very kind."

"You were fortunate, Richard. No, that isn't the
word. You made your own good fortune by your wisdom
and foresight. And that we were spared . . . I feel sure
we have you to thank for that."

"No, Uncle Ed. They were already farther than
they intended to come. And in a hurry to get back, because there's certain to be a battle—tomorrow if not today—somewhere very near."

Richard did not sleep that night. The ricks were
still smouldering; a change in the wind could bring
sparks toward the buildings. All night he patrolled,
until, an hour before dawn, Gideon came, persuading
him to get a little rest.

The day began under a heavy fog that caught and
held the sharp smell of smoke still rising from the black-

266

ened circles where the ricks had been. When the fog lifted, Geordie Spenser and two other boys set out on foot to go as far as the Forks, a safe five miles from the probable scene of battle, to gather what news they could.

They did not reach the Forks, nor even Trimble's Ford on the west branch. To their amazement, coming toward them on the Valley Road was what they took to be the whole British army, crossing at the ford and marching on up the tongue of land between the west and east branches. Thousands of men—infantry, grenadiers, light dragoons, Hessian jaegers, and officers with gold lace on their rich scarlet coats. A full hour they were in passing, under a blazing sun, dust rising all around them. When they were gone, the boys raced home with the news.

Intermittently through the day the sound of cannons reached Blue Meadow. At half past four it became continuous, not ceasing until dusk. Later, Geordie and his father, who shortly before sundown had walked to Willowfield seeking word of the battle, stopped on their return to tell what they had heard.

That portion of the British army the boys had seen crossing the west branch at Trimble's Ford, led by General Howe and General Cornwallis, had proceeded on to cross the east branch at Jefferis' Ford, outflanking the Americans and coming in on them from the north, while other regiments of British and Hessians remained in position on the west side of the river at Chad's. The battle proper had begun on two fronts with that burst of cannon fire at half past four. By nightfall General Washington's entire army was in retreat toward Chester. The British were in possession of the battlefield. Hundreds had been killed, a thousand or more wounded.

And again Richard did not sleep. For it was not yet over; every instinct told him that for Blue Meadow it was not yet over.

He had been having the girls sleep at the cottage; but that night he sent Bridget to Nurse's room to be near them, and told her to leave Brian and the baby with Cook when she came to the cottage in the morning, and to tell the girls they were under strict orders not to set foot outside the house the next day.

The night was hot and sultry; clear, but with a heaviness in the air. When the sun rose, there seemed a gray film over its red disk, though again the day promised to be one of sweltering heat.

In midmorning the dogs ran barking to the road. Richard followed.

Approaching from the east, halfway between the carriage drive and the bend, was a body of men, perhaps twenty in number. Rough bearded men, wearing hunting shirts, deerskin leggings and moccasins, and round wool hats. They carried long rifles, and each had hanging from his belt a small ax on the right, a hunting knife on the left, and from his shoulder strap a powder horn and bullet pouch. By their dress Richard knew who they were, for he had heard them talked of—frontiersmen from the west, the Pennsylvania Rifles, men so undisciplined, so unruly that General Washington himself, at the siege of Boston, said he wished they had never come.

Richard called the dogs back and stood waiting.

One of the men, a great strong fellow, was carrying another on his back. Two others were supporting between them one whose right leg, dark with dried blood, dangled uselessly. At their head was a tall red-bearded blue-eyed man who, as the British major had done the day before, introduced himself.

"Captain John Hogan, of the Eighth Pennsylvania! We want supplies!"

"Very well, sir." Richard spoke with easy outward calm. "We can give you supplies."

"And we want a horse and wagon for two wounded men."

"I'm sorry, we have no wagon. The best I can give you is . . ."

"You'll find one." The muzzle of the long rifle pressed against Richard's chest. "I've had my belly full of you damned Tories! Now get up to your barn and bring out a horse and wagon, or by hell I'll drop you where you stand!"

"Sir, I was about to say . . ."

"Richard! Richard!" Bridget came running. To stay safe inside the cottage, as he had told her, and from the window see this man hold a rifle to his heart? No, no, she could not.

"Go back, Bridget. Go back inside."

"No! Do they shoot you, they must shoot me too!"

"They aren't going to shoot me. They want supplies, that's all. And a horse and wagon."

"But the British took your wagon! Richard, these be evil men. They will hurt you. This one, this Irish red-beard . . ."

The "Irish redbeard" asked, "Who is this woman?"

"My wife, sir. Bridget, this is Captain John Hogan, of the Pennsylvania Rifles."

Blue lightning flashed in Bridget's eyes.

"For shame, Seán Ó hÓgáin! And what is one like yourself doing here, pointing your gun at the kindest of gentlemen, he being no man's enemy but ready and willing to help you as best he can? Does it be his fault that day before last the British came and took horses and cattle and sheep, and a wagon loaded to break the axles? Look yonder where they burned the hay ricks in the field, there being more than they could take, and they making sure not to leave it for General Washington. Mother of God! Be you without eyes in your head, like a thing that creeps always underground and so loses its sight for not needing of it? What is wrong with you at all that you do not know here be one with no ill in his heart toward you or the Sasanachs or anyone else in God's world?"

Long before Bridget's tirade ended, Captain Hogan lowered his rifle and stood leaning on it, grinning. Admiration was in his eyes and humble apology in his voice as he doffed his hat and said: "I beg your pardon, ma'am. Yesterday there was dust and gunsmoke all about, from noon to night, and I think until this moment my eyes have not been cleared of them. But now I see . . . Yes, now I see. And if there's any bit of help you and your fine young gentleman here can give us from the kindness of your hearts, we'll not ask for more."

"Ah, now," Bridget answered softly, "I did be thinking wrongfully of you, Seán Ó hÓgáin, by the roughness of your look, when I should have been remembering how on many of Ireland's greatest was just such hair as yours. Forgive, please. But see now, your wounded men . . ." Quick tears of compassion filled her eyes. "Ah, the poor brave creatures! May I not do for them, please, with tending of their hurts, and fresh clean bandages and all?"

"I would take it kindly, ma'am, for in the touch of your hands would be healing, that I know. But they're in a bad way, both of them, and such wounds are too hard for a woman to look upon."

"Richard?" She turned, pleading. "You know much

270

of these things. Could you not? They be suffering . . ."

"With your permission, Captain, I will treat their wounds. I've had some experience. With animals, chiefly," Richard admitted apologetically, "but I can help enough to let you get them safely to a doctor somewhere. If you will trust us . . ."

"I am not a man who has ever trusted another man," Captain Hogan said, "until now."

"Then bring them over to the kitchen, if you will. And it might be well if all your men come in from the road and make themselves comfortable under the trees. Over there"—Richard indicated a great white oak a hundred feet west of the drive—"the hedgerow will screen them from anyone passing by."

Captain Hogan gave orders to his men. They were to come in and take their ease over there in the shade while the wounded men were cared for. They were not to move from that spot. No man except those carrying the wounded was to approach this house, and no man at all was to approach the barn or the big house on beyond. Nothing anywhere on this place was to be touched.

"*Nothing*, you hear? And, by God, any man of you who thinks I don't mean what I say, won't *rest* under that tree—he'll *hang* from it!"

It was Richard's impression that no one doubted Captain Hogan's word. Certainly *he* did not; and though the threat diminished his fear of looting, it chilled him, and he wished it had not been made.

He asked what provisions they would wish to take with them.

"Not much. We need to travel light—and fast."

"Then you will hardly want an oxcart."

"God, no. We're scouts."

"Well, the only other thing I have to offer is a light chaise. It will carry your two wounded men, but little else. But it will let you make good time."

Captain Hogan appeared to be pondering a mystery.

"Yesterday," he said, "we followed the British across the ford down here a few miles, and up to the next one on the other branch. When the fighting started we were cut off—couldn't get back to our regiment. At daybreak we tried the northeast roads, but they were covered, so we came this way to circle around them. And not one single bastard anywhere would give us any help. Tories! This whole damned county—nothing but Tories! By the look of this place I took you to be the same." Bluntly he asked, "Aren't you?"

"We are neutral, sir. We do not like this war, nor any war. But armies are made up of men; and any man who turns to us for help, as one man to another, will not be turned away."

Richard went to the barn to have a word with Gideon, who received his instructions with unconcealed dismay.

"But she's yours! And your chaise!"

"We can spare the chaise better than one of the oxcarts," Richard said, "and the mare better than the oxen. As to the work mares—we need them; and besides, none of them would fit between the shafts. Go down through the woods and come back by the road, Gideon. But first, tell Cook to send food and cider down for twenty men, and two days' provisions for each to take along."

Now Richard went to his doctoring.

One of the men, faint from loss of blood, had a three-inch sword-gash on his arm, across the muscle and down to the bone. After cleansing the wound with

272

boiled water, and laying within it a thin cord of twisted linen threads extending an inch beyond—"So it can drain," he explained, "as it heals"—Richard stitched the gaping sides together. Bridget, under his direction—"Not too tight, better if air reaches it"—gently bandaged the wound.

The other man had been shot through the lower leg, the musket ball fracturing the bone. The leg had been crudely bound to a stick, but the jagged ends of bone were not together. Richard washed the wound, made a proper splint, set the broken bone, and with Bridget's help bound the splint firmly in place.

These ministrations, unhurried and thorough, took well over an hour. By the time they were finished, the scouting party had been fed; provisions had been brought down from the house for each man; and Gideon, back from his unhappy errand, was bringing harness for the chestnut mare.

The two wounded men, fortified with generous swigs of brandy, were assisted from the cottage to wait on the bench in the shade. The others, who had been sitting or lying under the big oak west of the drive, were now on their feet, stretching, picking up their rifles, preparing to leave.

Captain Hogan swept them with a look. "There's two or three I wouldn't trust not to steal from a blind man or murder their own mothers. But it's all right— no one's missing."

Satisfied, he crossed to the barn with Richard, who put the harness on the mare while Gideon morosely went to fetch the chaise.

"A fine animal," Captain Hogan said. "A beauty."

"Take good care of her, Captain, and she'll give you a fine foal in the spring. Her name is Gretchen, by the way."

Bridget for a minute or two stood watching. But she knew how fond Richard was of the red mare; and remembering the day the magic began—the day he came to meet the coach at Westbridge, and they drove home through the soft summer evening, in his chaise— she felt tears start, and turned and went into the cottage, not wanting to witness the giving up of these things he loved.

The kitchen was hot, for they had set the fire blazing to boil water. She had opened the door between the rooms, and the front door also, to let a current of air come through while they were caring for the wounded men. But now the door between the rooms was closed. That seemed strange, for she did not remember closing it, and there had been only a light breeze, not enough to have blown it shut. She crossed the kitchen and opened the door.

A man was in the front room. One of the Riflemen —a coarse ugly man with matted black hair and beard. He was at the desk—Richard's father's desk!—and had been rummaging through the drawers. He had in his hand a brass tinderbox, and she had seen him slip something else inside his hunting shirt. Now he stood motionless, staring back at her as she stared at him.

Indignantly she said, "Put that down! It be the Master's!"

"It's mine now." His voice was coarse and ugly, like his face. "And keep your mouth shut"—a long-bladed knife flashed in his hand—"or you'll get this across your pretty neck, my girl!"

In terror, Bridget turned and fled. She was almost across the kitchen, almost to the door, when something struck her between the shoulders. She felt it, hard and sharp; but felt no pain, only terror. She ran outside, screaming, "Richard! Richard!" and was halfway across the yard before she fell.

No one but Gideon, coming down the carriage drive, bringing the chaise, could afterward give a full account of what followed. Bridget couldn't, for she never knew. Richard couldn't, for he knew only that Bridget, whom he loved as he would never love another woman, lay bleeding on the ground and that beside her lay a hunting knife red with her blood. But Gideon saw it all, as a spectator sees actors going through their parts on a stage.

Captain Hogan, saying, "My God, my God!" picked up the knife—and well knew what men were armed with knives like that. Shock and fury held him rigid for an instant, until Gideon's shout, "There he goes!" dispelled the shock, leaving only the fury, cold and purposeful. Looking where Gideon pointed, he saw the man running across the drive to rejoin his fellows, who might be counted on not to give him away. He raised his rifle, coldly and deliberately took aim, and fired. The man dropped. Quickly but with the same deliberateness, he reloaded and fired again.

Richard, on his knees, held Bridget in his arms. He kept one hand pressed tight against her back, trying to close the wound, to stem the blood. Trying—though knowing it was useless, for he had seen that five-inch blade stained almost its full length.

She opened her eyes. "Richard—in the room—a dreadful man—but now with you—I be safe."

"Yes, Bridget. Yes, you're safe."

"Close," she whispered. "Hold me close. Do not let me go . . ."

"I'll hold you, Bridget. I'll never let you go. You'll always be right here with me, all my life."

"Richard, *a rún* . . ." The whisper trailed into silence. Her eyes closed. She lay limp in his arms.

Someone—Gideon—helped him to his feet, and he carried her to the cottage.

He heard Captain Hogan's voice speaking to him. Or was it someone else's voice, thick and rough with anger and grief and helplessness?

"I killed the bastard. But . . . Oh, God, I should have known, should have watched . . . What can I do, what can I say?"

Richard stopped at the door. And heard his own voice answering—or was that, too, someone else's voice, polite, dispassionate, far away?

"Do not concern yourself, Captain. It was not your fault. It is part of war—the slaughter of the innocents. Take the mare and chaise for your wounded men. Take the rest of your men and leave, please. You are urgently needed elsewhere, I am sure."

"But there must be something, some help I can give you . . ."

"You killed someone, did you say?"

"By God, yes!"

"Then all I ask of you, Captain—take care of your own dead. I will take care of mine." Richard took another step, but paused again. "One other thing. When you see General Washington, offer him consolation for yesterday's defeat by telling him of his moment of triumph here. Good day, sir."

Gideon closed the door.

Now it was over.

(11)

Early in the evening of the Sunday they left Blue
Meadow, Vincent and Jane reached Philadelphia. The
operation was performed the next day. During the following two days her life hung by the thinnest of threads.
On Thursday she showed improvement, very slight, but
enough to kindle the spark of hope into a small uncertain
flame.

That night, news of the Brandywine battle was
brought to the city, and through the night and the next
day scores of wounded men were brought to the hospital. Jane's condition continued to improve; but solely
by reason of her own vitality and its resistance to the
effects of the terrible ordeal she had been through, for
the influx of new patients so overburdened the hospital
that she was receiving little or no care.

On Sunday, at the invitation and insistence of
Cousin Elizabeth Peirson, Vincent had her moved to
Cousin Elizabeth's house, where under the best of care
her recovery seemed assured. As concern for what might
have happened—or might even then be happening—at
home, could now be put ahead of his concern for her,

early Tuesday morning he set out for Blue Meadow; on foot, for his team and wagon had been seized for the Patriot army.

The sky was heavily overcast, a strong cold wind blowing from the northeast. Long before he reached Westbridge rain overtook him, a veritable deluge released by the clouds that had been lowering for two days past. Soaked to the skin within minutes, he nevertheless continued resolutely on his way.

Another traveler, as resolutely pushing on in the opposite direction but stopping to exchange a friendly word, told him that only a few hours earlier the British had marched through, headed north toward the White Horse Tavern, and that he had heard General Washington was coming out the Lancaster road, and they were set to meet "over yonder near the White Horse," but he guessed they'd been rained out.

"Wish to hell they'd get it over with," he said in disgust. "Not safe for decent people even in their own houses any more. You hear about a woman being killed?"

"No. Where was that?"

"Other side of Westbridge, out beyond the Forks."

There were of course many places "out beyond the Forks." Nevertheless Vincent felt a sharp thrust of alarm.

"Did you hear the name?"

"No, all I heard, it was the day after the to-do at Chad's. Bunch of those backwoodsmen went through— a bad lot. Taking whatever they could lay their hands on, I guess, and the woman must've got in their way."

Wind and rain at his back, Vincent slogged on through the mud, not stopping until he came to Westbridge. Chilled to the bone, less from cold than from deep apprehension, he turned to the inn. He would have a drink, first; then he would ask for news.

Several men were inside, sitting around, drinking and talking. It seemed to him that a peculiar stillness fell on them as he entered, and that their eyes followed him as he crossed to the bar.

The innkeeper greeted him familiarly. "You look as if you've had a long wet walk, Mr. Stafford, and can do with a stiff one. What will it be?"

"A hot rum."

He waited. The stillness behind him remained unbroken. The innkeeper pushed his drink forward.

"Too bad about your brother's wife, Mr. Stafford."

Vincent lifted the steaming mug, looked at it, and set it down. He couldn't drink the stuff; he'd choke if he tried. He laid a piece of silver on the bar, pulled the soggy brim of his hat low over his eyes, turned, and walked out.

On through the rain and the mud. On across the fords, fighting his way through swollen breast-high water. To Willowfield, to the last ford, to the mill, to Blue Meadow.

He had been twelve hours on the road; it was now almost dark. And the gatehouse was dark; not so much as the gleam of one candle lighted the windows. But at the barn, through the open upper halves of the Dutch doors under the forebay, lantern light showed faintly. When the dogs ran toward him, barking, not recognizing him until quite near, Gideon appeared.

"Thank the Lord—oh, thank the good Lord, sir—you're safe home! And the Mistress?"

"Doing well."

"Ah, then, that's to be thankful for. You walked, sir?"

"Yes. Where's Richard?"

"Gone up to the woods to tend the beasts."

"Gideon—for God's sake—*how* is he?"

"Why, he's—he's all right, sir. That's to say—he's standing it. He . . . You've heard, then?"

"I heard Bridget was killed. Not what happened, or how, or . . ."

Tears streamed down Gideon's face as he told the story.

"Him doing all that for them, sir—doctoring, and giving his mare and chaise to carry the wounded—and that's how they turned around and did for him. I'd like to've killed the blackguards, every last man of them. When you think how he felt about her . . ."

"Where is she buried?"

"Right there, sir, there below the bank, just a little ways down from the cottage. He wouldn't have her put in the churchyard. I heard him tell Mr. Findlay no, she wouldn't like it there. He said when he dies they can be put in the churchyard together, but till then she'll stay right here. And he wanted to do it all himself, but Tom and me, we wouldn't let him. He hadn't any sleep for two nights, keeping watch; and then losing her like that . . . So we just had to set ourselves against him, sir, and go ahead and help, even though he said we shouldn't. We made a cedar box, and we dug the hole. And last night, when we knew this rain wasn't going to hold off much longer, we oiled a piece of canvas and put it over, so he wouldn't have to think of the rain going straight down through that loose earth. But . . .

"He's all right, sir. He's been going ahead with things . . . I mean the work, the plowing. He had us bring the teams down, he said it was safe now, nobody would come through this way again for a while. So Saturday, and yesterday, we got on with the plowing. He even plowed on Sunday, but he wouldn't let us."

"What about his children?"

"He keeps the little fellow right with him all the time, sir, no matter what he's doing. He fixed a harness and carried him on his back, plowing. And takes him along up to the woods and all. Except today on account of the rain he left him with Cook. And Mr. Findlay, he got a woman to come out from Westbridge—a wet nurse. She has our room—Tom and me, we're sleeping in the barn—and she looks out for the baby through the day. But at night, after everything's done, he brings it down from the house so they're together, the three of them."

"How are my daughters?"

"Well, it's been terrible hard on everybody, sir, from what I've heard. But the young ladies . . . I think it was Miss Findlay made them understand they mustn't take on too bad, since that would just make it the worse for him. So they've been bearing up, as I hear, and are in good health."

"Richard will stop at the house when he comes from the woods?"

"More than likely. Could be he's back now. And you shouldn't be standing around out here, sir, wet through like you are."

"I'll go up, now. Thank you, Gideon, for caring about us, and for everything you've done."

In dripping clothes and muddy boots, Vincent sought to enter the house through the summer kitchen. The door was shut and barred. He knocked. Inside, someone was moving about. The footsteps approached the door and stopped; but the bar was not lifted, and when he said, "Let me in, please," there was the sound of a hurried retreat. He knocked again. Now there were other footsteps, slower and heavier, and, "Who is there?"

"Vincent Stafford."

"*Ach, mein Gott!*" The door was opened. "Excuse, the girl did not know your voice. And it is orders—not to open unless we know."

"Very wise orders. May I leave my coat and boots here?"

"*Setzt, mein Herr,* and I will pull off your boots." Cook was searching his face. "The *Gnädige Frau?*"

He answered as he had answered Gideon, "Doing well."

She still searched his face. "You know of things here?"

"Yes." He took off his coat. There was another hanging on a chair back. "Richard is in the house?"

"*Ja.* Upstairs. He takes wood to your fire. Yesterday when the wind began blowing cold, he laid your fire, saying you might come." She set the boots aside. "You have not had your supper."

"Has Richard?"

"*Nein.* You will like it sent up?"

"No. As soon as I get into dry clothes, we'll have something here in the kitchen, if that won't inconvenience you."

Candlelight and firelight, warm and welcoming, shone into the hall through the open door of his room. Quietly he approached and stood looking in. Richard and Brian, their backs to him, were on their knees before the fire, watching little tongues of gold and orange flame lick the hickory logs.

"Pretty, pretty," Brian said.

"Yes," Richard agreed, "fire is beautiful to look at, but not to touch. We never, never touch it."

Brian nodded his understanding. "Hot."

"Yes, very hot. It would hurt you if you touched it. We make a fire to keep us warm and to cook our food. But sometimes, when we look at it, we see all sorts of

282

beautiful things in the flames. Beautiful colors and patterns and—dreams."

They were silent, looking into the flames.

"Richie."

Quickly Richard got to his feet and was smiling when he turned.

There was not enough light in the room to let Vincent see his face clearly; but enough to show the genuine warmth and gladness of his smile, and to show the lines and shadows, and to bring the thought, *God, he's as old as I am, and not yet twenty.*

What could they say to each other?

"A bad day with a good ending," Richard said. "It's great to have you home, Vince. How is Jane?"

For the third time Vincent gave the answer, "Doing well."

"You left her with Cousin Elizabeth?"

"Yes. How did you know?"

"Well, it would seem logical, and I always expect you to do the logical thing. When will you bring her home?"

"When she's fully recovered, and when it's possible to travel from place to place without losing one's means of transportation. That will work itself out. The thing now . . . Richie, if there were a single damned word to . . ."

"Vince, won't you let me help you out of those wet clothes and find dry things for you? I'm versatile, you know—I can be an excellent gentleman's gentleman."

While helping Vincent change, Richard told of the dragoons' visit, talking lightly of Geordie Spenser's narrow escape, of Red Earl's thoroughly predictable behavior, and of Major Halleck's pleasure in the bay colt and filly.

"I was sorry to let them go—they were a fine pair;

but because they were the most serviceable of the young ones they were the most likely to satisfy, and that seemed important."

"You did exactly right. Was it robbery or did they pay?"

"In between. Major Halleck regretted that he had neither the authority nor the means to pay what they were worth." Richard told of the hay ricks that were burned and of the one that was spared. "Uncle Ed's moving more hay to the clearing. We should all be able to get through the winter with what we have."

"You think we'll be visited again?"

"I'm sure of it. The British will occupy Philadelphia very soon, and will winter there. That may complicate things for you in getting Jane home, especially if the others stay close; but she'll be safe in the city. Where are Cousin Elizabeth's sympathies, by the way?"

"Under cover. She won't make the mistake of entertaining General Howe."

"Good. Because when the British leave in the spring, their Loyalist friends will have to leave with them, before the others move in."

The others. They were no longer to be acknowledged by name—those others—the destroyers.

Richard laid another log across the andirons.

Anxiously, Brian cautioned, "Fire, Rish. Hurt."

"I'll be careful, Brian. I won't touch the fire."

He straightened and turned. Vincent put an arm around his shoulders, somewhat roughly, and headed him toward the door.

"Come along, you two. Supper's waiting. I'll look in on the girls for a minute, then I'll be down."

September was over.

Two days after Vincent's departure from Philadelphia the Congress departed also, fleeing to Lancaster and from there to York, beyond the Susquehanna. General Cornwallis, with several battalions of British and Hessians, took possession of Philadelphia. General Howe and the main part of his army encamped at Germantown. General Washington was somewhere farther north, on the Skippack Road.

No reports reached Blue Meadow of any foraging west of the Schuylkill, and though it was learned that the British were bringing up supplies from Elkton, Maryland, under escort of three thousand men, Richard received this news with a shrug, and the fall work went on—the fields were plowed and harrowed and made ready for planting.

Early in October came word of the battle of Germantown; followed, later in the month, by word that part of the British fleet had come up the Delaware as far as Chester. Blue Meadow uninterruptedly went on sowing its barley, rye, and wheat; not until this was entirely finished were the oxen and work mares returned to the clearing. Attention was then turned to the cutting and shocking of the corn.

Richard, though unsparing of himself in doing his full share, had to accommodate his working hours and, to some extent, his work, to Brian's needs; for he would not, except on extremely rare occasions, allow his son out of his sight. With the coming of each day he took the baby to the house; then he and Brian went to the barn or to the fields. When cutting corn he took blankets with him, and for an hour in midmorning and again in the afternoon, snug in a corn-shock "home," Brian slept. As October advanced and the dark came early, Richard turned the cottage kitchen into a workshop where at night he set about making parts for a new wagon, working by the light of the fire long hours after Lavinia was asleep in the cradle and Brian in the pull-down bed.

They lived in the kitchen. The door between the rooms was kept closed after the weather turned cold, so that only one fire had to be tended. Once in a while Richard went into the front room, to go upstairs, needing an extra blanket or some article of clothing, and noticed how, though unused, it still looked lived-in and cared-for. There had been a crockery vase of Michaelmas daisies on one of the windowsills. They had lasted a long while, and even after they shriveled and dried and dropped their petals, he had not removed them. But one day he saw they were gone, fresh bright late-blooming marigolds in their place. He had of course also noticed that sometime during each day the kitchen was swept and made tidy, and had thought this Cook's doing; but when he thanked her she said, "*Nein*. It is the young lady. Riding home from her teaching she stops. She asks if you would mind. I tell her, why would you mind? It is good to have a clean house." So then he thanked Margaret; but with characteristic bluntness she, too, turned his thanks aside. "I'm doing it to satisfy my own need to do *some*thing, and less for you than for her. Either way, it's too trivial to be thanked for."

He did not make a headstone for Bridget's grave. Later—perhaps much later—he would; and would cut his own name as well as hers into the stone—his pledge that they would be together through eternity. But at night, in the stillness beside the fire, when the hour grew late and he laid the wagon parts aside, he worked for another hour carving from a piece of white oak a Celtic cross, which he would set in the ground where she lay. Bit by bit he chipped it out—the circle at the intersection of the arms, and in bas-relief the intricate design copied from a drawing in a book he had from his father's library. Too tired at last to trust his hand or eye, he fixed the fire for the night; and sometimes too tired to do more than take off his shoes, he lay down on the bed, and drew Brian close; and—sometimes—fell asleep at once.

On cold gray days in November, Brian could not stay long outdoors unless willing to sit huddled under blankets, for he had outgrown his warm clothes of the previous winter. Richard stitched together a pair of small calf-length woolen trousers roughly resembling his own; but these were of dubious benefit, since Brian was still very young, and trousers had not the practical convenience of petticoats. Cook knitted woolen stockings for him, and mittens, and a little jacket and cap, all of which helped, so that he bravely insisted, "Warm, Rish," even while shaking with cold, and wept at the suggestion that he stay in the kitchen with Cook and Lavinia instead of going to the fields or woods.

This situation eased one day when Vincent, having walked to Westbridge to leave at the inn a letter for Jane, found one from her waiting for him. Hers was dated some two weeks earlier, not long after she learned of Bridget's death (he had informed Cousin Elizabeth, but with the request that Jane not be troubled with the news until in better health). In it she told him she was well but still very weak and in need of being waited on; and as in that condition she would only be an added burden to them, it seemed best to accept Cousin Elizabeth's kind invitation to stay on. Of the tragedy she said nothing beyond asking him to convey her sympathy to Richard; but her letter ended with instructions to take from the rosewood chest in the third-floor storage closet any and all articles of warm clothing that would do for the child, as she supposed Richard would "now more than ever most unwisely insist upon taking him outdoors no matter how inclement the weather."

Along with Jane's letter, Vincent brought back the latest news of the war. General Washington had been moving his troops back and forth in the area north of Philadelphia; rather pointlessly, it seemed; but his presence blocked British efforts to obtain supplies from the surrounding countryside—which he, meanwhile, was systematically ravaging. In consequence, the British had turned their attention to the forts on the Delaware, taking them one by one, and the river was now open to their ships from the Capes to Philadelphia.

Richard listened, but had no interest in the activities of either army, beyond the potential danger they were to Blue Meadow. Foraging was widespread, as far west as Lancaster, and south into Delaware; but for some reason—perhaps the condition of the roads, which had been all but impassable ever since the September rains—the Willowfield area was passed by. Washington's men were desperately in need of clothing, shoes, and blankets; and orders had been given to "buy if you can; if not, take—especially from the Tories and the unfriendly Quakers and others notoriously disaffected to the cause of American Liberty." At Blue Meadow, all extra supplies of these desired articles not already hidden were removed from their usual storage places to closets which Richard disguised with false backs.

Despite the cruel justification given him to align himself with the "disaffected," Richard derived no satisfaction from hearing of the American defeats or the distress of the men without blankets and shoes. The truth was that he did not think of them as men, for he did not think of them at all—he had set up a wall in his mind, beyond which no thought of them could be allowed to penetrate. They existed; that was all. They were a vague outer force as impersonal and ruthless as the forces that govern the universe. They were simply "the others," without entity, without faces. The faces he would have had to give them were granted no admission behind that shielding wall. In dreams that woke him sweating or shivering or sobbing in the night, he saw those faces. Awake, by an act of will he shut them out.

Vincent, aware of the wall, was deeply troubled by it, for he saw that just as it served to shut out, so too it shut in. And it seemed to him that not only grief was sealed away behind that wall, but also some familiar and essential part of his brother. This controlled, self-contained, impassive Richard was not the Richard he knew. It wasn't only that all boyishness was gone, that this was not the Richard of the impetuous act and the quick unthinking word, not the Richard who ran when he could have walked, who sang at his work or, lost in daydreaming, forgot to work at all, who was sometimes negligent, sometimes too hasty, sometimes too slow in performance of a task, needing to be taught the error of his ways. What troubled Vincent was not that the boy was gone and in his place the man, but that this was a divided Richard. "He's standing it," Gideon had said. Yes, he was standing it. But divided in two; one part going on with the daily business of living; the other part withdrawn, insulated, and alone.

The wall was built of bitterness; and Vincent knew that for Richard to harbor bitterness was like taking into the body some foreign or poisonous substance that every tissue, every vein and nerve would by its very nature reject—or, unable to reject, would absorb with certainly injurious and possibly fatal effects. Richard could not by his own choice have an enemy, could not

289

hate or be revengeful, or even withhold forgiveness. Had he not, according to Gideon, absolved the captain of the Riflemen, saying, "It was not your fault"? The murder was one man's act; he had not put blame upon the rest. Then why the wall? *This* Richard could admit them; could even receive them, should they come again, with civility. Therefore it was for the seclusion of the other Richard that the wall was raised; the Richard he had been—young and vulnerable and generous of heart.

Not to anyone did Richard ever speak of the events of that day. Carefully, if any allusion was made, he evaded or ignored it. He had faced his loss alone, for more than two hours alone, until Edward Findlay, summoned by Gideon, intruded upon that terrible solitude. He had opened the door "looking haggard and pale," Edward related, "but calm and self-possessed, and thanked me for coming, and said no, there was nothing I could do, he would need no help, but if Margaret could spend the night with the girls he would greatly appreciate that kindness." He continued to face his loss alone. In two months, Vincent had not heard him speak Bridget's name. The book was closed, not to be reopened.

(12)

From farm to farm, ten miles north and ten miles south of the Lancaster road, word was passed—as if flashed ahead by signal light or carried by the wind— that a raiding party had come down from Valley Forge and was headed west, with orders to "forage the country naked." Inhospitable and already impoverished farmers hid what little they had left, and either hid themselves or with surly looks stood by to show the raiders their empty barns and empty storerooms.

A hundred foot soldiers, three mounted officers, and three wagons drawn by horses pitiably weakened by starvation, made up the company. Should the wagons be filled, other horses would have to be found to draw them. Or oxen. And there were no horses or oxen—the British had long since made off with all of them. Or, at any rate, there were none in any of the barns the frustrated raiders came to, though now and then a rider was sighted on the road far ahead, or on a snowy hilltop, watching their approach and then racing off to spread the alarm. Pursuit was useless; the pursued could outdistance the pursuers with infuriating ease.

Even the captain of the company, though well mounted on a fine chestnut mare, made no attempt to overtake those fleeing horsemen—"Damned Tories!" His mare was thin, but in passably good condition. And should be. Hadn't he, to feed her, paid those wily thieving farmers with silver out of his own pocket ten times what a sack of oats was worth, or a bundle of hay? And didn't he share with her his own ration of corn-meal, when there was any cornmeal to ration? Luckily a near-starvation allotment had reduced his own weight these past few weeks, or she wouldn't be up to carrying him, due as she was to drop a foal in the spring. If she was still alive in the spring . . .

On the third day out, the raiders left the Lancaster road, made a ten-mile swing to the south, and then turned east toward the village of Westbridge. From there, with as much as they were able to pick up, they would continue northeastward, completing their circuit, back to winter camp at Valley Forge.

They had so far picked up very little. The country had already been so stripped by both armies there was little left in it, and the inhabitants—even the damned Tories—were themselves suffering privation. A few sheep, a few scraggy cows. A few bags of meal, a few sides of bacon. With luck they might be able to double the amount on the way back; but even doubled there would not be one-twentieth enough to feed nine thousand men for one day; and not enough blankets and clothing for ninety. The needed goods were simply not to be had from this county, which had been gleaned long before. Worse than that, there were sections that had seen bitter fighting. Innocent people had suffered. . . .

Do not concern yourself, Captain. It is part of war —the slaughter of the innocents. Oh, God!

Shivering around their campfires, Captain Hogan's men passed the night in a narrow cleft between two hills, sheltered somewhat from the wind but not from the cold, nor from the snow that began falling in the early hours of morning. At dawn they melted snow over their fires to mix flour paste, and had for breakfast the same thing they had had for supper—"fire cake" baked on hot stones. Two inches of new snow had fallen by the time they set out again. They moved through that soft whiteness in silence, yet word of their coming ran before them, as well-heralded as if they themselves were announcing the fact with trumpets and drums.

There were a number of fine big barns and houses along the way. But, "We haven't enough to feed ourselves," the owners said of their empty cupboards; and of their empty barns, "The British were here," not adding that they had been willing enough to sell to the British, who paid with gold and silver, not with receipts and promises. Orders were to burn all corn, hay, and other forage that they could not for want of wagons bring with them. It would have been a pleasure to burn the barns, simply in revenge for their being empty; but Captain Hogan contented himself as best he could with cursing, and ordered his men to move on.

They came to a shallow creek some fifty feet wide between low banks bordered by meadows on each side. The road they were following went straight on. Another branched to the north, curving around the loop of the creek. The scouts said that road also would take them to Westbridge, but it was inferior, long stretches through forests broken only here and there by small farms. The rich farms, they said, were on the eastward road.

Captain Hogan found something familiar about

this spot: the Y formed by the roads, and the great U formed by the creek flowing west, then south, then beyond the ford turning back on itself. But he had passed innumerable rutted wagon trails, and had crossed only God knew how many meandering streams. One was like another; that was why it seemed familiar. He gave orders to ford the creek.

There were two farms; one on the north side of the road; the other, its cluster of buildings a half mile farther along, on the south. If he had ever seen those farms before, he did not remember them; again, the familiarity lay only in their resemblance to other prosperous-looking farms visited within the past hour. But on the first one stood a large red-brick house that gave him an uneasy feeling. Thank God, no—it was not *that* house, it was set much closer to the road, and the barn much farther back. It was only the design that was the same—the solid rectangle, the symmetrical spacing of the windows, the hipped roof—and the color of the brick.

An elderly gentleman, surprisingly cordial, came from the house to greet them. Yes, he could let them have a few things. Two sheep that had broken away and escaped from the British, who had not troubled to recapture them. Half a dozen sacks of shelled corn. One sack of wheat flour. Blankets? Clothing? Why yes, he could certainly find a few articles of clothing, and two or three blankets could be spared. Hay? No, the mows were empty, or nearly so; they might be able to fork enough together to half fill one of their wagons. Horses and cattle? No, he had not a horse or cow anywhere on his eight hundred acres—"They have been much in demand, you know."

The gentleman's amiable courtesy was such that

Captain Hogan refrained from expressing his opinion of Tories. Instead, he expressed polite gratitude for the things provided, wrote receipts for them, and went on.

His reception at the next farm was much the same. Cautiously but with apparent good will another gentleman offered as much as could be spared "without ourselves facing starvation." Again the barn was empty of almost everything. The wheat had been threshed a month ago, and the British had taken it. The corn had been husked; the British had taken that also. There was a cart, but no ox to draw it. Two blankets were produced, two old coats, a pair of breeches, three pairs of shoes. The gentleman regretted that General Washington's army was so distressed by the lack of these things; but no doubt the situation would soon be remedied—he understood that the Congress was making every effort to obtain the needed supplies through proper channels.

"The Congress be damned!" Captain Hogan retorted. "The only effort they're making is to keep their own worthless hides safe and warm!"

He ordered his men to move along, waited until the last of them were under way, then somberly followed.

Now the road lay between a hill on the left and the creek meadows on the right. And remembering that once he had followed just such a road, but in reverse, he found himself making a silent prayer: Oh, Christ, don't let it be *that* road. . . .

Snow-covered fields, snow-covered hills did not look as they had in September, when the aftermath of the summer's mowing was green, the wheat-stubble gold, the standing corn higher than a man's head, and the hot sun shining down over everything. Now there was only one great sweep of white, and a leaden sky from which thinning flakes continued to drift down. It wasn't the same.

But under him the mare quickened her step, though he had given no signal. Her head came up, her ears went forward. She whinnied. Ahead, the other horses plodded sluggishly along, indifferent to whatever had excited her. She whinnied again, tugged on the bit, and broke into a trot. He let her overtake and pass half the column before pulling her back to a walk. Beside him one of his Riflemen said, "I guess you know where we are, Captain?"

The big brick house, the big stone barn, the cottage under the pines . . .

Captain Hogan galloped to the head of the column, which had already halted at the entrance.

"Keep moving! We're not stopping here!"

But his lieutenant, pointing up the drive, presumed to argue. "There's a wagon—a big one! See the back end sticking out of that shed? They've got it jacked up—they've taken off the hind wheels to fox us. But they'll bring 'em out. And they'll bring horses, too, if I know *you*, sir!"

Furiously Captain Hogan shouted, "I say keep moving!"

He was having trouble with his mare. Determined to move in one direction only, she was sidestepping up the drive. He swung her around and put his heels to her. She promptly swung right back. Again she whinnied, and from the barn came a loud shrill answer.

"What did I tell you! They've got horses in there! And plenty more than horses, you can bet!"

"God damn it to hell, I don't care what they have! *Move!*"

"Friends of yours?" the lieutenant had the temerity

296

to ask; but had also the wisdom to turn his own horse to the road.

Slowly the column began moving past.

Long before the raiders forded the creek west of the Findlays, indeed almost as soon as they turned east the day before, news of their approach had reached Blue Meadow. Every farm along the road received complete details—how many men (twenty of them Pennsylvania Rifles), how many on foot, how many mounted, how many wagons, and the name of the officer in charge.

Everyone knew of Captain John Hogan. He had made a name for himself in recent months, foraging under the very noses of the British, cutting off their expeditions and taking their supplies; a bold and fearless man of dangerous temperament, designated hero or villain depending on which side did the designating. Beyond that, the name had no significance at Blue Meadow to anyone but Richard; for Gideon had not known the name of the officer that day in September; and Richard, never speaking of that day at all, had of course never spoken of his acquaintance with the now famous—or infamous—John Hogan. When word of the raiding party was relayed from farm to farm, and Edward Findlay, having heard much of the reputation of this man, came to warn the Staffords that a visit could be expected the next day, Richard received the warning in rather tense silence but without sign of alarm.

Blue Meadow had been twice visited by the British since Christmas. As with the Findlays and Spensers, on the first occasion most of their corn had been taken; on the second, their newly threshed wheat. Oats, still in the sheaf, were in the barn.

297

"Move your oats to the fields, by all means," Edward urged. "They haven't the wagons to carry any quantity—they will burn you out. I'll send my men over to help you."

Vincent, though agreeing that this would be a wise move, was attentive to his brother's silence.

"What do you think, Richie?"

And Richard said, "I think if we are all prepared to make a reasonable offering, with good grace, we have nothing to fear from Captain Hogan."

"My dear boy! They burned a number of barns along the Lancaster road. This man is ruthless, completely ruthless."

"Perhaps he is, Uncle Ed; but hardly so without provocation."

"And you think a reasonable offering will satisfy him?"

"From what you say," Richard answered, "he hasn't the means to transport very much. That should make a little seem like a lot."

"But this wagon you're building. They have three horses under saddle."

"If they take the wagon they can take most of the oats, which will eliminate the need to burn our barn. So don't worry about us, Uncle Ed. And for yourself . . . May I offer a word of advice? I think Captain Hogan is neither as ungentlemanly nor as heartless as represented. His appearance and manner are described as extremely rough and intimidating. Don't make the mistake of judging him solely by his roughness. I've heard it said that on a closer look it's possible to see in him a resemblance to some of the greatest of Ireland's leaders; and I remember my father saying that those leaders were in truth uncrowned kings."

When Edward left, Richard resumed his work on the wagon. Vincent watched for a short while in silence.

"Richie, are you planning to have the wagon ready for them?"

Carefully Richard cut a few thin shavings from a wooden pin.

"I'm planning to put the tires on in the morning."

"If they continue east," Vincent said, "we can look for them to come through in the morning."

"Yes." Richard fitted the pin in place.

Vincent asked, "What do you think we should offer them?"

"Nothing."

Now Richard turned, and Vincent saw his face— tight, strained, deeply lined; and his eyes—shadowed with pain.

"Captain Hogan won't stop here, Vince."

"My God! Are you saying . . . ?"

"I'm saying—conscience and decency won't let him." Richard swung Brian down from his perch on the wagon. "We'll have snow tonight. I think I'll take this fellow inside to warm up a bit, then we'll go tend the stock. It's going to be dark in another hour, the way it's clouding over."

In the morning, Richard and Gideon started up the forge and set about fitting the bands of iron to the wheel rims. The new snow—three inches by that time covered the old—deadened any sound of men or wagons moving on the road; but above the sounds within the shed—Gideon working the bellows, Brian running back and forth on a pile of boards—Richard thought he heard the whinny of a horse. He stopped his work and stood listening. When it came again, it was very close. From the barn Red Earl answered. And from the drive, down

299

beyond the cottage, as Richard took Brian in his arms and went outside, came the angry shout, "Move on, damn you, move on!"

Two men on horseback and a dozen on foot were at the drive entrance. Between the roadside trees Richard could see the rest—the long column slowly approaching and in obedience to that shouted command slowly passing by. Beside him Gideon was muttering imprecations; and Vincent, hurrying over from the barn, was saying, "By God, you were right!" But Richard's sharpest awareness was of only one thing—of something come back.

The past could not come back. The grave could not give up its dead. But part of the past was there; not in memory only, or in imagination; in reality; in the living flesh.

"That's Gretchen."

Drawn by some powerful force, something more compelling than any counterforce of reason or remembrance—anything that would have kept him where he was or led him to seek the refuge of greater distance—Richard started forward.

Vincent caught his arm. "They're going. For God's sake, let them go. Keep away from them."

"No, Vince. I have to speak to him. I have to thank him."

"*You* have to thank him?"

"Yes. He's being kind. He . . ."

"Well, considering what you have to thank him for, if there's any thanking to be done now, I'll do it. You stay here."

Vincent strode down the drive. But the force still drew Richard, and he followed.

Captain Hogan had succeeded in making the mare face the road. A third of his company had passed.

300

Grimly he sat waiting for the rest. Not one of the bastards would set foot on this place. . . .

"Captain Hogan?"

He looked down into the face of the man who had come from behind him and now stood at his stirrup. Older, heavier—not *that* face, thank God, though enough like it to give him a start.

"We want to thank you, Captain, for passing us by. My brother is especially grateful for your kindness. A few months ago, as you remember, he suffered an irreparable loss at the hands of one of your men. We are grateful to you for sparing us further loss."

"God's blood! Would any man do different?"

"Why, yes, some would. In war, men harden their hearts."

"A heart of stone," Captain Hogan said thickly, "would split wide open with thinking of what happened here. That girl, the sweetest creature in . . ." His voice broke against its own thickness. "How is he—the boy—your brother?"

"Here he is, Captain. See for yourself."

As Captain Hogan turned in the saddle, the mare, choosing to interpret the move as a signal, turned also, and with a little sound of surprise took two quick steps forward.

Richard put out a hand to her. "You'd never forget an old friend, would you, Gretchen?"

"Horse, Rish." Brian, too, put out a hand. "Horse!"

"Yes. This is Gretchen come back." Now Richard looked up. "You've taken good care of her, Captain."

In his thirty-odd years Captain John Hogan had been through many bad moments. That one last September was the worst; but he found this almost as bad, built as it was on the same foundation, and the whole picture so clear—so unforgettably, damnably clear. This boy with the deep lines in his face and the deep shadows in his eyes, lines and shadows that hadn't been there four months ago, this boy holding a child in his arms, a child with black curls, *her* child . . .

Words that he hadn't spoken aloud or in silence for years, burned in his mind. *Through my fault, through my fault, through my most grievous fault* . . .

It was too much. It was more than a man could stand.

Swinging to the ground, he slipped the bridle rein over the mare's head and thrust it into Richard's hand.

"Take her. I'll walk."

"Sir," Richard protested, "you can't do that. You can't give up a horse when . . ."

"The hell I can't! You think they'll cashier me? Let them! I'll keep the saddle"—he shouted to one of the passing wagoners to stop—"but the mare stays here, where she belongs!"

"Then we'll give you a replacement . . ."

"You'll give me nothing! I'm not asking and I'm not taking! God knows, if I could give back what I've already taken . . . !"

He jerked savagely at the girths, pulled the saddle off, dumped it in the arms of the astounded wagoner.

"*Horses!* What in hell do I want with horses? You know what's happening to them on those godforsaken hills? Starving to death by the hundreds—the ground frozen—there they lie—rotting carcasses all around the camp! Starving horses, starving men . . . Look at those wagons! Look what I have to show for three days on the road! How many will that feed? How many will it clothe? Men without shoes—everywhere they walk you can track them by the goddamned blood of their feet! Men without coats, without breeches, without blankets.

Sick, freezing, dying. Some run away, but most of the bloody fools keep hanging on. Why? Who in hell knows? General Washington writes to the Congress, and they sit on their fat backsides seventy-five miles away, never lifting a hand, saying the commissary will have things in good order before long. Before *long*! How long can a half-naked man live in those damned huts in this weather? How long without food in his belly? Till spring? Till the shad run up the Schuylkill? God!"

Captain Hogan wiped sweat from his forehead; sweat, on a bitter end-of-January day.

"Well, that's nothing to do with you. We'll move along."

Richard, listening to that violent outburst, missed not a word of it, though under and around the words the harsh voice was saying he heard other words and other voices.

There was nothing he did not already know in the picture drawn of the hardships being endured by the army at Valley Forge, for through the past month many such pictures had been drawn, though not from the same viewpoint, nor with passion. Those, deflected by the wall he had set up in his mind, had not touched him; had only brushed against the wall; had not been admitted beneath the outer surfaces of thought.

Armies are made up of men, he remembered his own voice saying. But that was before he built the wall.

In war, he had heard his brother say, *men harden their hearts.* But other things, too, made men harden their hearts.

The bloody fools keep hanging on. Why? In memory he heard the answer: *Through the ages men have been willing to die for the grand dream.*

Here was every physical comfort: warm rooms, warm beds, warm clothing, abundance of food—fresh

303

meat, eggs, fine white flour, and even imported luxuries —coffee and tea, sugar, lemons, Madeira wines. But on bleak winter hills only half a day's ride from Blue Meadow were men without food, without blankets, miserably existing in log huts that gave them less protection than the shelters he had built for horses and cattle.

Ah, the poor brave creatures . . . Richard, could you not? They be suffering. . . .

Something rose in him. He could not put a name to it, nor did he try; but it was like a fire springing up.

Richard, a rún—she was there beside him, he heard her soft voice, felt her take his hand—*these others need you. Go out to them. Go out and give to them for love of me. . . .*

The wall—of ice, not of stone—melted away in that instant.

"No—wait! Stop your men. Bring back your wagons. We have things to give you. You can refuse to ask, but you can't refuse to accept. We . . . Vince?"

He turned. The fire was all through him. Vincent saw it—the very fire of life.

"I can have the wagon ready in an hour. We can load it with oats. Oat straw is good forage, almost as good as hay, and with the grain in the sheaves . . . My three work mares—and maybe one of yours?—can pull it. We can fill their wagons with other things. We have so much . . . I know, only a fifth is mine—isn't a fifth mine?—but I'll make it up, I'll pay it all back. And if we run short we can buy—or borrow—Uncle Ed will help us out. We have to do it, Vince. We have to help. We . . ."

The young Richard. Eager, impetuous, thought leaping on thought and into words before the thoughts themselves were carried to completion. Vincent could

304

say nothing aloud, just then. But to himself: It's all right now. It's all right. If he lives to be a hundred, he'll die young.

Richard tried to read that silent searching look, but couldn't be sure it meant consent. Pleading, he said, "Vince, Bridget would want us to."

So Bridget was there; to be named; to be spoken of; to be part of the present. With that, Vincent brusquely took charge. Accustomed to telling people what to do, he had no hesitation about issuing a directive to Captain John Hogan.

"Hold your men, Captain. He's right—this is no time to put your private feelings ahead of the public good. We are well-provisioned here, we can spare you all you can carry, and meat on the hoof besides. Richard"—the same voice of authority—"put Gretchen in the barn. She's no longer a suitable mount for Captain Hogan. I'll provide one that is. Gideon can finish the wagon—send someone down to help him. Then go to the house, and strip every bed, every room, every closet, of every blanket and every article of clothing—coats, shirts, breeches, shoes, stockings—that can possibly be spared, bearing in mind that we can keep the fires up when the nights are cold. Be quick now—we don't want to put Captain Hogan to the inconvenience of a long delay."

Richard was quick. With wings on his heels and Brian in his arms, he ran from the barn to the house and upstairs.

"What are you *doing?*" the girls cried. And when he told them, they exclaimed in amazement, "For General *Washington's* men?"

"For men," he answered. "Men who must sleep without blankets to cover them, in little log huts, on the damp earth in the dead of winter. Men who sometimes have nothing to eat. Men who are cold and hungry and sick and suffering, but believe in a dream—and in General Washington."

"Oh," said Virginia, instantly willing to lend wholehearted support to any cause that had Richard's support. "Well, we can all sleep in *one* bed, Uncle Richard. They can have *our* blankets."

As fast as Richard stripped the rooms and closets, the girls carried armloads of blankets and clothes down to the front door, where the wagons stood waiting.

"*Gott in Himmel!*" said Cook. "Is the house itself gone mad?" But when she contributed a quilt, a blanket, and a thick knitted woolen shawl large enough for a bed covering, and he asked if she was sure she could spare them: "Can I not spin, *Dummkopf?* Can I not work the loom? Can I not sew and knit? Take! But it is you who must answer to the *Gnädige Frau* when she comes home, not me!"

Vincent, meanwhile, had gone to the clearing; and from there, taking his own saddle horse, had ridden down through the woods to the Findlays'. When he returned to Blue Meadow by the road, accompanied by Edward, and with Edward's men serving as drovers, he was at the head of a goodly procession: his own oxen; two carts, each drawn by a single ox (Edward's); twenty head of sleek young cattle (half of them Edward's); thirty sheep; ten fat hogs. One of the carts was already loaded with sacks of flour and meal covered by a dozen blankets; the other held a barrel of salted meat and a keg of rum picked up at the Spensers' in passing. Edward was riding one of his work horses and leading another, these to share the burden of the loaded wagons, which the half-starved and enfeebled horses of the raiders would not be able to pull through the snow.

Captain Hogan, who had never believed the story of manna from heaven, was dumbfounded. Nor did Edward's explanation—"My dear sir! If you could know what you've done! If you could know what it means to us to see Richard restored!"—make the matter any clearer.

"What *I've* done? I wouldn't have come within five miles of this place if I had known the road!"

"Ah, but that's it. That's the miracle. You were led here," Edward explained, "to be the instrument by which grief has been sublimated through giving, and by that he is restored."

Involuntarily, perhaps unconsciously, Captain Hogan made a once-habitual, now all but forgotten gesture; and with reverence, as he crossed himself, said, "Holy Mother of God."

The wagons were loaded and ready to go. Richard had brought the last things from the cottage. The secret storage rooms he had so artfully built were empty. All his own clothes were gone—his best coat (*Your fine Sunday coat, Richard!*), his riding boots, his tricorn hat, his homespun linen shirts and linsey-woolsey work frocks and trousers, everything except . . .

"Wait, Captain." Off came the hat from his head, the coat and waistcoat from his back, the shoes from his feet. "That's all, I guess."

But there was one more thing.

"Hat!" Brian exclaimed joyfully, snatching off his knitted cap and flinging it on the wagon.

Richard held him aloft. "Gentlemen, the first American Stafford!"

Slowly the train of men, beasts, and wagons got under way. Captain Hogan on a fine strong hunter— "He'll carry a hundred and eighty pounds all day, Captain," Vincent had said, "anywhere and over anything"— waited to fall in behind them. The snow had ended, the sky was clearing. An eternity had passed, it seemed to all of them, though the morning was not yet spent.

"You'll have a full moon tonight," Vincent said. "Will you try to push right on?"

"We'll try."

"Yes. Well, be patient with the oxen. They'll lie down when they're tired, and no power on earth can move them. But give them twenty minutes, and they'll get up of their own accord and go on. They're good honest beasts."

"We'll respect them, Mr. Stafford. And"—harshly— "we'll spare them if we can."

"That's good of you, Captain."

"Christ," Captain Hogan said. "I never knew what goodness was."

The last of his men were fifty yards down the road. He reined his horse to follow, but held back for another moment, his eyes on Richard and the child. He had a little trouble seeing them, and had to speak with more than his usual roughness in order to speak at all.

"For whatever it's worth from Seán Ó hÓgáin—may God bless you."

They watched him go; watched until the bend in the road took him and all the rest from their sight, and only the myriad footprints and the wheel tracks in the snow remained.

Richard was shivering.

Sympathetically, Brian said, "Cold, Rish."

"No, I'm not cold. It's just . . ."

But Vincent took a firm grip on his arm and led him to the cottage. "Get inside. And stay there until I find something for you to wear—if you've left anything."

The untended fire in the kitchen had almost burned itself out; but Richard laid sticks over it, and Brian blew on the embers, and soon a log was blazing.

Brian asked for tea. That meant warm milk with a little tea added for the sake of appearances. But there was no tea—the canister had gone with everything else, there was nothing on the cupboard shelves but a few pewter cups and bowls and the Dresden tea set. These and . . . far back in a corner, out of sight on one of the upper shelves, an ivory disk.

Long months since Richard had looked at it; long months since he could bear to. Now his fingers closed around it and brought it out. Still without looking—later he would look, but not now—he slipped it into a pocket in the waistband of his breeches.

"We'll use your mother's beautiful teapot, Brian. That will make milk taste like tea."

They went to the springhouse for milk, Richard still in his stocking feet—but he didn't feel the coldness of the snow, only the softness.

That softness blanketed the yard and the gentle slope along its eastern side and the whole broad meadow beyond, where the stream ran dark between snow-rounded banks. The sun was gilding the edges of torn clouds. Blue shadows lay across the snow; familiar shadows of trees and bushes, and the strange lovely shadow of a Celtic cross.

Epilogue

His great-great-grandchildren called him Father Richard. The neighborhood had long ago dubbed him Father Time.

He lived alone in the gatehouse at Blue Meadow Farm on the West Branch road, near the village of Willowfield. He had lived there, though not always alone, for a longer time than any but the very oldest of the villagers could remember: eighty-three years, since the day of his marriage at the age of eighteen in the autumn of 1775.

Many and various and unceasing had been the changes in the world around him. He had seen the thirteen colonies declare and win their independence, and now saw the spreading shadow of a still more bitter conflict to come, a war between the states, the North against the South. He had witnessed the inauguration of the first president of the United States, and had read of the inauguration of its fifteenth. The railroads had come, and steamships, and good broad roads to anywhere, and machinery of every sort to take the place of men. The frontier, which in his boyhood had been not far beyond the Pennsylvania mountains, was gone, all the great West had been opened, all the way across three thousand miles to the shores of the Pacific.

At Blue Meadow he had seen others come and go, had outlived his children, some of his grandchildren, some of his great-grandchildren. He was old, incredibly old, yet even more incredibly young. Once in a while he dined with his grandson and family at the big house as an honored guest, but usually prepared his own meals at the cottage, where he still tended his own hearth fires. He still rode horseback an hour or two every day unless the weather was extremely bad. He still carved wooden toys for Blue Meadow's children and their friends, his hands as steady and as deft as ever. And with his scythe at harvest time he still cleaned the edges and corners of the fields, after the big new McCormick reaper had done its work.

Near the gate cottage, just beyond the bank at the east side of the yard, was the slab of granite on which more than three-quarters of a century ago he himself had chiseled:

> Bridget Gallagher Stafford
> Dec 2 1757–Sept 12 1777
> beloved wife of
> Richard Gregory Stafford
> Oct 10 1757–

The last date would be cut by another hand.

But, "Father Richard is going to live forever," said twelve-year-old great-great-grandson Gregory.

"Don't be silly," fifteen-year-old great-great-granddaughter Lavinia admonished. "No one lives forever."

"*He* will. He told me so. He said someday I'll have a son, who'll have a son, who'll have a son, and as long as there's always one more son, he'll never die. He said life is a wheel that just keeps turning and turning. . . . "

"I'm afraid poor old Father Richard has wheels turning in his head."

"He has not! He always knows exactly what he's saying, and I always know exactly what he means!"

Young Gregory looked out across the fields, out to the hills and the far blue distances of earth and sky and time.

"Father Richard says *I am him*. . . . "